CHAPTER 1

July

I woke without the knowledge of who I was.

My identity was blank and flavorless, like tofu.

Or a character in a computer game.

Or page one of a sci-fi novel about space pilgrims waking up from space hibernation, about to embark on... space adventures.

Interesting, I thought, not panicked at all. *I wonder what this one is all about?*

I was in a soft bed, in a beige room, with sun coming in through white curtains. Not very creative, but not off-putting. Like a display suite for a new condominium project.

I was on my back, like a plastic doll in a package at a big box store.

Visible between my feet was a plain, white door.

The door burst open, and a young woman in a bath towel entered.

She gave me a cross look, rivulets of shower water streaming down between two auburn eyebrows.

"Mom, you'd better not make us late for Aunty Z's wedding like you were for my graduation."

So much expository information!

My mind reeled from the onslaught, the info dump, and...

I was back.

Zara Riddle. Librarian. Mother. Witch. Snappy dresser. *Spirit Cursed.*

"Not this one again," I said, my voice still croaky with sleep. "I want to play a different main character."

The young woman was my daughter, Zoey—half genie, part shifter, and wise beyond her physical years.

She swiped a bottle of green liquid off the bedside table—off *my* bedside table.

I tried to swipe it back, but she was too quick.

She shifted into her fox form while leaping to the top of a free-standing armoire.

With the bottle in her teeth, she appeared to be snarling at me.

"Give it back," I said.

She flipped the bottle into the air, and grabbed it in her hand, in human form again, sprawled horizontally in the small space between the armoire and the ceiling.

Something surprised me about her appearance. The towel she'd been wearing was gone, and she was dressed in underwear and a dress slip. Her hair, which had been dripping wet, was now dry. Messy, but dry.

Shifting into her fox form usually caused her clothing to get lost or mixed up. I'd never seen her use her powers to get dressed. She was growing more powerful and clever by the day.

"Very impressive," I said. "How exactly did you get clothes on?"

"Trade secret," she said.

"Did Pawpaw teach you that trick?"

Her hazel eyes sparkled. Yes. Her grandfather—my fox shifter father—had dropped a few tricks on his last visit.

WILDS OF WISTERIA

Wisteria Witches Mysteries

BOOK #16

ANGELA PEPPER

She read the label on the drugstore-brand cough syrup, then scolded, "Mom! This is full of disgusting chemicals!"

I stood on my tiptoes and grabbed the bottle back from my daughter.

"Too late," she said. "I already read the label. It's full of toxins, plus it says it's for occasional use."

"I read the label, too," I said, which wasn't true. "And I only use it on occasion... like on occasions where I can't sleep."

"Why can't you—"

The piercing cries of a healthy baby boy came through the beige wall next to us.

Zoey shifted back into fox form, and jumped off the armoire in a flash of red fur.

She trotted out of the room, calling out to the other people in the house with fox yips.

YIP-YIP-YIP.

Those yips, in that tone meant, "I've got the baby."

The baby's crying stopped immediately. Babies love familiar family members, and adorable fuzzy pets. My daughter could appear as both. Whether in human or fox form, she could soothe the baby in no time.

The baby was Fyrsil Fung, our newest family member. He was the offspring of my aunt, Zinnia Riddle, and her soon-to-be-husband, Ethan Fung.

There were more yips on the other side of the wall, then the sound of her human voice, singing a song of her own making.

Parental pride burst in my chest. She was so patient with the little guy. I'd been younger than she was now when I'd had a full-time baby of my own, but it still impressed me that someone her age could handle so many responsibilities—not to mention diaper changes—without complaint.

There was a knock-knock on the wall between us, and in a muffled voice, my daughter said, "I think you're officially running late, Mom."

I checked the time.

She was right, as usual.

I was in danger of making us late for my aunt's wedding—a wedding that most of us considered well overdue.

I'd be late, just like I had been late for Zoey's high school graduation. And multiple Sunday dinners with the family. And everything else I'd been invited to over the last twelve months.

My constant tardiness had even gotten back to my vampire mother. She was still traveling the world, staying in mansions with her famous undead friends. She hadn't tired of her young protege Xavier Batista, her companion. The other members of my coven were casually betting on whether she was going to adopt Xavier or marry him. The age gap only made the local witches more intrigued. With my mother, an age gap would never have kept her off a man she wanted, but I also knew her taste in men, and her taste was *not* Xavier. Their friendship was more like mother and son, and in spite of my jealousy—a feeling that surprised me—I was happy for them that they had each other. Or so I said to anyone who asked.

Why wouldn't I be happy she had a new son who wanted to be around her? A good person wants their loved ones to be happy. The world can be a lonely place if you're on your own.

My phone rang.

It was my mother.

Speak of the vampire.

Without so much as a hello, she demanded, "What's this about you not being ready for Zinnia's wedding?"

"I would be ready if people would stop ransacking my room, questioning me about my sleep habits, and phoning me."

"Honestly, Zarabella, must you always be so dramatic?" In a quieter tone, away from the phone, she said, "Of course it's happy hour. Why don't you check that clock on the wall? If you can't read the numbers, try removing that colorful paper money someone left stuck to it."

"Mom, I thought you stopped drinking."

"I did no such thing. I simply trimmed it back to one day per week."

"Mm hmm."

"Don't be snippy with me. I told you before, and I'll tell you again. Either move away from that little town of yours or don't. But don't punish everyone else for your indecision by moping around."

"I'm not moping around!"

"It's past noon, and you're still in pajamas."

How did she know what I was wearing?

I ran to the window and yanked open the curtains.

Sitting on the ledge on the other side of the glass was a blue jay. It had been peeping at me through the crack in the curtains. It continued to stare at me, unperturbed.

I knelt down and stared into its beady eyes.

"Stop spying on me," I said into the phone—the bird familiar relayed mostly visual information. It could be used for audio, but not nearly as easily as a phone.

"Someone needs to keep an eye on you," said the voice on the phone. "Speaking of eyes, why are yours so puffy? You look like a passport photo, but in real life."

I ended the phone call, waved goodbye via the blue jay, and closed the curtains.

If Zirconia Cristata Riddle wanted to get on my nerves, she'd have to spring for airfare. Then I would tell her in person that she was wrong about my indecision. I was fully committed to my life in Wisteria. I just needed time to get back to my usual speed.

But I would make more of an effort to be punctual, to act like I wanted to be there.

Starting today.

I skipped the shower—it would only make me later—and cast a dry shampoo spell over my whole body.

Was it supposed to tingle? Did that mean it was working? I hoped so.

I yanked open the doors of the armoire, which served as the only closet in the room.

The armoire burped.

Uh... the armoire burped?

I closed the doors carefully, then opened them again.

Another burp.

My first suspect was our local wyvern.

"Ribbons, is that you?"

No response, telepathic or otherwise.

I cast a threat detection spell. It only illuminated the clothes hanging in the armoire. There were no creatures, wyverns or otherwise, inside.

The only thing that looked different from the last time I'd been in there was something sitting at the bottom.

It was a cardboard box, and it was labeled "Nun-Chuks and Nun Habits."

The handwriting was my own, which shouldn't have been too concerning, except I recognized this specific box, and this box *didn't exist*.

The last time I'd seen that box, it had contained the old thrift store pots and pans I'd moved to Wisteria with. The pots and pans I'd unpacked, and used daily, right up until they'd been lost, along with everything else in the house, thanks to the explosion.

How could the box be here?

My shoulders tensed up. They were still tingling from the dry shampoo spell, so my tension was extra noticeable.

I used my thumbnail to break the seal of the tape, then I slowly lifted the cardboard flaps.

A scent rose up. Not a magical one. Just the smell of colored sculpting clay.

6

I relaxed my shoulders.

What a silly goose I was, getting worked up about a mysterious box that didn't exist.

I was wrong about the pots and pans. This particular box had never contained kitchen cookery, so I hadn't bothered to unpack it two years earlier. These were my craft supplies, exactly as I'd packed them so many moons ago.

As for the Nun-Chuks and Nun Habits label, I'd played a little moving trick on myself, labeling my boxes with nonsense labels so I'd be forced to unpack every single one of them instead of just the basics.

Obviously it hadn't worked.

I dug through yarn, glue, googly eyes, and more.

The tingling of the dry shampoo worsened. Was I being watched? I checked the window. My mother's blue jay spy had flown away.

How could my crafting stuff be there?

Even if I hadn't unpacked the box—even if I'd left it unopened in the attic, it would have been lost with everything else.

I pulled out a ball of elastic bands, and gave it a bounce.

Still springy.

There had to be a logical explanation.

Maybe the box had been out on loan to my coworker who loved crafts—Kathy Carmichael. Maybe she'd returned it earlier that day, when I'd been comfortably ensconced in my cough syrup nap.

Since I didn't have time to ponder every single weird thing that happened in my life—especially not that afternoon—I kicked the box back to the shadowy recesses of the armoire, grabbed my bridesmaid gown, and got dressed.

I put the final pin in my hair using a hair-tidying spell as I gently knocked on the door to Zoey's room. It was Ethan's study, which he'd allowed her to take over temporarily. I was in the guest room, which hadn't yet received my aunt's decorating touch. The decor in the room was actually a point of contention between the two. And good for them. They had one more thing to iron out once they were married—something with low stakes they could use as a practice run for conflict resolution before bigger calamities happened. Not that I wanted them to experience calamities, but they were inevitable, even for people who weren't supernatural.

"Zoey?" I knocked again. "I'm here to help you finish your hair. I know you can do it yourself, but soon you'll be off to college, and I'll miss out, I mean you'll miss out..."

There was no answer.

I opened the door. The room was empty. She'd folded the wall bed back into the wall, and it didn't even look like a bedroom at all, with nothing but Ethan Fung's desk visible.

The room darkened, as a cloud passed over the sun outside.

The house was incredibly still and quiet, like a tomb. This was the house without any people in it. This was what the house was like when we were out for the day, or when we ceased to exist. Left like this, it would only take a few years for the rain to come in from above, and the ivy to come in from the sides, and then the woodland creatures...

A horn honked outside.

I ran to the window and looked out.

A long, black limousine was parked in front of the house.

The house was empty because Zoey and Fyrsil were already waiting in the back.

I ran outside barefoot, holding my shoes in my hand, extremely aware of my tardiness.

"It was Gigi," I said as I climbed into the limousine. "Gigi phoned, and she had one of her dirty birds doing dirty deeds, peeping in my window."

Zoey gave me a flat look.

"It was Gigi," I said again.

"Oh. Well, I'm sure everyone at the wedding will understand us starting late if you just explain to them that a *bird* was looking in your window."

"It doesn't sound like a good reason when you say it like that."

"No? What if we exaggerate, and make it two birds? Two turtle doves."

"I don't like your attitude today."

She turned and looked out the limousine window. We were rolling slowly through the neighborhood Ethan Fung had chosen for his house. It was a new suburb on the edge of town, with extra-large lots and big houses with ample room around them and absolutely no character. You really see the value of a porch when you're in a spooky suburb where residents act like it's a crime to be seen on the front side of your home.

My daughter had three loose tendrils of hair—the perfect number to cast a hair-tidying spell on.

Magic has a mind of its own, and magic loves the number three.

I reached for them.

She swatted my hand away like it was a weapon.

I held my palm out. "You've got three loose curls. Let me fix them for you."

"Leave them alone," she said. "Fyrsil likes to have a few curls to play with."

"Babies pull on hair. They yank. Hard. That's why so many new moms cut their hair short."

"I don't mind." She leaned over the baby, who was buckled into his car seat. He was a wily wriggler, so we'd had to reinforce the safety straps.

Fyrsil grabbed one of the loose red tendrils in his chubby fist, and gave it the gentlest of tugs.

Zoey glanced my way. "See? He's just a baby. He won't hurt me."

I snorted loud enough to startle him. He stared at me with big eyes and an open mouth, sucking in air to let out a wail.

"Tsshh," Zoey said, distracting him with her fingers.

He didn't wail after all. Our limousine continued on its course, gently rocking us from side to side, which most babies found soothing, including our new family member.

"You're okay," Zoey cooed at the baby. "Cousin Zara makes funny noises sometimes. Like a zoo animal."

"Don't say that."

"Then don't make animal noises."

"Not that. I mean don't say that I'm his *cousin*."

She arched one eyebrow at me.

"It's not normal," I said. "Our age gap is too wide. When we introduce ourselves as cousins, people have all sorts of questions and then corrections. For conversational purposes, I'm his *auntie*. I've always wanted to be an auntie."

She blinked repeatedly. "It's not normal? *Normal?*" More blinks. "Who are you, and what have you done to my mother? Since when did you ever, for a single minute, want to be normal?"

"I know, I know. It turns out normal isn't just a setting on the dishwasher. It's also... a way of saying that... well..."

"Yes?"

I reluctantly spat out a conclusion I'd been grappling with recently.

"It's also a way of saying that you don't always have to be difficult for the sake of being difficult."

Zoey looked puzzled as she wiped spittle off the baby's chin. She really was wonderful with him. He would miss her so much when she left for college in the fall. It wouldn't be fair to him. She ought to stay in town a few more years. For Fyrsil's sake.

"I think you're trying to trick me," Zoey said without meeting my gaze. "I think you're lying about trying to be normal."

"Lying? I beg your pardon?"

"Maybe not lying. Just being selective with your word choice."

"Are you trying to hurt my feelings?"

As I said the words, I heard my mother in my voice, and it echoed in my head. *Are you trying to hurt my feelings?* It was something she always said, as though me just being myself was all about finding new ways to upset her.

My daughter frowned. "I think... you're trying to guilt me into staying here, and I wish you wouldn't, because I don't want there to be an undercurrent of bad blood between us when I do leave."

"I didn't use the word normal to *trick* you. My word is my bond, it was not premeditated."

She appeared to be unconvinced.

I shrugged. "Maybe it was subconscious. Or maybe you finally got to me. All these years of you trying to get me to be normal have finally paid off. It's a shame you don't have a younger sibling who will benefit from your hard work. It's a shame you won't be around to enjoy the fruits of your labor."

"And here we go with the guilt trip." She made faces at Fyrsil, pretended to nibble on his fat cheeks, then baby-talked to him, "Auntie Zaza is a funny lady. You love Auntie Zaza, don't you?"

"Zaza? Really? Do you think Zaza is so much easier for a baby to say than Zara?"

Fyrsil looked at me and said, "Zaza."

I gasped in surprise and delight. He'd not started speaking yet. This was a magical moment. His first word was... my name!

"Zaza," he said again, clear as a bell. "Zaza!"

Zoey clapped her hand over his mouth. He happily babbled against her fingers.

"Oh, no," Zoey said. "We can't tell anyone about this."

"He's only ten months old, Zoey. This is good news. I hate to say this, because you were a wondrous child, perfect in every way, but you weren't saying anything that sounded like a word or a name until you were a rather embarrassing fifteen months old."

"But he should be saying Mama, or Dada, or the name of anyone but you."

"Anyone but me? What's that supposed to mean? I take care of him. I take my turns. You know. When nobody else is taking care of him. When it's... my turn."

She fidgeted with his clothing, a tiny tuxedo that was only staying clean thanks to some spellwork by the whole coven.

She said, "Maybe we imagined him saying it. Or maybe he's already forgotten. Fyrsil, can you say Mama? Mama?"

She pulled her fingers away from his mouth.

He gave her a long, steady look, then said, "Zaza."

"It's my fault," Zoey said glumly. "I've been talking to him about you. He learned it from me."

"What do you mean, you've been talking to him about me?"

Her cheeks flushed. "Never mind."

"Zaza," he said again.

"Zara," I said. "With an R."

"Zaza," he said. "Zaza. With an R."

Zoey looked like she might start crying. "Oh, Mom, you have to stop. They're not going to like this. Auntie Z has had such a hard time, and the house is so crowded. I think this could put her over the edge."

"The only way to get him to stop is to teach him swear words," I said. "Do you want that?"

"No."

"Zaza," he whispered with a grin.

"Shh," I said to him. "Let's keep this one under wraps, kiddo. Let's work on it for a few more days before we surprise your parents, okay?"

One of his eyes closed without the other one. Did he just wink at me?

The limousine stopped.

We were picking up another bridesmaid, or, as we had been calling her, the Maid of Dishonour.

It was Margaret Mills, my aunt's best friend and my fellow coven member.

She was standing on the curb, and entered the limousine while chewing us out for being late.

Zoey and I rolled our eyes at each other.

It was just like a person who was typically fifteen minutes late herself to be upset when someone else was running behind by a few minutes.

Margaret's wiry hair was springing with unfocused magical energy.

I hoped we would all be able to get through the big wedding day without casting spells on each other.

CHAPTER 2

The wedding would be at an unconventional venue: Wisteria City Hall.

It had started as a joke, with both Chief Fung and my aunt threatening to elope at City Hall whenever anyone pressed for details. But then someone had suggested they look into the new facilities on the third floor.

The third floor had been home to a board room, which the Permit Department used to discuss reports about other reports. The room, however, had recently been relocated to another floor, and the space was merged with the former offices of the Property Taxes Arrears Collection Services. That department was moving out of the building and across town to an undisclosed location due to ongoing turf wars with another undisclosed department.

This new third floor space was available for special events, and it was the exact right size for a not-small-but-not-large wedding.

I only mention all the building details for the benefit of those of you who are fascinated by goings-ons at our local municipal buildings. Your tax dollars at work!

Our limousine arrived at City Hall.

We stepped out, and Zoey took Fyrsil—still clean and handsome in his tiny tuxedo—to join the rest of the

15

wedding party on the ground floor, in the pre-wedding staging area.

They'd taken over the whole Permit Department, since it was the only other extra space in the building that didn't require a special events permit to have been filed months in advance. The WPD required, oddly enough, a post-use permit, which I guess makes it technically more of an apology than a request. That's all I know about that, so don't ask.

Margaret Mills and I went up to the third floor to check on the premises.

Margaret looked very round in her bridesmaid dress, despite it having been given extra darts by a tailor.

Margaret wasn't overweight, just short and solid. The beige fabric of her bridesmaid dress merged indistinctly with her frizzy hair that was currently tinted a nebulous shade that was midway between gray and brown, a sort of beige.

She looked like a real force of nature—a tumbleweed —as she charged around the newly-remodeled banquet room, tut-tutting about table placement and linens.

"Zara, did you ever think you'd see this day?"

"They did a nice job," I said of the renovation contractors. "But I can't compare, since I don't know how it looked before. I always paid my property taxes on time, or at least close enough that I didn't get in trouble with Collection Services."

"Not that. I mean did you think you'd ever see Zinnia as a blushing bride?"

"I'm not so sure *blushing* is the right word to describe Zinnia."

"It's a shame your mother couldn't make it. Probably for the best. Zirconia is always taking the credit for talking sense into Zinnia about the marriage, even though everyone knows it was me." Margaret puffed up her chest, looking even more like a tumbleweed. "I know Zinnia better than she knows herself. I knew she was pregnant with the little bear cub before anyone did."

That wasn't true, but I let it go.

"Yes, it is true," Margaret said. "I knew way before you did."

Margaret had read my mind, which was such a Margaret thing to do. She claimed that she had no control over it, and that she wished she wasn't psychic at all. She didn't like hearing other people's voices in her head. She tried to keep her appearance drab and neutral to avoid unwanted comments from random strangers. *Everyone thinks they're a judge on a reality TV show*, she'd told me more than once.

I kept my head down, and my mind on my bridesmaid duties. I had nothing to hide, but I still didn't want my thoughts wandering over to Margaret's head.

I checked that the seating arrangements matched the wedding organizer's plans.

"People are just going to sit wherever they want," Margaret said with a huff. "That's how people are. Nobody respects rules anymore."

So much for me keeping her out of my head.

I wondered how long Margaret would keep reading my mind telepathically, and talking to me as though we were having a normal two-way conversation.

"All day and all night," Margaret said.

I could have some fun with this. I focused all my imagination on a visual thought: a big pitcher of fresh, cold lemonade.

"Stop making me thirsty," Margaret said, then "I smell something."

I imagined the scent of fresh lemons, limes, grapefruit, oranges, and even bergamot.

"Not your imaginary lemonade," Margaret said. "I smell cheap cough syrup." She stared at me.

Cheap? It wasn't that cheap.

"You need a boyfriend," Margaret said. "You'll sleep much better with something warm beside you other than a cat."

How dare she speak that way about Boa?! And besides, the cat had taken to sleeping in the nursery, on her special pillow that was heated by electricity. We'd had to purchase it to keep her out of the crib and off of the warm baby. We trusted her not to harm him, but it triggered something in us to walk in and see her sprawled over him, disrespecting his personal space the way she did ours.

Maybe what I needed was another cat—one who was loyal only to me.

Margaret said, "If you want someone loyal, Barry has a new intern I can introduce you to."

Barry was Margaret's boyfriend, or boyfriends. He was two genius inventor brothers who shared a single body.

Margaret went on. "He's not much to look at, and he's terrified of all shadows that are fifty percent longer than their source objects, but he's very loyal, and completely unable to detect sarcasm. He'd be perfect for you."

I was speechless—at the mouth level. Margaret Mills was as good a matchmaker as she was a caring friend.

She stomped one hoof-like boot on the floor indignantly. "And that's exactly the kind of sarcasm that would fly right over his head."

I shook my head. What would my family ever do without her?

"You'd be short one Matron of Dishonor," she said with a wink.

More like short one *short* Matron of Dishonor.

She put her finger in the air. "I let you have that short joke, Zara. I set you up on purpose with my word choice. I used to do improv, you know. In college. Our troupe was the MacGuffins, and we were very good. We could have toured the world."

I wiped some dark lint off a tablecloth. A world-famous improv group? They'd have been the first.

"I was funny before I had kids," Margaret said. "Don't make that horrible face at me."

What horrible face? I thought my makeup was very tasteful.

"That long, sad face," she said. "The poor-old-me face. The face that looks like the physical embodiment of all that sighing you do lately. Both of which are putting a real dampener on the coven's energy. I didn't want to say anything, but now's as good a time as any." She huffed up her tumbleweed chest and put her hands on her hips. "The coven is planning an intervention for you."

I stopped straightening up the tables, and stared at her.

Margaret's frizzy hair began moving with a mind of its own, the way it did sometimes. The beige frizz on her forehead gathered itself together into a single curl that shot straight out, like a rhino horn.

An intervention? For me? That made no sense. I'd gone through a few bottles of cough syrup lately, and before that I'd been ordering frozen cheesecake delivered on a subscription service, but the other witches regularly did so much worse.

"It's about your long face," Margaret said.

That didn't sound like the sort of thing people had interventions for.

"They're worried that you might conjure one of those buttfaced Pain-Body Cacodemons, like your aunt did."

I would never intentionally do such a thing.

"That's the thing about those critters," Margaret said. "They don't care about your intentions. You've seen one. It doesn't even care about symmetry. It had five paws, or seven, depending on if you count the warty things. And if there's one thing they're drawn to, it's a DITD Witch."

I didn't know what she meant.

"A Down-in-the-Dumps Witch," she said with an eyeroll, as though I should have known what she meant.

Now she was just making things up to irritate me. Had she been talking to my mother? Was she acting on someone's behalf?

Margret waved a hand, dismissing my unspoken suspicion.

"If anyone at the coven asks why I went ahead and talked to you on my own, tell them you tortured it out of me," Margaret said.

I flexed my fingers. Did she want me to leave bruises to corroborate her story?

"Zara, you need help," Margaret said, her irritating voice sounding almost friendly.

I didn't need help.

"You do," Margaret said. "It's practically been two years since..."

Since what? *Say it.*

Her expression faltered.

I dropped away the thin veil of privacy that had been shielding her from my next layer of thoughts, my innermost feelings.

The iron gates opened, and I released the deep, dark core of grief and blackness that was always at the center of me now, weighty like the heavy metals at the center of the planet.

Margaret's eyes glistened. Her eyelids puffed. Her hair coiled and uncoiled.

Another wave of dark matter flowed from me to her over her psychic hotline.

She grew shorter, wider. The seams of her wedding dress made a noise under the strain.

Something changed inside me. A light pierced in through cracks.

Relief.

It was a relief to let her have my pain.

Was this what she wanted? Was this the intervention?

Sign me up. She could have all of it.

Softly, she said my name.

"Zara."

Then sternly.

"Zara!"

I felt my name more than I heard it. My pulse was rushing in my ears.

Along with the relief, something else was coming unstuck at the bottom of my soul.

I wouldn't be able to get through the day if I let it all out.

I had to leave.

Could I leave? Would I curse us both if I walked out feeling how I did?

Margaret held up a finger, indicating for me to hold on a moment.

She performed a counterhex, and gently separated us by the psychic tether that had formed.

As the darkness whipped back into me like a cursed yo-yo, Margaret returned to her regular size. She was unharmed, but ashen-faced.

"Go get some fresh air," she said. "I'll finish checking the place settings by myself."

Something had changed between us.

She had become a witness to my pain, to the grief that had not yet resolved.

I didn't want to ask, but my soul did.

How bad was it? Would a buttfaced Pain-Body Cacodemon be coming for me? Was I putting the whole coven in danger, the way Zinnia had?

"I don't know," Margaret said. "But we've bought you some time."

A tear leaked out her eye.

Now I felt bad for giving her some of my darkness.

She pulled a cloth handkerchief from her bra—it was a spell.

"It's okay." She dabbed her eye, and waved for me to go. "If anyone asks, I'll tell them these are happy tears. It's a wedding, after all. A beautiful day."

I turned and left before I could ruin everything.

If I didn't get myself together, people were going to start wishing I would be even more late for things. Late enough that I missed them entirely.

CHAPTER 3

I paced up and down the empty stairwell with my thoughts.

Margaret Mills could have been more sensitive, but she had made her point. I wasn't dealing with my grief as well as I could be.

Zonking myself with cough syrup to sleep as much as possible wasn't the answer. Whenever I woke up, everything returned.

Spreading my pain out by making others miserable didn't make me feel better, either. It simply compounded my Survivor's Guilt with even more guilt.

My coping methods had been failures.

On my third time up the stairs, my head cleared. The answer was suddenly obvious.

I just had to take better care of myself.

I could start by eating, since I couldn't remember the last meal I'd had that wasn't consumed after dark, in bed.

Where could I find food? I didn't dare leave City Hall without permission. I was still in my uniform, and officially on duty as a bridesmaid.

Zoey had an assortment of snacks with her, but they were for the baby. As much as I liked a handful of O-shaped cereal now and then, it wasn't worth getting my hand slapped.

I exited the stairwell and went directly to the building's cafeteria. Their food was fast and cheap, bordering on experimental, but I had limited options.

Zara tries to be a good bridesmaid. Zara keeps her phone and her fireballs fully charged at all times on the Big Day.

I grabbed a cafeteria tray, got in line, and told the woman in the hairnet to dish me up "as many carbohydrates as it's legal to serve one person."

She gave me a stack of macaroni and cheese casserole with a side of chocolate-dipped mini breadsticks. Ah, chocolate-dipped mini breadsticks. The mid-day nap inducer I didn't know I needed.

The food had an excellent sedative effect, as intended.

I would balance it out later with some protein, maybe a hearty stew, but this was a start. I was eating in the light of day, and using utensils.

One hour and a second helping of chocolate-dipped mini breadsticks later, I was calm and collected for my aunt's nuptials.

I met up with the others on the ground floor offices of the Permits Department.

My aunt's coworker, Dawna Jones, swiveled around on her office chair and said to me, "Oh, hey Margaret. You're needed on the third floor."

"Dawna, it's me, Zara."

She did a double take. "Girl, I was just messing with you," she said with a fake laugh.

"You don't need to spare my feelings by lying. There's no mirror down here, so you have to be my mirror. Do I look like a tumbleweed?"

Dawna picked up a deck of cards and shuffled it nervously rather than answer. She was also a bridesmaid, and wore the same dress.

Dawna Jones and I had very different appearances. Her skin tone was as dark as mine was pale, but the dress wasn't flattering on her coloring, either. What skin tone was the dress made for, anyway? Blue?

Gavin Gorman, who was sitting across from her in his usual work chair, said, "Ladies, if the look you're going for as a bridal party is Wild West, then you've succeeded, because you both look like tumbleweeds."

Dawna kept her eyes down as she tossed a series of playing cards across her desk in a quick pattern.

"It's a curse," Dawna said, interpreting the cards as only a card mage could. "This is bad news. Something could happen and ruin the wedding. What are we going to do?"

"Ask the cards," Gavin said.

She dealt out more. "Oh. That's weird. Zinnia isn't cursed at all, or the Chief. It's just us, the bridesmaids."

Just then, there was a loud groan from the former office of Karl Kormac.

It was followed by a HARUMPH, and then Karl Kormac emerged from his former office, which was still basically his office.

Karl was a sprite, like my coworker Kathy, his first cousin. I received regular updates about Karl from both my aunt and Kathy.

The older man had finally turned sixty-five and taken the retirement he'd talked about so frequently. However, just like his diet of imported junk food, retirement didn't agree with him. He dropped into the office all the time, snooping through the paperwork on other people's desks, and then commandeering their most complex projects so he had an excuse to keep coming in.

Karl fit the stereotypical image of a male sprite from the illustrations in the magical tomes. He was blustery and full of gas, never quite fitting into his ill-fitting suits, which were both too small and too large at the same time.

Karl looked over Dawna's cards, which were just regular playing cards, and said, "What's this about a curse?"

"Look at us," Dawna said. She got up and stood beside me. "We look like tumbleweeds, boss. Who did this to us? Do you know anyone who'd want to stop this wedding from happening?"

Her former boss pulled his brown trousers up high over his belly.

"You girls are overreacting as usual," he said. "This whole department has been a mess since I retired. Between the hysterical womenfolk and all the unauthorized overtime, I'm surprised we haven't been shut down and moved across town."

Gavin chimed in with, "The womenfolk around here do get hysterical, boss."

Karl rubbed all of his chins thoughtfully. "Ladies, did those dresses come from a department store?"

"Of course they did," Dawna said. "That's the only way to get the same dress in different sizes."

"The wedding isn't cursed, but the dresses are," Karl Kormac said with all the authority of an older, respected sprite. "Everyone knows that. Even the nothing people know that." By nothing people, he meant non-supernaturals who knew about magic but couldn't practice it.

"I didn't know," Dawna said.

Karl let out a HARUMPH. "It affects eighty-seven percent of commercially-purchased bridesmaid dresses."

Dawna said, "Now that I think about it, that number seems low."

"I'll just un-curse us then," I said, quickly casting a minor anti-hex to take out some of the unflattering wrinkles.

"Don't," Karl said, but it was too late.

My spell inverted on its own—as spells occasionally do—and the wrinkles that should have disappeared spread out. The inversion had not been intentional, so technically it was what we called *bad juju*.

Dawna looked down at herself and said, "Eww!"

In frustration, I cast the anti-hex again with double power.

The wrinkles worsened. The bad juju was in full effect.

Dawna whimpered, "Someone have mercy and unzip me from this thing."

Gavin started toward her, hands ready, but she staved him off with a stern look.

The magic pooled in my palms, ready to go.

I broke out in a cold sweat.

Calm reason set in, and I let the magic dissipate, uncast.

That was a close one.

Every witch ought to know that the third time is the curse as often as it's the charm; if I'd cast that third spell, the wrinkles on the dresses might have spread to our faces.

I explained it all to Dawna, and apologized.

"Don't hex yourself up on my account," Dawna said. "If our dresses are the worst thing about this wedding, it will still be a better wedding than most of the ones I've been to. Remember when Carrot's genie fellow melted into a puddle..." She trailed off, presumably remembering that Carrot's fiance had once been closely connected to me. Not only had he been holding a torn-off piece of my soul when he melted into goo, but he was also the father of my daughter, the source of her genie powers.

"Oops," Dawna said, wincing.

Karl lost interest in our conversation. With a final HARUMPH, he slipped away, heading into Zinnia's office to snoop through her papers. He wasn't very sneaky about it, groaning as he sat on her chair and rummaged through her filing cabinets.

Gavin, who'd never stopped sucking up to his former boss, went to join the sprite in his snooping.

Once the two of us were alone in the main room of the open-plan office, Dawna gave me a sad look. "How are you doing, girl?"

I shrugged. "Margaret Mills gave me an intervention. She thinks my long, sad face is going to bring us all certain doom."

Dawna fidgeted with the neckline of her ugly tumbleweed dress.

"You know about the intervention," I said.

"Yeah, but there's nothing certain about the doom of the future," she said with a smirk. "Things will probably clear up for you, in time."

"What do you know about my future?"

She tried to hide her smile but couldn't.

"Dawna, have you seen something about me in one of your card readings?"

"Only that your fate line is about to intersect with someone else's."

"What? Who? How?"

"If I tell you, it might change things." She covered her lips with two very long, tumbleweed-colored fingernails. "I may have already said too much."

She turned back to the cards on her desk, shuffled them expertly, dealt them out yet again, then smirked at me as she mimed zipping her lips.

I pointed at her. "This is why you aren't invited to the coven. Nobody likes a smug psychic."

She laughed and gathered up her cards, unbothered.

The door to the office opened swiftly, and the wedding planner yelled at us to stop gossiping and get to our places.

CHAPTER 4

The wedding organizer was our fellow coven member, Maisy Nix.

Maisy was a striking woman, and the tallest of the witches at six feet two inches, or even more in heels.

She was instantly recognizable and well known around town, mostly as the owner of our local coffee chain, Dreamland Coffee.

The loss of our levitation powers had grounded Maisy's second job, the secret one, fighting forest fires from above, flying on her broomstick.

Since she liked to keep busy—most witches do—and didn't have any kids to chase around, she'd started a side business running special events, including the Riddle-Fung nuptials.

When I reported for duty on the third floor, Maisy looked over my dress, and grumbled under her breath that I was a walking disaster.

"It's a curse," I explained. "Karl Kormac says there's a known curse that affects commercially-made bridesmaids outfits."

She used her long, slender hands to manually press on the wrinkles, which only made them worse.

She tried her hands on Dawna's dress, and had the same result.

Maisy gave us both a shared dirty look—as though we'd done this on purpose—then turned on her heel and stormed off to be disappointed about something else.

Dawna and I giggled about our dress wrinkles—what can you do but laugh? We touched up each other's makeup, then got ready to walk to the altar in our assigned processional order.

Dawna was paired with her on-again-off-again boyfriend and coworker, Gavin. He looked impeccable in his tuxedo, though his pants were too snug as usual.

I didn't have an obvious counterpart, so Maisy had loaned me her own guy, groomsman Humphrey.

Humphrey was Maisy's pet—or boyfriend, or animal familiar, or whatever. He was a komodo dragon when he wasn't in his two-legged form, as he was today. The guy wasn't entirely human, yet he was a person, or close enough.

Humphrey gave me one of his sweet-but-blank smiles. He took my hand and placed it in the crook of his arm. It was a tender gesture that wasn't lost on me. I could feel his bicep through the suit jacket. I couldn't recall the last time I'd felt a man's bicep. It was nice enough.

When would I touch another nice bicep?

Dawna had said my fate line connected with someone else's, but the cards could be vague. The cards might have been referring to this moment, to me simply holding Humphrey's nice arm. It wasn't *not* a connection of fates.

Humphrey said, "Hello, pretty lady."

"Hello, handsome fellow," I said right back.

"We are friends."

"Yes, I suppose we are more than acquaintances by now."

"You are wearing the same dress as several other ladies."

"You have a keen eye, Humphrey."

"The only thing that makes the dresses look different is your bodies underneath them. I like your dress second best."

"Thanks for the honesty," I said. "It's almost as good as a compliment. You've cleaned up decently yourself, my fine fellow. You don't look at all like someone who eats dead flies off the windowsill like they're raisins."

"Shh. That is a secret."

"I won't tell anyone," I assured him.

Over by the altar, the classical musical quartet, which included my daughter on her harp, began playing the first song.

The music was ethereal, with only the occasional awkward note from the young musicians marking it as distinct from a prerecorded, professional track.

I watched my daughter's hands closely. She was making her awkward harp notes—the wrong ones—on purpose. She must have been doing it to fit in with the other three musicians, to not outshine them. I hoped they were more easily fooled than her mother.

The song reached a high point, lifting the spirits of everyone gathered for the celebration.

What a perfect moment in time this was. If only we could use a genie time bubble and freeze this moment to make it last.

The music was elegant, the air smelled of fresh flowers, and the whole venue sparkled and shimmered. It didn't even feel like we were inside City Hall, except for the view out of the windows, which faced a lush lawn and Pacific Spirit Forest beyond.

Maisy sent us the signal.

Humphrey and I proceeded down the aisle as planned. We took our places on the altar.

There were happy smiles all around, and a few sniffles in the audience.

Carrot Greyson was wiping her eyes. I caught her attention to give her a look of encouragement. It felt like my job. She and I had the unfortunate bond of being kinda-sorta widows together. She forced a toothy grin to let me know her tears might be happy ones.

The music swelled, every note perfection.

Margaret Mills walked up with Barry Blackstone at her side. Barry must have been nervous. His eyes lost coordination with each other. The two brothers who inhabited his body had to be fighting over some internal navigational controls. To his credit, his feet didn't falter.

Margaret made eye contact with me. This time, I shielded my mind against her psychic intrusions.

I hadn't communicated with her since our talk, but I hadn't stopped thinking about what she'd said. The others really had been planning an intervention, there was no doubt. Margaret only fibbed about the same things she lied to herself about—that she followed her own rules, was never late, and didn't deserve any of the punishments life threw her way. She could and would lie, but not to me about the coven.

She took her place beside me, her expression as stiff as the single rhino-horn curl on her forehead.

From the edge of the room, Maisy Nix gave us one enthusiastic thumb up over her clipboard. So far, so good.

The music stopped, and the silence felt sudden and eerie, as though everyone gathered had drawn in a breath at the same time.

The doors opened, revealing the beautiful bride.

The next song began. Zoey played all the right notes, as did the others.

Zinnia Riddle entered slowly. Step, pause. Step, pause.

She wore a shade of cream that glowed with soft undertones of green and gold. Her thick, red hair was swept up in a twisty, complicated style, and adorned with a covering that wasn't a veil or jewelry but something in between. Glittering gems and sparkles fell around her like rain.

She was accompanied by a gentleman in a perfect-fitting tux. Her father—my grandfather—had been gone for years, so she was accompanied by this man, whom I'd never met. He was Zinnia's former mentor.

And he was surprisingly dreamy. In the days leading up to the wedding, she'd described him to everyone as a "dear, old friend." I'd assumed he would be in his seventies, but this guy didn't look a day older than the groom.

I had a hard time taking my eyes off him. And the ladies seated on the rows of folding chairs were having similar difficulties, especially Carrot. Zinnia's mysterious mentor was, in the vernacular of the local teens, a *frosty cupcake*.

The ceremony started smoothly.

It continued to run smoothly.

To my absolute shock and amazement, nothing went wrong in the first half.

Sometimes in Wisteria, it felt like any crowd over a dozen people would result in someone getting murdered or turned into an inflatable groundhog-shaped parade float. But, to everyone's relief, the wedding vows didn't turn into warfare or even a spell-off.

The room grew warm from all the gathered bodies.

I actually nodded off, sleeping on my feet, until Margaret rudely elbowed me awake.

I sent her a psychic blast: *Time already for another intervention?*

Her rhino-horn forehead curl twisted to a sharp point as she blasted back: *It's your turn to sign the paperwork, you silly OCW.*

She cast an extra magical jolt to my buttocks to get me moving faster. This, in spite of the fact we all pledged to cast no magic whatsoever that day. Sure, I'd broken the rule trying to unjinx my dress, but that wasn't nearly as bad as what she'd done—in my opinion.

I paused before picking up the fancy fountain pen, earning two more magical bites on my backside. Those ones hadn't even come from Margaret. Maisy was giving me furious eyes over her clipboard.

The papers were largely symbolic, but with a few unusual additions—a stack of special permit applications from a few floors below.

I asked the room, "What's this one all about?" I knew a good opportunity for levity when I saw it, and my butt could handle a few zaps. "A Form 320PDQ? Is this anything like the 320QVC for selling copper-colored garments over broadcast television? I really ought to get my lawyer to look this over."

My joke failed to elicit any laughter from the crowd. Tough room.

The groom, Chief Ethan Fung, cleared his throat and gave me a *just-try-to-do-the-right-thing* look.

I'd seen that look on his face many times lately.

Since the Riddles vacated the Cerulean Lagoon Hotel, I'd been living in his house, under his rules. At first, I'd thought he was only *pretending* to be a stick-in-the-mud about hanging up jackets on your assigned hook by the door. However, he was surprisingly anal about home organization. He'd lived as a bachelor for many years, developing his own systems.

The Chief was having a tough time with not just one Riddle woman under his roof, but also two more. The three of us ladies had seriously tested his ability to adapt. He did have limits. The man could change into a giant Grizzly bear by magic, but he couldn't change his morning wakeup routine.

I didn't want to upset him again. Not like earlier in the week, when I'd "helped" him with his soup stock by pouring all of it down the sink while straining out the soft bones and mushy carrots.

I shut up, did the right thing, and signed all the papers as a witness. Today wasn't about me. None of the days had been about me for a long time.

Next, Gavin from the WPD stamped everything in triplicate.

Finally, the groom's elderly great-uncle—who was either 94 or 104, depending on who you asked—said a few words.

There was a huge cheer when the formal part of the day finished.

Energetically, everything flipped over and reset, like a giant hourglass.

Maisy Nix's coffee baristas swept in and changed the room. She'd closed both Dreamland Coffee locations for the day to secure her team for the event. They moved all the chairs to the tables, adjusted the lighting, and brought in even more flowers.

Maisy announced that the light luncheon would be served shortly.

She also said people were welcome to stay beyond the speeches and cake service, but the room had been rented for another wedding for six o'clock. The party, if it lasted, would have to move elsewhere. Maisy didn't spell it out, but everyone assumed we would make our way to Dreamland Coffee to close out the evening.

I checked the time. It wasn't anywhere near six, but I felt like I'd lived through a day and a half. As for staying up, I *could* imagine myself dancing all night—it wasn't unimaginable—but the idea did make my shoulders slump, like my arms were made of brass.

I gave myself a little pep talk.

Zara tries to be a good bridesmaid. Zara stays away from the wine, and paces herself appropriately. Zara does not shove the other single women out of the way when the bouquet is tossed.

I took my seat in my assigned spot for the luncheon, which was technically more of an early supper, as Gavin Gorman had already mentioned a dozen times.

The bridal party had been mixed in with the other guests—an idea of Maisy's—so I was at a table with strangers, far away from my daughter. Half of my table worked in construction, and knew my aunt through the permits department. The other half were administrators from the police department, plus a redheaded nurse, Shari Heminger.

Shari Heminger.

It hadn't clicked in before, but that explained why I'd been placed at that specific table. It was to keep an eye on Shari. The springy-bodied, freckle-faced nurse had been romantically linked to Ethan around the time he and my aunt were secretly... also linking. She'd been smitten with him at one time. Was she still?

In between the various speeches and toasts, Shari would turn and talk to the architects and builders at the table, and laugh louder than anyone in the room.

Yes, she was still in love with Ethan. Nobody laughed that loud at bad puns.

I watched her as she stared at my aunt with a deep longing to trade places with her.

This was partly my fault. There had been a day that I'd talked to Shari at the hospital. I'd foolishly encouraged her to pursue Ethan. Was it my fault she was still hung up on him? Partly. I'd used magic to encourage her.

Talk about a close call. What if my meddling had been successful? What if those two had fallen in love, and there had been no baby Fyrsil?

I was worrying through imaginary scenarios when there was a sudden crackle and pop on the back of my neck, like a static shock.

Magic.

Had there been any point at all in the whole coven agreeing to not cast magic at the wedding?

I scanned the room to see which witch had cast the forbidden spell.

Margaret Mills had her rhino-horn curl pointed at me as she mouthed *your face. Fix your face.*

As much as I hated having her psychic messages intrude my head, seeing her mouthing at me from across the room was just as bad.

What was wrong with my face? Had I been making the long, sad face that the other witches found so troubling? The intervention face?

I forced a smile.

After only a minute, the smile hurt my face and soured my mood.

Wasn't it enough that I was dressed like a tumbleweed? Did I have to look thrilled about it, too? This was ridiculous. A bridesmaid's duties, like those of a witch, or a mother, truly had no end.

For the next hour, I kept the painful smile on my face —not that anyone at the function would have noticed.

Friends, work colleagues, and even distant relatives milled around me as though I was invisible.

And why wouldn't they?

The star of the afternoon was my aunt, the newlywed, and her very proud husband. In third place was Fyrsil, whose baby tuxedo was still clean, and who babbled happily as he was passed around and squeezed.

Everything was going exactly how it should.

Nothing about the day was about me, the beige tumbleweed. Not boring, cursed, trouble-causing me. People were wise to ignore me. I was, after all, notorious for leaving a trail of destruction behind me wherever I went.

I got up and wandered over to the punch bowl.

Pro tip: If you're feeling sorry for yourself for being ignored at a social function, you can always mingle with other malcontents near the punch bowl.

I stood by the punch, and watched everyone as though behind a wall of thick, bulletproof glass.

Aunt Zinnia looked so lovely in her dress, which fit perfectly. It must have been drawing fit magic from the inverse of the hex on the bridesmaid dresses. That actually made a lot of sense. Nobody cursed anything for no good reason.

Seeing her looking so radiant on her special day made me painfully happy for her and also equally sad for myself.

The photographer turned his lens on me. I self-consciously smiled harder.

Zara tries to be a good niece. Zara knows there's nothing less pretty than a single woman sulking around at another woman's wedding.

Another single woman, Shari Heminger came over and joined me at the punch bowl.

Shari was, objectively speaking, a ten-out-of-ten, a very attractive redhead. She was a nurse, too, so she had that caring energy around her.

"I'm so thirsty," she said as she filled a cup.

Of course she was, after all that extra-loud laughing at the table to convince everyone she wasn't still hung up on Ethan Fung.

She handed me the first cup, then filled her own.

"Penny for your thoughts," she said, her faux-serious tone sounding exactly like Bentley's genuinely-serious tone when he had asked the question many times.

For an instant, it was as though he was there with us, channeling through Shari.

I snapped at her, "No!"

She recoiled, and turned to go.

"Wait," I said. "I'm sorry, Shari. I didn't mean to snap like that. It's just that *penny for your thoughts* is something... someone used to say to me."

She stayed, but didn't look too comfortable about it. "Was it that detective guy you were dating? The mysterious one?"

I nodded.

"What was his deal, anyway? I used to see him feeding the blue jays in the park."

"Theodore Bentley was a friend to all the woodland creatures. He kept peanuts in his pockets at all times."

"I haven't seen him around. Did he get transferred?"

"Something like that."

We sipped our punch.

"This is a nice wedding," Shari said. "I'm so happy for Ethan. He's such a good guy."

"Are you happy for him? Really?"

She shrugged. "If you love something, set it free." She gave me a coy smile. "Have you ever had Dawna Jones do a tarot card reading for you?"

"Tarot? You don't believe in stuff like that, do you? It's all superstitious nonsense."

She shrugged again. "It makes as much sense as anything in this crazy world."

"And what did Dawna's tarot cards tell you?"

"That my life path is going to cross with someone else's life path soon."

I snorted. Was Dawna giving that reading to everyone, or just the single women in need of hope?

"Dawna's the real deal," Shari said. "Nobody in this town can get a winning scratch-off ticket because they always go to her."

"She's lucky, all right, but that woo-woo she gave you about paths crossing is pretty generic."

The ten-out-of-ten redhead looked down, blushing. "I know it's silly, but I think being here today, seeing Ethan and Zinnia so in love, and everyone gathered together... I feel like I can believe in love again." She glanced up and held eye contact with me. "What do you think? Is love real?"

"Is love real? *What do I think?* I'm not really the thinker. That's my daughter's job, but..." I swirled my punch, oxidizing it to release the scent of an unexpected magical ingredient: alcohol. "Shari, I *think* this punch has been spiked with rum, and vodka, and possibly something else." I took another sip. "Is that creme de menthe? What kind of monster would spike a punch with creme de menthe?"

"I know," Shari said, smiling. "The catering is genius."

"This is a Humphrey move," I said. "His tastebuds aren't like ours. He's so weird about flavors."

"Weird but good. Your friend Maisy is going to get so much business from this." She rubbed the rim of her glass with her finger. "Speaking of Maisy, and her friend Humphrey, what's his deal?"

"Humphrey? Trust me. You don't want to know. Plus he very much belongs to Maisy, if you catch my drift."

"Oh, I know that. I was just wondering if he had a brother, or a cousin. There's something so unique about him. So simple, and pure."

"He's unique, all right. Even if we did find a cousin, since when do you trust me as a matchmaker? I'm the one who encouraged you to go after Ethan, and look where that got you."

"Every story has a happy ending, eventually."

Really? Every story? As a librarian, I happened to know that was not true at all. But I knew she didn't mean it literally.

Shari said, "Are you moving out this month or next? I just moved apartments, and it was terrible trying to find a place."

"What do you mean? You know something about us moving? Is the Chief looking at bigger places? We could use another bathroom."

"I saw Ethan for his physical workup at the hospital last week. He said he felt really guilty about kicking you out of his house. That's probably why his stomach ulcer is acting up."

He was kicking me out of his house? This was news to me. As was this stomach ulcer of his.

I replied, "Oh, did he? Sounds like you two had quite an informative chat."

"Sorry if that was confidential," Shari said. "I blame this punch, and whatever's in it, for giving me loose lips." She wavered from side to side, mildly inebriated. "I should get back to our seats. I'm so glad we're at the fun table. Are you coming now?"

"That depends. Do you think anyone would miss me if I didn't return at all? If I turned myself into a bat and flew out of here?"

She laughed, as though I'd made a joke and not a serious hypothetical proposition. Yet she hadn't laughed earlier that afternoon, when I actually had made a joke over the paperwork. Too little, too late.

I handed her my mug of boozy punch.

"Babysit my drink for me, and we'll talk later."

Her eyes brightened. "Ooh, girl talk!"

"Girl talk," I agreed.

She went back to our table of people who could only be considered "fun" when compared to hospital patients at death's door. Perspective was everything.

And I left the party.

Not after transforming myself into a bat—I didn't have even half the ingredients for that spell, plus creme de menthe made my Witch Tongue unreliable.

I left as myself, Zara Riddle, woman in search of an apartment for rent.

CHAPTER 5

It was late afternoon in July, so of course it was sunny outside, but the brightness still surprised me. I felt the same disorientation I did walking out of a movie matinee, and I hadn't even eaten my weight in buttered popcorn.

I also sneezed a dozen times.

Was that new? A dozen sneezes was excessive. Was this a side effect of the cough syrup? Had it interacted with the creme de menthe from the punch? Maybe I did need an intervention.

A tiny, dirty tornado—a dust devil—formed over a manhole cover on the street. It swirled toward me, then passed over me, getting grit in my eyes and causing a second round of sneezes.

The manhole cover lifted up, and a town employee emerged in his reflective safety gear, coughing. He looked around, his gaze passing over me without stopping, and then he went back down into the hole, closing it behind him.

No more dust appeared, let alone a dust devil.

It was odd, but not anything that warranted my meddling, so I turned and walked away.

The sun warmed my bare arms and the top of my head as I wandered over to the back lawn.

Here was the solution to my eviction. The lawn!

Not literally, but I would sit in the sunshine today, and naturally recharge while I thought of something.

Once I figured out my housing situation, I would be a dutiful bridesmaid, reporting back inside for whatever disaster was almost certainly unfolding by now. Probably dirt devils sweeping through the third floor. Fingers crossed the cake would be okay.

My dress bared my shoulders, and the sunshine felt like bliss on that area that was usually covered. I settled back on the ticklish green grass, stretched out, and closed my eyes.

My dear, old friend Sleep took me for a magic carpet ride. I dreamed about the playing pieces from board games: plastic figurines, dominoes, and dice of all shapes and sizes.

I was rudely awakened by a man in a beret and camouflage clothing.

Seeing him looming over me was exactly as jarring as you might imagine. Why the camouflage? Was he in the military? Were we at war?

He had a French accent, and said, "Hello! Hello! I am waking you up!"

I'd met plenty of French people, and they weren't all abrasive, but this one was.

He repeated, "Hello! I am waking you now!"

"Tell me something I don't know, like who are you? And how did you get here?"

"I am zee wedding photographer. I have flown here from Paris. In an airplane."

"No, you didn't. I met the wedding photographer."

"I am him! If you met me, you did not! If you met me, that man is an imposter!"

"Calm down. Are you here for the two o'clock wedding or the six o'clock?"

"Yes! Six o'clock!"

"Okay, then I haven't met you."

"This is what I say to you!" He shook one fist at me. "Now please go! You are ruining everything. You are all over my beautiful green grass."

"And you're standing in my napping sunshine, so I guess that makes us even. Why don't you shoot your pictures around me? It's a huge lawn."

"No. I have secured the entire lawn for this time period. I have a permit, and I am authorized, whereas your recreation here is unauthorized." He pointed at me like he was scolding a dog. "You must now, how you say, take a hike!"

Take a hike? Who did he think he was talking to?

I'd send *him* on a hike. On a hike to pick up his eviscerated entrails.

While plotting a grisly murder I could pin on Ribbons, I happened to glance down, and the photographer's tone made more sense. My cursed dress had gone from tumbleweed to trash bag. Thanks to the dust devil, there were loose leaves, empty fast food wrappers, and even a banana peel affixed to my wrinkled brown dress.

I understood exactly what was happening, and I was deeply offended on behalf of whatever group of people the rude man had mistaken me for.

"My dear sir," I said, trying not to sound insane and failing instantly with my word choice. "My good man, Mr. Photographer, Sir, there is no permit that allows you to remove a member of the public from a public recreation area."

"Is that what you say? But then how do I have... this?!"

He pulled from the pocket in his camouflage jacket an official document from the Wisteria Permit Department that permitted him to do exactly that. It had been signed off on by Gavin Gorman, plus there was a signature smear of orange cheese-puff dust from Karl Kormac.

"I am evicting you," the man said. "Go and make recreation somewhere that is not my beautiful green lawn!"

I glanced around, just in case I needed to fireball first and ask questions later. Unfortunately, there were witnesses.

Standing in a group nearby, watching our interaction with some amusement, was the wedding party the French man was there to photograph. They were the second party, the one that would have the third floor after six o'clock.

The bride was Liza Gilbert, a pretty, young blonde with fashionably thick eyebrows and light makeup. She worked in my aunt's office on the ground floor, which explained how she'd known to get every permit possible.

The groom was a young man who looked exactly like her ex-boyfriend Xavier Batista, except—if I'm being honest here—better looking. He looked like the computer-modified after photo in a before-and-after advertisement for exercise equipment that tones your physique while saving you valuable dollars on gym memberships.

I was glad Xavier wasn't there to see the girl he'd been so smitten with marrying a better-looking version of himself. That would feel... well, it might feel like if Shari Heminger was marrying someone I had fallen in love with. Terrible.

Liza Gilbert squinted at me, shielding her eyes with one hand against the bright sunshine, then squealed in surprise, "Hey, Zara! Hey! How's it going at the other big wedding? I hope your aunt can forgive me for not being there, but I'm sort of busy!"

The photographer eyed me warily and said to her, "You know *this*? This disgusting creature?"

Nobody could say *disgusting* quite like the French. Again, not *all* French people, but... you know.

"She works at the library," Liza explained to him.

He wrinkled his nose. "That explains everything." He waved his hand from side to side in a slash. "She can NOT be in the photos! No way!"

"I don't want to be in your photos anyway," I said to him. "No offense," I said to Liza.

Liza gave her bridesmaids some instructions, and all of them ran up to me eagerly, like a group of chipmunks— a *scurry*—right down to the excited sounds they were making.

The scurry of bridesmaids had a wheeled suitcase full of emergency cleaning supplies. They had been forewarned and well-armed with lint rollers, a sewing kit, and even a handheld vacuum cleaner. They gave my dress and shoes a manual cleaning that was just as thorough as my top spell might have been.

Next, the bridesmaids cleaned each other, since some of my dust devil debris had transferred to them and their peach-colored bridesmaid gowns.

"Perfect job, girls," Liza said.

They made more chipmunk noises, then scurried away to the nearby gazebo, along with the photographer, leaving me alone with the bride-to-be.

Liza stepped closer to me.

I took two steps back, so that anyone walking by wouldn't fear for the beautiful bride's safety around the lady in the crinkled-up garbage bag dress.

Liza said to me, "It's funny how my bridesmaids' dresses keep looking worse while mine keeps looking better." She winked. "It's a real mystery."

I replied with a knowing air, "It's no mystery to those of us who know all about the hex on commercial bridesmaid dresses."

She closed the distance between us again, and plunked her hand on my arm like a boat dropping anchor.

In a hushed tone, she asked, "Is everything under control up there?"

"You'll get your room at six o'clock," I said. "Don't worry. When I stepped out for fresh air, it was still in excellent condition. No scorch marks on the walls, no cacodemon doodie in the chandeliers." None of us had ever seen cacodemon doodie, but that summer it had become a popular term in the supernatural community to describe anything unpleasant.

She nodded and bit her lower lip, showing the first sign of wedding day jitters. "I'm sure everything will be fine, as long as nobody uses the elevator. Everyone made a pledge to only use the stairs. Some of my girls don't know about portals, so I had to make up a superstition." She glanced up at the tall building whose shadow we stood in. "Have you heard from your mom lately?"

"Xavier is alive and well," I said, answering the question she hadn't asked. "Does he know about...?" I nodded at the gazebo, and the Xavier lookalike in the sharp tuxedo.

"I wrote him a letter, but he didn't write back."

Of course he didn't. Why would he? Liza had strung along poor Xavier for years. He could do better than her. He was a good kid, when he wasn't pouting about being a Nothing Person.

The photographer waved desperately to get our attention, and yelled, "Hello! Hello! I am short one bride for my stunning composition!"

Liza and I air-kissed goodbye. We kept an extra margin of air so I didn't mess up her makeup or transfer any hexes, and she ran off to be photographed.

As I watched the group pose on and around the gazebo, my heart dropped. Not really—I wasn't a vampire, so I couldn't move my heart by an inch or two to avoid a staking—but sometimes it felt like my heart wasn't where it was supposed to be.

Liza kept pretending to go limp, as though the whole thing was such an imposition. Such an ordeal.

Poor thing.

To be young and beautiful, and getting married, with your new life ahead of you.

The density in my chest was punctuated by a sharp pain. Nothing fun and magical, just regular ol' angina. It wouldn't hurt me immediately, but I did need to get my circulation moving.

Words echoed in my head: *The heart is a rose.*

The heart is a rose. What did that mean?

I remembered a woman's dying words: *"We think we have free will, but we don't. Everything we do is predetermined by a bunch of chemical signals running through a lump of fatty meat. We think we're making choices, but we're not. We just do whatever this thing makes us do."*

She'd pointed to her temple, her brain.

And yet she'd also been talking about the heart, comparing it to a rose.

What had she meant?

And why could I remember her dying speech perfectly when I couldn't keep track of a list of five things I needed at the grocery store?

Ah, life's mysteries. Too many to investigate. Too few to fill a book without some artistic license.

I looked over my shoulder at the City Hall building.

The old building had too many floors and windows to have a face, and yet it did have a face, and today that face looked long and uninviting.

Did I really need to go back inside already? The windows on the third floor weren't broken, glowing unnaturally, or bursting with tentacles.

Perhaps I would go on a little walk to oxygenate my heart. And build up my appetite for wedding cake.

I did need to find an apartment, and the neighborhood around City Hall was one of the older ones, with plenty of large century homes that had been converted to apartment buildings.

I could start looking online tomorrow, with a broad search, but everyone in Wisteria knew the best way to find a hidden gem was to walk around and look for the signs. The *For Rent* signs.

CHAPTER 6

One nice thing about my beige bridesmaid dress was it didn't impede movement.

I covered a lot of ground quickly, and I enjoyed seeing all the large houses and the sturdy, mature trees stretching to high-five each other over narrow streets.

Unfortunately, I didn't find very many For Rent signs.

So much for my plan to find myself an apartment by serendipity.

I would try one more street, then turn back.

The next block was actually quite different.

It had the same large, old houses—mansions from a bygone era—along one side, but the other side was a lovely patchwork of community gardens.

I'd heard of these gardens, yet I'd never seen them in person.

They looked somewhat wild but well loved and inviting.

I knew the community gardens were an area of recreation that was open to the public, though harvesting materials was limited to its members.

Unless Liza Gilbert's cranky photographer had a permit to remove me, I would be welcome to wander through.

I crossed the street, looking for a logical entry point into the garden, so I didn't trample any delicate plants. I found a cedar arbor covered in roses, and passed through it sideways, careful not to disturb the delicate flowers.

I wandered down a path, and through a field of tall sunflowers that were not yet in bloom.

I didn't see or hear any people, which didn't strike me as that odd, until I encountered a table with a white tablecloth. On the table was a glass pitcher full of what appeared to be ice—only twenty percent melted—and lemonade.

The garden was peaceful, with only the sound of nearby pollinators buzzing from flower to flower, and the joyful laughter of small children playing in the nearby park.

Had this lemonade stand been abandoned by those same enterprising children who'd learned the valuable lesson that the secret to a lucrative business was location, location, location?

There was no pricing for the lemonade listed on the front of the table.

I called out a tentative, "Hello?"

No response.

A crow landed on the arm of a nearby scarecrow, and greeted me with a loud CAW!

I didn't like the look of the scarecrow.

I hadn't thought much of them until the night of the tornado, when the Wizard of Oz had been playing on the television. I'd shown up at my aunt's house in the midst of the storm, and she'd compared me to a scarecrow. Something about a lack of brains. And Bentley. My Bentley. She had called him... the Tin Man.

Except he wasn't the Tin Man, because the Tin Man met the wizard and got himself a new heart, and he got to live.

Last October, the town had held their annual pre-Halloween parade featuring scarecrows. It was bigger than ever, due to the recent decision to officially include zombies, whether they displayed the minimum seventeen stalks of straw poking out of their clothing or not. And I had only stood along the parade route for the first float before I'd been reminded of that terrible night. It had upset me so much that I'd sat out the other parades.

So now I didn't like scarecrows.

Some will say that people can't change, but it isn't true. You can always find new things to be scared of.

I decided I wouldn't run from this scarecrow. It was just a single scarecrow, safely elevated on a stick, and it wasn't even a zombie.

The bird cawed again, defying the scarecrow along with me. We had that in common.

When it cawed a third time, I replied, "And a good caw to you, too, my fine crow. Is this your garden?"

The crow winked at me with one black beady eye, then the other.

"Ribbons?"

The crow didn't move.

I laughed out loud. "Sorry. It's just that you remind me of someone else. But do I know you?"

The crow didn't appear to do anything.

But that didn't mean it *wasn't* doing anything.

"Mother? Have you upgraded your spying eyes?"

The bird didn't even blink.

If I could get my hands on it, I could get some answers. But with no levitation powers, and the majority of my bread-and-butter spells needing adjustments, I had few options.

There was one spell that might reveal who the bird was, if it was a shifter.

I had barely dabbled with it since the time I'd used it on my foxy father.

I cupped my hands together. I felt that good feeling of my power rising, pressing on my skin from the inside like rushing water straining against a dam, cracks forming in the concrete. I was so much more adept at the Witch Tongue that my controlled voice was inaudible.

Cease your mischief now. I command you.

I rolled the spell into a ball, and manually lobbed it at the crow.

My aim had been improving, and I hit the creature dead on.

The spell washed over the crow.

Now it would return to its human form, breaking the wood arm of the scarecrow as it fell to the ground.

Except it didn't.

What the crow did do was turn from black to white. Then it took off from the scarecrow with a panicked flapping of now-white wings.

Oh, fluffernuts.

I looked around to see if anyone had witnessed that. I was still alone, to my relief.

I was even more lucky that the crow hadn't been a shifter. I could have gotten the whole coven in trouble with the DWM.

If my luck held up, the only fallout would be a new crow with albinism living in town. Just one white crow who didn't like me at all. I'd dealt with worse.

All that magic casting had made me thirsty.

I went to the table, and poured myself a glass of lemonade.

Sitting face-up on the table was a small white note. The glare from the sun had hidden it from me until now.

The sign that read:

Help yourself.

The lemons are grown here, in our community garden.

We are now taking applications for our newest plots - no experience necessary!

Tours today, every hour on the hour.

The lemonade was delicious.

Had the lemons really been grown there? I didn't think our climate was warm enough to support citrus.

As I poured a second glass, I heard human voices—adults—chattering happily.

A group of five people were weaving a path through the gardens toward me.

They were in no rush, stopping to admire various flowers in bloom, making ooh and aah noises.

I felt a bit like an intruder, a lemonade thief, so I gave them a little wave.

All five people returned my wave with enthusiastic, whole-arm waves, and began charging in my direction.

I was so surprised, I had to check behind myself to see if an ice cream truck advertising free drumsticks had pulled up. There was nothing behind me.

The five people surrounded me, all talking at once, asking questions and introducing themselves.

It was the exact opposite of the treatment I'd received at the wedding, which felt like some distant memory by now.

There was a flurry of noise, and handshakes, and the latin names of flowers being thrown around, then all five of them asked, in unison, "Will you join us?"

Would I become a member of the community garden?

By that point, I had sipped their lemonade, and it was exactly as fresh as it looked.

I couldn't say no.

CHAPTER 7

Time passed quickly in the community garden. There's a reason we don't have many clocks outdoors—nobody would believe them, even if they were running on time.

My new friends were so excited about showing me everything that grew there, and I was so happy to be a part of their group, that I completely forgot about my wedding duties.

When I did finally remember, I excused myself and ran as fast as I could back to City Hall.

I climbed the stairs to the third floor, breathing heavily, my bare feet dirty and grimy, and my kitten-heeled bridesmaid shoes in one hand.

It was not quite five o'clock, but my party had already left.

Maisy's employees were there alongside some City Hall cleaners, cleaning and preparing for Liza Gilbert's event.

Only one member of the Riddle-Fung wedding party remained.

It was my aunt's new husband, Chief Ethan Fung, and he was sweeping up something sparkly.

I put my shoes back on for safety, and tried to take the broom from his hands, but he resisted handing it over.

"Brooms are technically my domain," I said. "Don't be a grumpy bear. Let me do my duties."

He bristled at me calling him a bear, but he let me take the broom. He did, however, keep the dustpan. That would work. We could work as a team.

"This looks like safety glass," I said of the sparkling debris. "What did you break?"

"Me? I didn't break anything," Fung said. "But there was a wild animal who wanted to join the party. It broke through that funny window."

He pointed to a tiny rectangle of brightness on the exterior wall. It was Wisteria's smallest window, barely larger than a playing card. And it was missing its glass.

I jumped to an assumption about which wild creature had done the deed.

"Sorry about that," I said on his behalf—I always took the blame for his bad deeds anyway. "I'll get Ribbons to pay for a replacement. You might not believe this, but he has pockets somewhere on him, and he carries money at all times."

"It wasn't the wyvern. It was a mutated wild bird."

I focused on sweeping up the glass, and said nothing.

"A white crow," Fung said.

"Are you sure it wasn't a pigeon? Or a seagull?"

"It was definitely a crow. And it seemed to have a grudge against a particular type of human. It swooped all the women with red hair. Poor Shari was beside herself with fright. Do you happen to know anything about this sort of phenomenon?"

I kept sweeping, moving on to other areas that didn't need sweeping.

"We did catch the poor creature," he said.

I sighed with relief.

"And humanely euthanized it," he finished.

I stopped sweeping.

"I'm actually relieved that was the worst thing that happened," he said with a light chuckle. "You should have seen it, Zara. The women were shrieking, hiding under the tables, and all the men banded together like they were going into battle. All over a bird."

A pair of men walked by us, carrying the tiny pane of replacement glass for the window. They were each carrying one side, each using both gloved hands, but only their thumbs plus one finger because there was such limited space.

One of the men self-consciously explained without being asked, in a gruff tone, "It's regulation. A minimum of two employees must have their hands on a replacement pane at all times during transport."

Fung said with equal gruffness, "Your professionalism is not unnoticed. Thank you, gentlemen."

To me, Fung said, "We should probably get going to Dreamland, so the Gilbert girl can have her room. She didn't order two grooms, plus I'm already spoken for." He grinned proudly.

"Congratulations," I said.

"Thank you."

He gave me his elbow, and steered me to the door.

"Sorry I disappeared for a bit," I said. "I was..." I didn't say the part about looking for an apartment. Should I even tell him I knew he was planning to evict me?

He patted my hand. "I'm sure you and your good deeds were needed elsewhere. Did I ever tell you how proud I am to have you in my family?"

"I can safely say you have not."

"Well, I am. A man can pick his bride, but not his in-laws. That's up to luck, and I feel very lucky today."

"Even though I accidentally cursed a crow, turned it into a white-feathered monster with a vengeance for redheads, and almost ruined the whole day?"

There was a pause—he hadn't been certain I was the cause of the incursion, but he wasn't shocked by the revelation, either.

"Accidents happen," he said.

"Is there anything else you want to tell me?"

The elevator doors closed. I hadn't noticed we'd walked right into the thing. I felt uneasy.

Fung said, "Is everything okay? I'd like to keep my arm unbroken today."

I released his arm and shook out my hand.

"Just nerves," I said apologetically.

We reached the main floor, and the elevator doors opened. Everything looked the way it should.

We walked out of the building, and past the incoming wedding group.

Fung repeated my question back to me, "Is there anything you want to tell me?"

I gave him a big smile. "Just that I'm really grateful to have you in the family. We're the lucky ones. And I love living in your house. I know it's been chaotic, but things will settle down when Zoey goes off to college, I promise."

"Mm hmm."

We got into a waiting taxi, and headed toward the second party location.

I was pretty sure that he knew that I knew about the planned eviction, but I'd already confessed to the white crow, and I didn't want to ruin his interrogation skills by offering up too many confessions voluntarily.

Plus, maybe if I didn't bring it up, he'd forget to evict me until it was too late, and he'd come to appreciate having me around.

On the drive, we made small talk about the wedding.

He didn't bring up our living arrangements at all that night.

Not even after the white crow, which assumed had been killed, made a surprise encore appearance.

The cursed creature flapped around terrorizing absolutely everyone until Humphrey, bless his lizard reflexes, grabbed it from mid-air and ate it in two bites.

CHAPTER 8

September

I made it to September without being evicted.

My daughter left for college in late August, and the only thing positive about that was that it left more space in the house for me.

I still had my job at the library, and could easily afford my own place, but there was nothing on the market that appealed to me.

My insurance company had finally paid me for the hole in the ground that had once been my dream house, but even with that chunk of money for a down payment, I couldn't find anything half as nice.

Renting was the best way to go. Or the *only* way to go, given how the local real estate agents had blackballed me. Even when I disguised my voice, they refused to take my phone calls. Word had gotten around I was a fussy client. Was it my fault I'd been spoiled by my first house?

As summer changed to fall, I'd been lucky to keep a roof over my head, but then toward the end of September, just as the leaves on the sugar maples changed color, my luck ran out.

That Saturday, I opened the front door as usual, letting myself into Fung's house. It was also Zinnia's house, but it still had all of her husband's rules, so I still thought of it as his.

I had baby Fyrsil in my arms, and he tried to "help" by pulling my jacket back on while I tried to pull it off.

After some wrestling with his pudgy baby arms, I got my jacket hung up on my assigned hook.

I sighed happily as I put my dirty rubber clogs in the assigned spot for clogs.

I was tired, but it was a pleasant tired, earned from a full day of gardening with my helper.

My new routine for weekends was to babysit Fyrsil by taking him out in the mornings so his parents could relax or tidy up.

Then I took care of my many tasks at the community garden. The baby got plenty of fresh air and sunshine to help with his development, and I kept my mind off missing my daughter. Zoey must have been having a spectacular time immersing herself in big, thick college books because she didn't call home nearly enough.

But I was making the best of my situation. Life was moving forward. I could measure it by the rise and fall of the annuals in the community garden.

My aunt came to meet us in the front entryway, drying her hands on a dish towel. I couldn't see every room, but the house had the energy of a home proud of itself after a good cleaning.

Zinnia's hazel eyes widened in horror at the sight of us. We were a bit more dirty than usual.

"I can barely tell it's you under all of that," she said crossly. "I ought to take a picture to show our book club." There was no book club; that was what we called the coven around impressionable ears.

"Take a picture if you want. We can do up a calendar to send Zoey, so she doesn't forget about all of us."

"You two look like a couple of Himalayan Pink Skunkapoo fresh out of hibernation."

"Is Skunkapoo the plural of Skunkapus?"

My aunt continued frowning while drying her already-dry hands with the dish towel.

"It's not a flattering comparison," she said.

"But not inaccurate, given that I do have a pouch."

I had fashioned the front of my sweatpants into a fabric pouch for carrying baby Fyrsil. The Himalayan Pink Skunkapoo carried her offspring for up to three years within her pouch, three times longer than her non-magical relatives, the kangaroo. My elastic waistband would only last another month or two, given the baby's growth rate.

Aunt Zinnia took Fyrsil out of my sweatpants pouch, revealing a baby-shaped clean patch on the front of my shirt.

She held him away from herself so he didn't transfer filth to her clean blouse.

"Dirty, dirty, dirty," she said, more to him than to me.

"It's technically mud, not dirt," I said. "The baby drool mixes with the dust, and forms a paste."

Fyrsil blew muddy bubbles and said, "Zaza. Zaza."

Since the wedding two months earlier, he hadn't learned any other words or names besides mine.

It would be an understatement to state that this was a sore point within the household.

"That's right, *Mama*," I said. "Mama. Mama's got you, muddy boy."

Zinnia didn't believe me that Zaza was just a sloppy pronunciation of Mama. She hadn't believed me the previous hundred times, either.

The baby squealed, "Zaza!" He gleefully used one chubby fist to paint a streak of filth on my aunt's clean tea towel.

"Sorry," I said. "I would have pre-washed us both with your outdoor shower, but it's getting a bit chilly. Plus your creepy neighbors enjoy watching me a little too much."

"We don't have an outdoor shower," she said. "Is that why the garden hose is always turned on?"

"The garden hose isn't the only thing that gets turned on when I take an outdoor shower." I pretended to make a comedy rim shot in mid-air. "I'm talking about your creepy neighbors," I said.

"They're not creepy," she said. "They're a perfectly lovely couple."

"They collect dolls," I said.

"Nobody's perfect. We ought to allow other people their idiosyncrasies as they allow us ours."

"Some of the dolls are ventriloquist dummies."

My aunt looked as disturbed as she ought to be. "Oh, dear," she said.

The baby squealed again. "Zaza!" He reached for me.

"Zaza? That's a fine idea," Zinnia said sweetly to her son. "Zaza got you muddy in her garden patch, so Zaza can clean you up."

"Sure." I began casting the appropriate spell to transfer the dirt from his pudgy body to a nearby mop bucket, twisting my tongue in a practiced motion.

The air went SNAP, CRACKLE, POP, then a very anticlimactic FIZZ.

My aunt had shut me down with her own counterspell.

The energy whipped back up my arms, hexing me with an instant dull headache.

And then, with a ZZIF, then a POP, ELCKCARC, PANS, the spell inverted fully.

Bad juju incoming.

All the grime that had been sitting in the mop bucket—the grime from all of my aunt's cleaning efforts—rose up into the air in a tidal wave, and splashed onto me.

I spat muddy water out of my mouth.

"Aunt Zinnia! What was that for?"

"No m-a-g-i-c," she said, spelling it out so Fyrsil might not learn *magic* as his second word.

"Not even a little—"

"No."

"But it's so much faster and—"

"No."

"But you just did your own—"

"Zara Riddle, I ought to dose you with witchbane to teach you a lesson, since you seem to have forgotten your teachings. You're as bad as Margaret Mills, thinking that perfectly sensible rules don't apply to you."

My jaw dropped. "How dare you. I'm nothing like Margaret."

We faced off for a tense moment.

Then she said in a low, careful tone, "I know about the white crow."

"He said he wouldn't tell you."

Her eyes narrowed. "So, it was you."

Tricked and busted. I said nothing more, lest I incriminate myself further.

I gently took Fyrsil from her, and held him to my chest like a human shield. It wasn't the bravest move, but all was fair in love and war.

Zinnia used the muddied tea towel to clean her hands. And then, without another word, she grabbed the now-empty mop bucket, and left.

The baby gently tugged on the three loose tendrils of hair I'd started leaving down for him to play with.

"Mama is disappointed with us," I told him. "Can you say Mama?"

"Zaza."

"If you insist on saying my name, it's Zara, with an R."

"Zaza wit' Rrrr."

"Shh." I whisked him down the hallway to the bathroom before he shouted it from the top of his lungs.

I ran the water for the bath, and stripped off my muddy outer layers. When I climbed into the tub with him, I kept my underwear on, since there weren't enough bathrooms in the house and people or cats were always bursting in.

I'd barely settled into the tub when Boa, our fluffy white cat, shoved open the door. She didn't like water, so she jumped onto the sink counter to keep a safe distance. She groomed herself while watching us with her watchful eyes.

Fyrsil and I dropped most of our mud into the warm water.

We were laughing and making bubble castles when two more house-pests showed up.

Ribbons, our resident telepathic wyvern, flapped in by air.

He dumped his son into the bath water like a tugboat emptying a garbage scow in ancient days gone by—or from recent history—*recent* being relative to the ancient wyvern's age.

Then he perched on the tub's water spout, like a skinny bird with a seahorse-shaped head, iridescent green and purple scales, and a long, snake-like tail.

"Perfect timing," I said. "Put those big nostrils to use and heat up this water. Easy on the mint flavoring, I don't want to prune."

"You look even more pale and puny when you are in water, Zed."

He was a telepath, like Margaret Mills, except less insulting to my intelligence.

He spoke directly into my mind in his vaguely "European" accent. Other witches reported hearing him differently than I did, but my version was a pastiche of B-movie vampires, local actors playing wealthy British aristocrats in stage plays, and movie mafia bosses.

"And a warm hello to you, too." I used my hand to make a current in the water to direct RJ, his sharp-taloned offspring, away from the human baby. "How's it going with the little sentient can opener who flies around with you?"

"Every minute of raising offspring is the worst torture a creature can withstand. As we learn the truth of this, the extinction of all creatures of intelligence is inevitable. Babies are the cure for advanced civilization."

"But they are pretty cute."

We both watched as Fyrsil and RJ played one of their baby tub games. RJ kept popping up from the bathwater with bubbles on his head, and Fyrsil smashed him back underwater with his baby fist.

After a few minutes, Ribbons said, "Something sinister is happening with the dirt, Zed."

I splashed the water. "It's just a little garden dirt in the water, you superstitious old catcher's mitt."

He reacted visibly to being insulted, hopping up and down on the spout while blowing ribbons of colored steam from his nostrils.

"Vile creature, I will wear your entrails as a hat and vest. I will parade around this fly-over town in my Sunday best, taking compliments from all your vile human friends."

"You will not, you cranky, unmoisturized undercarriage of a wildebeest."

"At least I am not soft and stupid like an ice cream sundae with an extra scoop of stupid."

"You would look cuter if you weren't inside out."

"You would look cuter if you were." He flashed the talons of the hand-like claws on his wing-arms. "Let's find out."

I splashed him with water. He snorted a plume of fire, turning the water to steam. The steam was dangerously near the back of Fyrsil's head. Near enough to singe a single baby hair.

It was all fun and games until the baby got hurt.

I reacted without thinking, striking the adult wyvern with the back of my hand.

He hadn't expected it, and my backhand sent him flying off the spout.

He would have hit the wall if he hadn't landed against Boa, wings spread, face-planting into her fluffy side.

The cat reacted instantly and violently, skittering her way across the sink, sending toiletries flying onto the hard tile floor.

There was a horrendous clatter, and the cat was gone, out the door.

A broken hand-held mirror spun like a top for several seconds, throwing broken reflections and years of bad luck all around.

Ribbons went into attack mode.

I felt his fury in my mind. He was operating on pure instincts, and ancient rage.

I had to act quickly.

With a quick castling, I encased him in a protective spell.

I'd been practicing the spell for just such an incident. In spite of the danger, I was pleased with myself that I'd popped it off better in real life than I ever had any of the times I'd practiced it on inanimate objects.

My aunt came running in to see what all the commotion was.

She shoved me out of the way and scooped up her son. She held him tightly to her chest, breathing heavily.

Her eyes flashed with terror, and then anger as she took in the scene:

Muddy water on the walls.

Smashed toiletries all over the floor.

Ribbons squirming inside a pulsating ball of semi-transparent jelly.

And RJ, the world's newest and least house-trained wyvern, perched on the edge of the tub, shrieking in the high-pitched tones that caused gastrointestinal distress in humans.

Through clenched teeth, my aunt said, "Zara, what did I tell you about m-a-g-i-c?"

"I can explain. It's not what it looks like."

"Really? Because it looks like you did something to make Ribbons attack, and you had to quickly cast that jellyball spell before someone got hurt."

"Okay. Maybe this is all exactly what it looks like."

The small wyvern's shrieking was having a terrible effect on my guts.

I reached out and calmed him down by letting him chew on my fingers. His baby teeth were sharp, but my flesh would grow back thanks to my witch powers.

Aunt Zinnia shook her head. "I never planned to have children at this point in my life, much less two, or three, or four."

I shrugged. "Life doesn't always work out how you plan."

She pointed her finger at me and spoke slowly. "You. Zarabella Diamante Riddle. Are. Hereby. Evicted."

Then she pointed her finger at Ribbons, who was emerging from the jelly bubble with a telepathic blue cloud of naughty words, and said the same curse to him.

"You. Ribbons Alexander Kittipoo Wyvernus. Are. Hereby. Evicted."

She said it to RJ as well, and then she finalized all three evictions with a setting spell.

As the compulsion settled over me, I knew she meant it, and that I would obey her command.

Ribbons and I exchanged a look.

No more jokes or insults. This was serious.

We would all need to be gone by nightfall, or suffer terrible, painful consequences.

CHAPTER 9

Monday, October 1st

6:30 pm

I carried my only cardboard box of belongings down the lovely, tree-lined street to my new home.

My friend, Frank Wonder, was gallantly carrying my suitcases for me.

Moving in wouldn't take long. My box was the craft supplies I'd discovered back in July. Everything else I owned—some clothes and a few toiletries that hadn't been destroyed by the cat—fit inside the suitcases.

Frank watched with amusement as I struggled to get through the doorway while holding the awkward box. He had offered to carry the box, too, but I'd insisted on lugging it myself.

"Zara Riddle, you are as stubborn about doing everything yourself as you are adept at the Dewey Decimal system."

Frank and I worked together at the Wisteria Public Library. Not all of our references were librarian-themed, but it did creep into our daily speech.

"Thanks," I said over the box with a huff, blowing off a residue of dirt.

Frank led the way through the common area, past the mailboxes, and up the stairs. He didn't ask which floor, he just ran up the steps two at a time, as though my suitcases weighed nothing at all. He was extremely fit for a man pushing sixty.

When we reached the doorway to my apartment, which was on the third floor, I said, "Either the doors in this place are shrinking or this box is growing."

Frank scrutinized the door with a furrowed brow. "That's not a standard-sized door. It's actually quite small."

"I love it," I said. "I love older buildings with all their quirks. That's where the magic is."

He looked up and down the hallway. "At least the hall carpets have been cleaned."

"Have they? It's hard to say with that pattern."

He took the key from my hand, unlocked the door, and waved me in.

The place looked more tired and dusty than when I'd first viewed it, but all apartments behaved that way.

Frank barely glanced around before crossing his arms in judgment.

I dropped the cardboard box to the floor with a thunk that echoed in the unfurnished space.

I closed the door, and double-checked the protective spells I'd cast that morning when I'd picked up my keys. The wards included a noise cancellation spell to keep interior conversations private. Anyone on the other side of the thin walls would be able to detect us speaking, but the conversation would be triple-scrambled and double-muffled.

Frank continued judging.

"Zara, I don't know about this place. I still don't understand why you couldn't stay with me in my condo. I'm a very fun roommate."

"Frank, you know perfectly well why I couldn't stay with you."

He rolled his eyes. "I'm sure there weren't *that many* ghosts."

"Your building, the so-called former candy factory, was the Wick family's pest control headquarters for decades. They used it for experimental poisons and inhumane traps. It was worse than the cafeteria at City Hall."

"Ha ha," Frank said.

"And before that, it was a prison for the criminally insane. And before that, it was... you don't even want to know."

"But you're a witch. Can't you do your little exorcism thing on the ghosts?" He looked vexed. As vexed as his beloved building was hexed. "You said it was only mildly haunted once you got inside my place."

"Your place is lovely," I said. "You have nothing to worry about. And I'll still come visit you every chance I get."

Frank looked up at the room's light. It was an ornate brass fixture, well over a hundred years old, and original to the building.

The three-story former mansion, which was currently split into apartments, had been built during a special seven-year period in which it was the law in Wisteria that every new home be built in a decorative style. That decorative style was so fancy, it made Europe's *La Belle Époque* look downright dowdy.

Even the plumbing pipes, which were mostly obscured within plaster walls, were decorated with embossed patterns on the outside as well as—rumor had it—the insides.

Frank stood on his tiptoes and ran his fingertips lightly over the old fixture, sending cobwebs fluttering down.

"This can't be original," he said. "It's electric, and it would have been gas at the time. Hmm. But the arms are facing up, not down." He squeezed one of the chandelier arms, like a doctor examining the finger of a fascinating patient. "I wonder if it was retrofitted for electricity about a hundred years ago." He couldn't take his eyes off it. "Zara, whenever you upgrade the dim lighting in this room to something more contemporary, I'd be happy to take this dirty, old thing off your hands."

"Nice try, Mr. Burnside."

His last name was Wonder, not Burnside, but I was making a joke.

Doc Burnside, not the one from the 1990 film *Alienator* but a different Doc Burnside, was a character from one of our favorite shows, *Rebel Relic Renegades*. It was a space opera about a motley crew of salvagers racing to secure the galaxy's priceless historical artifacts.

In the show, Doc Burnside was a silver-haired prankster who ran the spaceship's library when he wasn't acquiring artifacts for well below their auction value. He was a fan favorite, and it was no coincidence he resembled the real-life Frank Wonder. Frank had sold his likeness rights to the network for a comfortable chunk of change.

My dear friend giggled about being compared to his fictional double. The happy sound of his voice activated my unfinished spellwork, and cleared out the rest of the room's cobwebs. The corners sparkled.

What would I ever do without Frank?

He was my rock.

He had taken me in after my eviction from Ethan and Zinnia's house, and he'd been a fun roommate—for about three days.

On day four, I found out why he lived alone. It wasn't just one thing, but an assortment of quirks and peccadilloes that made Ethan Fung's rules about where to put clogs seem downright reasonable.

I still adored Frank, but the only way to protect our friendship was to not share a roof with him. That's why

I'd exaggerated my feelings about the ghosts and ghouls that lived in his exposed brick walls.

Frank wheeled my suitcases into the sole bedroom. The room had been a storage closet in the original mansion, and still felt like it.

He insisted on helping me unpack, which took all of ten minutes.

We arranged my limited wardrobe in the room's freestanding wardrobe. It was the only furniture that had come with the place—probably because there would be no way for the landlord to get it out through the small doors.

"You need furniture," he said when we were done. "You need one of everything."

"Don't worry about me. I'll get everything sorted out on the weekend."

"It's Monday today."

"I know what day it is."

"You need a bed, and you need it right now."

"I've got a sleeping bag."

"You do not."

I pointed to the brown fuzzy thing hanging in the wardrobe. "That extra-long jacket is also a sleeping bag. See? You can zip all along the bottom."

Frank was not impressed. "But you still need a bed, or a cushion, or at least a thick rug."

"I can sleep on the floor just fine."

"Zara Riddle, you cannot sleep on the floor. Come back to my place. Just for tonight. We'll start shopping tomorrow morning on our coffee break. I have free delivery with several companies."

How could I tell him I was planning to call in sick to work the next day? All the better to sulk alone in my empty apartment?

"Sure, we can shop tomorrow," I said.

Empty promises were so easy to make, they practically made themselves, like cobwebs or dust bunnies.

I grabbed him by the shoulders, turned him around, and steered him to the front door.

He said over his shoulder, "We'll look online to preview, then go in person after work."

"Sure, sure. Get out of here and forget about me." He was resisting my efforts to get him out. Didn't he understand that I just wanted to be alone? I'd gone from being afraid of being alone to wanting it to start immediately. It was my new life, after all.

He grabbed onto a piece of wood trim and held on.

"Frank Wonder, if you don't leave right now, I'll cast a spell to make you forget everything you know about me. I don't have much here for ingredients, but I could whip up a bookwyrm using a few—"

"GACK!"

Frank ran out into the hallway and disappeared in the stairwell. In his rush, he'd dropped a single pink flamingo feather. Shifters were funny that way.

I closed the door.

I was alone in the apartment.

Alone.

I reached out with my mind for Ribbons, but he was out of range.

That figured.

The wyvern probably wouldn't show up until I'd stocked the kitchen with his favorite syrups. Maybe if I only bought healthy food, he'd never figure out where I lived.

I was alone.

Alone.

I checked my phone. The last message from my daughter read: *I'm busy right now, but I'll phone you in one hour.*

The message was five hours old.

I stood with my back against a wall. There was nothing to sit on, so I slid down the wall until my butt hit the hardwood floor.

I wouldn't be alone for long, because soon my companion Grief was there.

Grief wasn't like Death, which merely peeked in from time to time. Grief was like—

Something buzzed.

I jumped to my feet, my hands tingling with magic. I could form a fireball if need be. The devil had taken our levitation powers, and screwed up most of our spells, but I could still lob fireballs at monsters with as much strength as I could chuck a snowball, and that wasn't nothing.

The buzzing thing buzzed again.

It was an intercom unit next to the front door. Not an original feature, obviously, but quite old, with yellowed plastic on the panel.

I pressed what I assumed was the one-way communications button. It was orange, and whatever text it had once been labeled with was long gone.

I spoke into it. "Hello?"

A familiar voice crackled back over the old speakers.

"It's just me," Frank said. "You forgot something in my car."

I knew I had not forgotten anything, but I pressed the other button, a small black one, to buzz him up anyway. He would try even harder to convince me to come back to his condo for the night, and I would go.

Resigned to my fate, I went to the bathroom to re-pack my toiletries for the night.

When I emerged from the bathroom, I found a half-dozen of my dearest friends funneling into my apartment through the tiny door.

Two of them were carrying a petite sofa I'd admired at a consignment boutique the week before.

Frank gave me a bashful look. "I know you didn't want a housewarming party, because it irritates all the neighbors right when you're trying to make a good first impression, but..."

I shook my head to keep from crying. "But you couldn't help yourself."

"At least I invited all your neighbors," he said with a grin.

Sure enough, right behind my half-sister, and the end of the sofa she was carrying, were some new faces. My neighbors. One of them was carrying a whole, steaming pie.

The last person in the door was a beautiful young woman, casually beautiful in jeans and a hoodie from her new college.

"Zoey!" I threw my arms around my daughter.

"Sorry I didn't phone you," she said into my shoulder.

The tears that had been brewing all day, or maybe for months, came out all at once.

This was my new life now.

CHAPTER 10

Tuesday, October 2nd

I woke to the sight of thin blue stripes. It was the bottom side of a mattress, as seen through wood slats.

There was a bed underneath me, and a bed above me; I was the filling in a bed sandwich. I was the jam, and peanut butter, and cheese, and pickles, and... I was hungry.

Hunger was a positive sign, a sign of vitality.

I'd slept suspiciously well, considering it was my first night in a new space.

I stretched out like a starfish, touching all five—not four—bedposts with my fingers and toes. It would take a few nights to get used to their unequal placement.

The bunk bed had been part of my surprise housewarming party the night before. Frank Wonder had gifted it to me for the apartment's only bedroom. It was a custom build, and he had gone through no small amount of effort to commission.

What a sweetheart. Sometimes his pranks were annoying, but this particular one was nothing short of heartwarming.

It was no coincidence I'd wound up renting that particular apartment. It had seemed so lucky that I'd been on a walk with Frank when we'd bumped into the property manager right as they were putting up an advertisement for the apartment. But it was more Frank than luck.

He had masterminded everything. He'd already viewed the place three times before I'd ever stepped inside, including once to take measurements for the bunk bed.

In hindsight, it should have been obvious. Frank had known which floor to walk up to with my suitcases. He hadn't demanded a full tour the minute he'd walked into the place, running from one corner to the next, peppering me with questions and decorating suggestions. He hadn't done any of the things that a friend does when you move into a new place.

My beautiful new bunk bed had a larger sleeping space on the bottom than the top, but I couldn't tell you if the mattresses were double, twin, or queen-sized, because neither were rectangular. The entire thing, including the mattresses, was truly custom fit to the odd-shaped room. No two edges were parallel, and one corner had been cut out to accommodate some utilities that ran through the room. Hence the five bedposts. Even the sheets and duvets were custom made. The pillows were completely standard rectangles, but still—Frank assured me—high quality and hypoallergenic.

I crawled out of the lower bunk quietly, careful not to wake my daughter on the top bunk. *Her* bunk.

I got dressed in the bathroom, which was spacious relative to the other rooms.

The bathroom had been carved out of a larger space when the house first gained indoor plumbing. Some of the original built-in shelves remained along one wall. They were dark hardwood, the perfect size for books. The size of the shelves was—just like my score getting the place— no coincidence. My entire apartment had once been the mansion's private library. No wonder I felt so at-home.

The kitchen was small but efficient. There was no microwave. The big appliance that I'd thought was a microwave was actually a combination toaster and can opener. I'd never seen anything like it. The fridge and cupboards were already full of groceries, thanks to a thoughtful housewarming delivery by the Fungs.

The Fungs.

My aunt, once a Riddle, was now a Fung.

Technically she was a Riddle-Fung, but when I talked about the three of them as a family unit, I called them *the Fungs*. Their new slogan was, "We're a whole lotta of Fung." Or so I'd been pitching them. The slogan, like so many of my household management tips, hadn't caught on.

I whipped up a breakfast of avocado dip, sausage rolls, baked beans, and barbecue short ribs.

Okay, I didn't whip up anything. It was all leftover party food, but I did unfold the space-saving fold-away table to create an eating nook, and I arranged the leftover cartons attractively.

By the time Zoey crawled out of bed, there was still enough left that she couldn't tell I'd been nibbling for hours.

"There's so much protein here," she said with wide, grateful eyes. "I should come visit more often."

I had to correct her. "You should come *home* more often."

She chewed her lower lip as she loaded her plate. "Mom..."

"You have your own bunk here. And it's permanent, not like the bunk beds our old house used to make sometimes. It's your very own bunk, because this is your home, too."

She kept her gaze lowered. "I think... never mind." She lifted her chin. "It's an excellent bunk. Mr. Wonder really is the best."

"He is."

"He knows what's best for you."

"Sometimes."

We ate in silence, then to the hum of the ancient refrigerator, then silence again.

Zoey separated the bits of shredded ham from her baked beans while she ate.

Normally Boa would have been swishing around our feet, pestering us for her share of ham.

But she wasn't there. The Fungs thought it would be best for her to stay at their house, where she had free run of a spacious yard. Plus the little ham-disposal-unit had just enough brains to be useful. She could protect Fyrsil from non-magical creatures smaller than herself, such as toads, which were strangely aggressive in that neighborhood.

Zoey took an audible breath, then ate the stack of set-apart ham in two bites.

She said, "I miss—"

"Boa. I know. I miss her too, but at least we can eat ham in peace."

"No. I miss Marzipants."

A chill washed over me from right to left. Grief in the form of a breeze. Someone had opened a memory window, and let Grief in.

Marzipants was gone.

It was easy for me to imagine him living his life at my aunt's house, but he wasn't there.

Marzipants, the noisy budgie who'd traveled across the country with a lawyer to live with us, was gone.

The little bird who'd gone from annoying house-pest to beloved family member was gone.

The squawky brat who loved to play hide and seek, even though he was terrible at it, was gone.

He had passed away of natural causes around the time of the Fung wedding.

"Little birds don't live forever," I said to my daughter.

It was true, but, judging by the reaction I got from Zoey, it had been the exact wrong thing to say.

Her eyes welled up, her freckled cheeks reddened, and she abruptly left our fold-down table for the bathroom.

I'd screwed up.

She didn't come back out for an hour, and when she finally did, she looked no different from when she'd gone in.

I asked her brightly, "Do you have any ideas for today?"

Frank had arranged for one of the library's volunteers to cover my shift.

I only had one day with Zoey before she had to get back to her school and her classes. She was attending a regular college, no more magic than any other. I mean, it magically wicked away tuition and fees more readily than a hex, but it wasn't technically magic.

Her best friend Ambrosia had gotten into the same school, and they were the only two supernaturals as far as we knew. It was actually a relief to me to know that whatever trouble they'd be getting into would just be the regular college-aged stuff.

Zoey shrugged with fake nonchalance. "We can do whatever you want. I don't care."

I don't care.

It stung to hear those words. That particular phrase was so casual on the surface, so normal for a teenager going on twenty to say, yet it spoke volumes.

I don't care.

Three little words that underlined how young and busy she was, and how old and lonely and dull I was by comparison. It stung because it spoke to the truth; her being there was a favor to me, not her.

I bit back my emotions and pretended to survey the space for the decorations it needed.

I actually did need a few things.

Curtains would help with the echoes. And pictures for the walls would cover their bareness. And why not a clock? I could use one of those clocks that ticks loudly for a few minutes a day, right when you need something to ground you in reality and pull you from your fantasies. For when the old humming refrigerator wasn't up to the task.

"Shopping would be nice," Zoey said, as though she could read my thoughts, which she couldn't—not like Margaret Mills, anyway.

Then she said, in the same neutral tone, "I can't remember which day Marzipants died. Was it before or after the wedding?"

"After," I said confidently, though it was a lie. The truth was, we'd all been so busy, we hadn't noticed. He might have passed the day before the wedding, then not been discovered until the day after.

Not to be a bummer, but—full disclosure—his unwitnessed death was yet another item on my list of things to feel bad about.

For, you know, when I was running short on things to feel tortured over.

"That Marzipants was a real character," she said with a heartbroken smile.

"He was a special bird," I said. "Bless his little spirit, wherever he is."

"Can we?"

"What?"

Zoey took my hand.

I was shocked by the sensation of her skin on mine, by the physical presence and the warmth of her.

But of course I was.

She'd been away a full month, an eternity for a parent.

We'd spoken plenty, so my ears had heard her voice, and my eyes had seen her face in pictures, but I hadn't touched her in all that time. I hadn't felt the familiar skin that had once been formed from my own, inside of me, always part of me, yet always very much and very independently hers.

She held my hand, then she closed her eyes, and she said a prayer for Marzipants.

He returned to life in my memories.

Find me, I heard in his little bird voice. *Find me!*

I had found him.

I had found him on his back, with his toes curled in the air.

Forgotten and alone.

My daughter prayed for our dear old Marzipants' little soul, and my heart broke a bit more.

CHAPTER 11

Saturday, October 6th

My daughter left on schedule, and I spent my first few nights alone in my new place. I didn't love it, but I didn't hate it. The wyverns hadn't found me yet, so my groceries seemed to be lasting forever.

The transition was likely easier since I had some continuity in my other activities. I'd been busy at the library by day, and busy in the community garden by night.

That first Saturday in October, I walked to the community gardens feeling lighter than I should have been, like I'd forgotten something. I didn't have Fyrsil with me. I'd been there plenty of times without him, but it would be my first Saturday without my little muddy buddy tucked into my sweatpants.

Mrs. Paisley Puddikin looked up from her pile of dirt and greeted me warmly in her always-loud British voice.

"Zara! You silly girl, you never knock me up!"

Tentatively, I said, "I, uh, try not to."

She got to her feet, pulling off her gardening gloves. "You never come visit and knock on my door. I'm right across the street from you, love."

"You are?"

"Of course! Aren't you in the Mystery Mansion?"

"That's funny. It sounded like you said Mystery Mansion. I'm actually renting in the old... oh."

The family that built the house had been the Mysters. Of course people called it the Mystery Mansion.

It didn't help that the old Dutch Colonial revival with a Beaux-Arts twist had two tall windows that looked like watchful eyes. Considering how much it resembled famous horror movie houses, *Mystery Mansion* was a pretty benign nickname.

Mrs. Puddikin must have found the look of realization on my face hysterical. She laughed like a horse, whinnying away with her prominent front teeth on display, for a full minute.

"I'm glad I could provide you with some entertainment, Mrs. Puddikin."

"Call me Paisley. Mrs. Puddikin sounds like a loud, old British lady with big buckteeth." She laughed again until she had to wipe tears from her rosy cheeks.

You gotta love people who can laugh at themselves. I'd been trying to get my own sense of humor back to full strength, and I hoped Mrs. Puddikin—Paisley—would rub off on me.

She composed herself and looked me over. "You've lost some weight there, love. One pudgy baby's worth. I do hope everything's okay with the little fellow."

"He's got swimming lessons today."

"So he's teaching already then, is he?"

"No, he's... oh. Ha ha." I picked up a shovel, and pushed the tip into the soil. "Need some help?"

"Yes. Just as soon as I remember if I'm digging up or planting." She walked over to a wheelbarrow full of tulip bulbs. "We're digging up," she said with confidence. "If we don't get the rest of the bulbs out before winter, the rabbits will turn this patch into an all-you-can-eat salad bar. They are strangely voracious around here, and don't get me started on the local toads."

"Aye, aye, captain."

We dug, hand-tilled, and weeded for several hours, finally stopping for tea a few hours later. The tea was served piping hot from a ceramic pot, a special blend of Paisley's making, fermented with a strain of lemon balm.

The other members of the community garden group came by to chat and drink tea on their way to other sections of the garden.

There were only six of us in total—the five who'd recruited me, plus me.

Paisley had privately confided that the other four were troublemakers, and that she was the only sane one in the group, and thus was happy to have a sane ally in me.

The next day, another member had taken me aside in private and given me the exact same speech. And so forth on the following day. Each member thought they were the sane one, but only I knew that the honors belonged to me. Probably.

I'd been warned that the spring would be the most contentious time for the group. However, if we had enough patience and love, we'd get through it, and see the fruits of our labor come summer. It was a good metaphor for life.

There were a few troublemakers in the group, though.

As I had watched them fight bitterly over variegated strains versus unvariegated, I'd been grateful that none of them knew about magic, let alone had their own powers. Oh, the damage they might have done.

I also learned a new saying: One person's weed is another's prize specimen.

On a personal level, connecting with the earth, with my hands in the soil, did make me feel more... *it's a cliche, but it's true...* grounded.

Paisley and I finished our tea break, then pulled up the remainder of the tulip bulbs. We'd finished not a moment too soon. A trio of bunnies scampered through the dug-up patch while we were taking our second tea break.

"Close call," Paisley said.

Another trio of bunnies came running through.

I asked, "Are we on a bunny superhighway or what? How have I never noticed all the bunnies?"

"They have underground tunnels," she said.

"You mean burrows?"

Her eyes twinkled. "These are more than mere burrows, love. They've got tunnels."

Yet another trio bounded through, hopping right over our feet as though we weren't even there.

"I've heard of the tunnels," I said. "My house fell into a sinkhole connected to the tunnels. What do you know about them?"

"People say you can walk in at one end, and show up somewhere else in town an hour before you left."

"Really?"

She laughed. "You know how people in this town are. Full of wild stories." She stopped laughing and tilted her head toward mine, in the universal old-lady gesture that indicated a shocking story was about to come from her lips. "You've heard about the treasure, haven't you?"

"Can't say that I have." That wasn't entirely true. I'd heard about treasure, and seen it with my own eyes. But that had been deep underwater, at the bottom of the ocean. And I'd had Chessa Wakeful's spirit inhabiting my body at the time. Mrs. Puddikin couldn't have known about that.

"They say it's everything that every treasure is known to be. Everlasting life. Fame beyond imagination. Riches without measure."

"Does it have a name?"

Mrs. Puddikin took a step back. "Why would it have a name?"

"Legendary treasures need legendary names. Like the Arc of the Covenant. Or the Sarcophagus of Menkaure. Or the... uh... Vessel of the Remainder." I'd had some personal experience with the last one. It had been ingested by my half-genie daughter, and had been incorporated into her. Technically Zoey had become a living Vessel of the Remainder, holding the balance of the world's souls, blah blah, end of the world stuff. I tried not to think about it.

"I've never heard of that last one," my fellow gardener said.

"Probably for the best. Ancient artifacts aren't nearly as much fun as they sound." I quickly added, "According to the books I've read about them. We have quite a selection at the library."

A group of five bunnies ran over our feet.

"We'd better get these bulbs stored away safely," Mrs. Puddikin said.

"How many bunnies are down there in these tunnels?"

Her eyes widened. "So many," she breathed. "In the darkness, there are chambers where it looks like dark waters, but it's just their eyes. A sea of dark eyes."

I actually shuddered at the idea of a sea of rabbit eyes glinting underground. I liked bunnies, but even cute things could be terrifying in large numbers.

I had to ask, "Have you been down there yourself?"

She laughed loudly. "Why would I ever go down there, love?"

"I don't know. To find the treasure?"

She laughed even louder. "I'm an old woman. I'll stick to my gardening, up here where it's bright. I'm not some old fool who'd go hunting after a treasure. Not like my dear old husband, bless his soul."

"So, it was your husband who told you all about this legendary yet unnamed treasure. What else did he tell you?"

She began loading the delicate china cups back into her wicker picnic basket. They clattered noisily. She wasn't taking the usual care to pack up that she typically did. She snapped shut the basket.

"I think that's about enough nonsense for one day," she said.

"When I'm at the library next week, I can see if there's anything about this local treasure."

"No need," she said. "It was all poppycock made up by my husband. He was foolin' around on me, love. Had another wife in another town."

"So, there's no treasure down there, guarded by an army of bunnies?"

Her face wrinkled, and her eyes glistened with tears. "I wish it were true, Zara. I really do."

"I'm sorry about your husband."

She shook out her gloves. "Nothing to be done about it now." She shook the gloves aggressively, then wrung them. "Walk you to your front door, love?"

"Hmm." I tilted my head from side to side. "Honestly, I'm not ready to go home yet."

"Having a hard time adjusting to being on your own? I remember when I was alone for the first time in forty years. The days felt so much longer." She started pulling her gloves back on. "I could garden a little longer. We still have sun."

"Don't let me keep you from getting home."

"Home to what?" She waved at the plants around us. "This is as much my home as anywhere."

She picked up her tools, and we trimmed back the laburnum as well as some especially crabby crabapple trees.

While we worked, I kept looking across the old train tracks, at an area we called the Wilds.

She saw me looking, and said, "You're thinking about getting wild and crazy, aren't you, love?"

"Someone should do something about the Wilds."

"Do it." She flashed her eyes at me. "Do it."

I grabbed the sturdiest of the shovels. "I'm doing it."

"You're doing it?"

I marched through the tidy patches, over the old train tracks, and into the most overgrown, least civilized area. She followed me.

"I'm doing it," I said as I dug my shovel into a dense green mass.

"You're doing it," Paisley Puddikin squealed, clapping her hands. "You're a true gardener, Zara! We've thoroughly corrupted you. Yay!"

I dug again. And again. There was no sign of progress. Shovel after shovel, under the green mass of leaves was only more green.

I began sweating profusely from my efforts. All of our lovely cups of tea leaked out my pores.

I paused and rested my chin on the shovel.

"There's no use," I said. "I'm not even hitting dirt. Look at my shovel. Not one speck." I waved across the Wilds. "We need heavy machinery for this. Something with big teeth. Something that runs on stinky diesel, and goes beep-beep-beep when you back it up."

Mrs. Puddikin shook her head. "You know the rules."

I did know the rules.

The other members of the community garden were vehemently opposed to machines in the garden.

My partner in crime, however, was a touch more pragmatic than the others, perhaps from her many years of running a successful clothing and home goods business, The Chintz Boutique.

I said slyly, "What if something were to... hypothetically happen with heavy machinery in this general area? Say, when there are no witnesses around?"

Paisley chewed her lower lip with her extra-large front teeth.

"I don't know, love. Do you mean hypothetically after dark?"

"That is the best time for things to happen without witnesses. Hypothetically."

"And do you also mean hypothetically tonight, when the other members are out of town at the Heirloom Tomato and Ketchup Festival?" She winked.

"Oh, is that where everyone is?"

Her eyes bulged, and darted from side to side. "You didn't hear it from me. And you certainly didn't hear that they'll be gone all weekend."

"Interesting."

I gave the greens at my feet one more whack with the shovel. Not only did I not hit dirt, but the plants seemingly grew back stronger. Were these magical plants? They had to be. Nothing else grew like that, not even Morning Glory.

Mrs. Puddikin dug into her carry-all bag, rummaged around, then handed me a tattered business card for a heavy equipment rental company.

"They rent out machines by the hour," she said. "I'm not brave enough to run something like that above ground, not with my terrible depth perception, but... well, I've said enough, love."

She saluted me goodbye. Salutes were something the group did with each other to avoid touching dirty hands. As a bonus, it transferred the dirt onto our foreheads and faces so that anyone we bumped into later in the day would know we were serious about gardening.

I watched her disappear behind the big, yellow sunflowers.

I tucked the equipment rental card into my pocket. I wouldn't be renting an excavator or even a mini skid steer, cute as they were.

I was a witch, and not just a theoretical witch on paper. I was a powerful witch, and I had plenty of spells that I'd been aching to use on the community garden. Until now, I'd always had a baby with me, or other people around. But tonight was different.

There was a cackling.

Witchy laughter.

It was me.

The sun would be setting soon, and the dark cover of night couldn't come quickly enough.

CHAPTER 12

One Hour After Sunset

I'd never been a prep cook at a restaurant, but I did have the perfect spell to make that job a breeze.

It was a blade spell, modified specifically for chopping carrots.

And since my daughter and I had an aversion to using knives to chop veggies—vegetable chopping never happens on a TV show or movie unless the person with the knife is about to lose a finger—I had plenty of practice using the spell.

Now, technically my carrot-dicing spell wasn't meant to be used in a garden, but carrots *were* roots, and the plants I was dealing with had similar thick roots, so I figured it was my best option.

I figured that once the plant roots had been diced, cubed, and julienned, I'd use a rake to quickly gather the severed stems.

The Wilds would soon be The Tames. Or something else that didn't sound like a famous river in London.

As I entered the community garden, darkness was my cloak. I cast a checking spell to make sure nobody was watching, and then I wasted no time casting the carrot-dicing spell.

The first sounds began below my boots.

POPPITY-POP.

POPPITY-POP?

That wasn't right. It should have been SNAPPITY-SNAP.

The POPPITY-POP continued beneath me.

It definitely wasn't a SNAPPITY-SNAP.

The sound spread out in a ripple around me, and gradually faded away. The power level I'd used would only extend six feet. If it worked as intended, I'd simply cast it repeatedly while walking up and down the wild patch.

After the spell subsided, I knelt where I'd been standing, at the epicenter, and used a hand spade to dig up a sample.

To my disappointment, the root of the plant I pried out was whole, unbroken.

I compared it to the sample I'd dug up before the spell.

The root had changed. It was no longer shaped like a skinny carrot. It had multiple jagged lines around the circumference, and bulged between those lines, like a knobby finger.

Had the root adapted to the spell, changing its shape to evade chopping? That had never happened in my kitchen.

I set the root on the ground in front of me, and watched carefully as I cast a tightly focused carrot-chopping spell.

My magic diced the carrot-like root into perfectly-even chunks, ideal for stewing. The green part wilted. All was working as it ought to.

I placed all the parts together, waiting for it to Dr. Frankenstein itself back together in the moonlight.

A minute passed.

Nothing happened; the plant did not reconstitute itself.

That meant the spell itself wasn't the problem, so it had to be some other variable, like the soil, or the fact the root wasn't visible to the spellcaster, yours truly.

Now what? I'd been so certain the blade spell would work that I hadn't considered many backup plans.

Of course if I'd still have levitation powers, I'd have simply used that.

Losing that one ability really drove home the fact that levitation was the simplest fix for ninety-nine percent of life's inconveniences. It unlocked most doors, literally and metaphorically. That did explain why the devil—a young man named Atom Wick—had taken it from us.

If only our coven hadn't taken the risk of banishing him. Now we were living with the consequences.

If I'd had all my old powers, I'd be able to clear that garden patch in an instant. I would be heading home by now.

Instead, I fantasized about putting a curse on Atom's head. He deserved a big, angry boil on the middle of his forehead. But cursing him only made him stronger, and it also made him keenly aware of the curser.

He hadn't been around much since the night of the tornado, and I wanted to stay off his radar.

Even so, I wasted plenty of time thinking up curses to ruin his good looks, sweating with each flash of anger. Now I was shivering in the cool evening air of autumn.

What was I doing out there, all alone, in the untamed corner of a community garden? Waiting for some sort of divine guidance from a higher power?

A familiar psychic voice entered my mind.

"What are you doing, Zed?"

"Isn't it obvious? I'm making the world a better place."

"You speak in riddles, hence the warning of your name."

"What?"

"I named your ancestors, Zed."

"Did not."

"Many years ago, I named them Riddle so that I would know to avoid your bloodline."

"But you do the opposite of avoiding us, so that can't be true."

"Then tell me what is true, Zed. Why have you summoned me to these grounds? These dank warrens?"

"I didn't summon you."

"You did."

"Did not."

"Did."

"Not."

"I was summoned!"

"Hey now!" I yelled back. "There's no need for that."

He sulked in the darkness, wherever he was.

"Show yourself," I said.

He remained in the darkness.

"Ribbons, you're not afraid of me, are you?"

He didn't answer.

"I'm not going to hurt you," I said. "We've been over this. I didn't mean to hit you that day in the bathtub. I was worried about your steam around the baby, and when I reached out, it was pure instinct. Just like you when you went into attack mode."

The wyvern continued to sulk in the darkness. He would need more time.

I dug up another version of the weed, replanted it partly in the dirt, and tried the carrot-dicing spell.

It went half SNAPPITY-SNAP and half POPPITY-POP.

Next, I tried a spell for making appetizers with celery sticks.

That didn't work, but I wasn't surprised. Nobody liked celery sticks, and nobody liked that spell.

I tried a spell for removing sticky tape, then tried it with some extra stank on it.

That removed the outer husky layer from the root, and I thought I was good to go with the carrot-dicing spell next, but it was no more effective than when I'd started.

Ribbons finally showed his green scaly self, flapping into the pool of moonlight I'd gathered around myself. He landed on the handle of a pitchfork stuck in the ground.

"It takes a powerful creature to make magic look easy, Zed."

"Thanks."

"Not you. You make magic look difficult."

"Why are you here, anyway? Shouldn't you be on the mountain with RJ? Hunting for adorable furry things to eviscerate?"

"My son is at swimming lessons."

There was a snip to his tone that discouraged me from pressing for details. There had been custody issues involving the hatchling's mother, who made her home in another dimension. I knew better than to offer my sympathy, let alone my opinion. Ribbons didn't want a referral to my lawyer, and he didn't want my opinion on the matter.

"Since you're here, let's play a game," I said. "How many of these plants can you yank out of the dirt in sixty seconds? I'll set a timer, and see if you can break my record."

The wyvern responded by holding absolutely still on the pitchfork handle, except for his tongue, which he used to lick one eye and then the other. He made an audible SLURP. I still didn't know why he licked his eyes. He had tears, and eyelids.

"At least stay quiet while I cast the next spell," I said.

He did.

I prepared to cast my aunt's beloved spell for perfectly round melon balls.

The scoop action could be an effective way to sever the plant roots and loosen the soil at the same time.

I realized, as I shivered in the night air, that it was a much better match of a spell than the one for vegetable chopping. Naturally, I was low-key furious at myself for not thinking of it sooner. Sometimes I had too many choices.

I let loose the melon ball spell.

The ground beneath my boots didn't go SCOOPITY-SCOOP as it should have.

It went, once again, POPPITY-POP.

Now I was furious at myself for even expecting it to work.

And why would it have worked? It was a spell for melon balls. I was trying to use it on unidentified weeds, growing underground. Who or what exactly did I think I was? The beginner's luck I'd experienced at the start of my time as a witch had gone to my head and made me overconfident.

I grabbed a shovel and started digging. If I worked all night, I could dig a big hole to jump into, then pull the dirt on top of myself, and just die already.

Was this what a Down-in-the-Dumps witch did when facing failure?

If so, then I was the living embodiment of a DITD witch.

"Remarkable," said the wyvern in my head. "Your valiant attempts to overcome your own towering ineptitude are truly remarkable, Zed."

I kept digging and growled back, "Don't tempt me to backhand you like the crap-talking, misshapen tennis ball you are."

"Not even in the dimmest light do I resemble a tennis ball. Your metaphor is as sloppy as your Witch Tongue."

"Keep it up, and I'll build myself a special tennis racket so I can hit you around the court until your sharp edges are smoothed away."

He used his little mouth to let out a creepy wyvern chuckle. He was enjoying my threats of violence. He had gotten over the bathtub incident and we were... whatever we were again.

Under his watchful beady dyes, I stopped digging my grave.

I couldn't be a DITD witch. I had people counting on me. My landlord, for example, would wonder where the rent payment was.

Plus I had responsibilities to my fellow community gardeners.

It wasn't much, but it was better than a dirt nap.

I used my shovel to wrestle another plant from the soil, and examined the root. This one was more rootlike than ever. The knobs had sprouted accessory roots, which also had new shoots growing upward.

I wasn't killing plants, I was propagating them.

I said out loud for dramatic effect, "I'm not killing plants, I'm propagating them."

Ribbons hopped down, grabbed a rooted plant by the stem, and tugged. When the plant came free, he fell backward onto his pointy tail, exposing his underbelly to me.

His little underbelly was glittery and pale in the moonlight. It was more adorable and tempting than even a cat's belly.

I reached over and gave it a tickle.

Just a little one.

The wyvern's limbs flew outward in helplessness.

He was ticklish!

I tickled a second time.

He curled away from my hand, rolled into a ball, then flung himself into the air like a swarm of bees.

I knew murderous rage when I saw it coming at my face.

I had to cast the jelly bubble again.

It was good I'd been practicing.

Minutes later, after he wrestled himself free of the glowing jelly, we went through the usual routine.

I begged his forgiveness while he detailed the ways he ought to wear my body parts as garments.

"Vile witch, I will use your strong red hair as a loofah for scrubbing the scales of my undercarriage."

"You wash yourself, Ribbons? In what? The sewage treatment plant?"

"You would not understand my smell if I gave you a new nose and adequate sinuses. You humans, you have too much face."

I snorted. "I have too much face? Is that the best you've got?"

"Arguing with you is like force-feeding sorrow to a Wallflower Ghoul. You enjoy it too much for it to be enjoyable for me."

"I don't *not* enjoy it," I admitted. "Now help me figure out how to remove these weeds, if you're so clever."

He waddled over to one of the holes in the dirt we'd made, squatted over it, left a steaming deposit, and then flew away.

I called after him, "Don't go away mad, but do go away."

He hated to let me have the last word, so I expected he would be back again like a boomerang, but he didn't return.

I was alone again with the weeds.

I probably shouldn't have tickled his belly. But he did need more practice controlling his rage if he wanted to be in the same room as Fyrsil again—not that Fyrsil needed another bad influence in his life.

A chilly breeze brought the scent of the wyvern's fresh deposit to my nose.

I nearly gagged.

I relocated to a different part of the garden. I still caught a few whiffs, but it reminded me to be grateful that since I no longer lived with a cat, I no longer had a litter box that the wyvern could use for his business when he didn't feel like going outside. That was probably the main reason he hadn't been by the Mystery Mansion.

Back to the task at hand. Taming the Wilds.

I brightened my working light a little bit, and examined the dense vegetation in that area.

Over here, the plants had variegated leaves, and the roots that were closer to beets than carrots.

I ran through the same series of spells, hoping for better results.

The beet-like plants responded by lengthening themselves a full inch above and below the soil.

So much for those spells.

I moved away from the fruit and vegetable category, away from office supplies, and onto a spell normally used to regrow hair, fur, or feathers.

Once again, I found myself questioning my thought process.

Why hadn't I tried that one first?

The regrowth spell had terrible side effects when used on humans. It thickened hair above the skin, but at the cost of weakening the roots.

In my situation, the side effect was the main effect I was looking for. If I could force all the vitality of the plants into the part above the surface, the roots would atrophy, and yank out easily.

Could I remember the incantation order? I hadn't cast that spell since Halloween the year before.

No.

It had been two years ago.

That was the year Zoey had been dressed as Marzipants for our house party. I'd used the spell to fill in the bare patches of her feathered costume.

Last Halloween, she had dressed as...

We celebrated by...

I couldn't remember. We hadn't gone to the Monster Mash at Castle Wyvern. I knew that much. What had we done?

I shivered again.

I saw myself the way a passing ghost might see me.

It was three o'clock in the morning, and I was kneeling in an overgrown patch of community garden, trying to do something that didn't even need doing.

What difference did it make whether that area was weeds or something we'd intentionally planted? A weed was just someone else's prized specimen.

I decided against casting the hair-growth spell. It might have been the perfect solution, or it might have made everything ten times worse.

It wasn't like me to walk away from a problem in need of a solution, but I was living a new life now. A life where I didn't go looking for trouble.

I got up and headed home.

Back to the Mystery Mansion, back to the third floor, back to my modest little apartment with the library in the bathroom.

I fell into the asymmetrical bottom of my bunk bed, and slept fitfully.

I dreamed of bony hands reaching for me, reaching through walls and floors and ceilings, reaching for me and everyone I knew.

I woke from the nightmare and sat up with a start.

These were no ordinary nightmares.

Something did have a hold on me.

It was the Wilds. The patch of garden that didn't want to be tamed.

I had to do something about it.

I would not be able to rest well until I'd turned every inch of topsoil, and rendered it civilized.

With that fact acknowledged, I fell down into the soft bed and slept deeply until morning.

When I fully woke up a few hours later, I knew what I had to do.

CHAPTER 13

Sunday

I watched from a safe distance as the big, green truck pulling an equally big trailer arrived at the community garden. The trailer held something more powerful than the feeble gardening spells I'd been frustrated with the night before: a mini skid-steer.

Mrs. Paisley Puddikin stood next to me, wringing her hands and making tsk-tsk sounds.

"I'm sure he knows what he's doing," I said.

TSK TSK she said.

The driver, an old man with wildly-tousled white hair, gave us a thumbs-up signal as he navigated through a tight spot in a fence.

TSK TSK went Mrs. Puddikin.

"Then again, maybe he doesn't know what he's doing," I said. "I guess I see a guy like that, with silver hair, or white hair, and I just assume that whatever he's currently doing is something he's been doing his whole life. Kind of a big assumption, really. You can judge a book by its cover, but not a person."

She tore her gaze off the truck, and blinked at me. "Speaking of silver hair, how is Frank Wonder? He used to buy up all my vintage paisley menswear, but he hasn't been in to see me in ages."

"Frank went through a bit of a style makeover," I said. "He's out of the vintage and the pink hair. He wears tailored suits. Even his pranks have become classier. He found me an apartment, furnished it, and threw me a housewarming. I'm not sure it even qualifies as a prank."

"But no more paisley?"

"Maybe in a tie? He's done with corduroy, too."

"But what did *paisley* ever do to him?" She looked offended on a personal level, and maybe she was. Her name was Paisley, so it figured she'd have some feelings about people rejecting the pattern of the same name.

"Maybe you could entice him back with a more subtle version of paisley."

She went from looking offended to horrified. "There's nothing subtle about paisley. It comes from the Zoroastrian symbol of a cypress tree. It represents life itself. There's nothing subtle about life itself."

"Is that why your parents named you Paisley?"

She pulled her head back abruptly. "Of course not. That would be ridiculous. I'm named after the Scottish town, of course."

"Of course," I said.

I could be agreeable when I wanted to.

"Not the town in Ontario, Canada," she said. "Or the one in Florida, or Oregon, or Pennsylvania, or South Australia."

"Of course," I agreed again.

The engine noises filling the usually-quiet garden changed tone. The truck had stopped alongside the railroad tracks, ready to unload.

We walked over.

The driver told me I could unload the rental myself for practice as my first lesson, so I hopped onto the trailer, and climbed into the little machine. The cab was very small, and felt more like a golf cart than my car, but I could work with that.

The driver lowered the back gate of the trailer, turning it into a ramp.

He gave me a few instructions, plus a pair of safety headphones, and I drove it down the ramp.

The controls were more complicated than a car, but logical enough. It could go forward and back, steering left and right on its tank-like tracks which skidded across the ground. The front-end loader mechanism was on its own set of controls. Everything was clearly labeled. If only everything in life came with such clear labels.

The driver said to me, "Heavy machinery suits you, Ms. Riddle."

"I bet you say that to all the girls."

He grinned and winked. "I do. And it's always true." He was quite flirty for a guy in his nineties.

"Thanks again for renting this to me on such short notice."

"No trouble at all," he said. "Park 'er right here when you're done, and I'll pick 'er up first thing Monday morning. You don't need to be around, but don't get too attached and try to take Betsy home with you. She's already rented out for the week."

I patted the hood. "I'll take good care of Betsy."

"Her full name is Betsy-Boop-Boop. You'll understand why after you've had 'er in and out of reverse a few hours. That reminds me..." He ran back to the big, green truck, and came back with a second set of safety headphones that he handed to me. "Make sure Paisley wears these if she's helping."

I would. I could cast mini sound bubbles to protect my ears, but I would also wear my headphones to be less suspicious. Sometimes non-magical solutions were better than magical ones. Like, for example, renting excavation equipment instead of losing my mind or hexing myself in the moonlight with failed spellwork.

"Betsy has a new seat warmer," he said, showing me how to switch on the coil for the heated seat.

I thanked him again, and the driver, who I suspected was also the owner of the equipment rental company, went over to chat with Mrs. Puddikin.

I actually pulled out the grimy, rain-warped instruction manual—there's a first time for everything—and read through it.

The driver and Mrs. Puddikin continued talking, in hushed tones I couldn't hear.

Was the old fellow hitting on her? What a champ.

They turned their backs to me, so I couldn't see how she was taking what I assumed were his best pick-up lines.

I finished reading the instruction manual.

I looked up as the big, green truck and trailer were driving away.

The sun was about as high overhead as could be in October.

Here we were, out in broad daylight, just me, my co-conspirator, and our rented mini skid steer.

If our fellow gardeners weren't out of town at the Heirloom Tomato and Ketchup Festival, judging the new relishes and chutneys, we'd have been in big trouble. By the time they found out, it would be too late. I would take all of the blame, since I was still new enough to claim ignorance of the rules.

Mrs. Puddikin stopped wringing her hands and gnashing her buck teeth long enough to make us a fresh pot of tea. Years ago, the community garden had heated water on a wood fire, but they couldn't keep up on all the town's permit requirements without a full-time administrator, so they'd switched to solar. On a clear day, our panels generated more than enough energy to boil a kettle.

We sipped our cups of piping hot tea, and stared at Betsy.

Mrs. Puddikin said, "We are going to get in so much trouble when the others find out."

"I'm sure they'll find a way to forgive us when they see how much we've been able to expand the garden. It's like making new land."

I finished my tea, climbed into the machine, switched on the heated seat, and fired up the engine.

Ah, power.

I hadn't felt that much raw power under my control since Atom Wick took our powers.

I put Betsy-Boop-Boop in what I thought was Drive.

She went BOOP BOOP BOOP, and backed up over our best patch of sunflowers.

I took her out of Reverse, and put her in Drive for real.

That went slightly better, but not great. Power was hard to control, in any form. Power begged you to put the pedal to the metal well before you were ready.

I eliminated some daisies that hadn't done anything to deserve it.

"The steering is a bit stiff," I called over the engine noise to Mrs. Puddikin.

She yelled back, "Is that why you can't drive it in a straight line?"

I didn't have any excuse for that.

She dove out of the way, even though I hadn't come anywhere near her.

I headed for the wild patch, cutting an accidental swath through the rest of the wilted daisies.

They'd grow back.

Daisies were just like the Riddle family. Tougher than we look.

CHAPTER 14

The Next Saturday

October 13th

I parked my car, Foxy Pumpkin, in front of the tall red-brick building known as The Candy Factory.

It was my first visit since I'd stayed there on Frank's couch, and my first time seeing the place fully decorated for that year's Halloween.

The residents had spared no expense, adding to last year's already-impressive display. It looked like Hell had thrown up all over the place. There had to be over a dozen skeletons on the front lawn, plus more climbing up the facade of the building. Some were human skeletons, but the majority were creatures both real and mythical. The skeletons were the traditional white, except for a grouping on the lawn. They were a flamboyance of flamingos, and they were hot pink, even though they had no feathers. It was so wrong, but it felt so right.

Everything was lit by endless strings of lights in white, orange, and purple. A thick fog had rolled in that morning, and its presence gave the decorations a perfectly spooky ambiance, but the building itself did most of the work.

I still had Frank's spare key, so I let myself in. Now that I didn't have telekinesis for easy door unlocking, I'd gotten to be a bit of a spare-key hoarder. Let that be your warning. Don't give me a key if you want it back.

The Candy Factory's communal brass mailboxes were the same style as the ones in my new place, but the fancy chandelier in the foyer was much more lavish. We had a cheap modern dome light, the round kind with the threaded pin in the middle—the type that people called a *boob light*.

The building's hallway and stairwell gave me a wave of claustrophobia with a side of nausea, but once I was through Frank's dark wooden door, I was relaxed again.

His apartment was lofted, with a high ceiling, brick walls, and exposed wood beams. After a few weeks of living in my much cozier apartment, it felt like an aircraft hangar by comparison.

A few of Frank's other friends were there already, fussing over the brunch items. They were a colorful, fun group, even though none of them knew about magic, much less had powers. Being around them was like being in the garden—they made me feel grounded. Of course I didn't tell them that. Most people wouldn't take it as a compliment, even though it was about as good a compliment as a person could get.

Frank handed me a mimosa, and said, "There's just a splash of champagne in these. We don't need anyone throwing up on the hay ride."

After brunch, the group of us were going to the annual Wisteria Hay Ride. I'd been once, the year before, so I knew what to expect. It started like any regular hay ride, with a horse-drawn carriage full of hay bales for seats. Then, once the ride passed through a covered bridge, actors and volunteers in costumes jumped out of their hiding places to give thrills and frights. The ride continued through a series of tableaus. Last year's tableaus had been too gruesome, so the Permits

Department had withheld this year's permits until the organizers had agreed to use fake corn-syrup blood instead of—I hesitate to tell you this, lest you think poorly of our town and its people—actual blood from a slaughterhouse.

I finished my mimosa, and asked for a refill.

"Don't worry about me getting motion sickness," I said. "I have a very strong stomach."

"It wasn't the motion that got everyone sick last year," he said.

"Right. Well, I'm sure the corn-syrup blood won't smell nearly as bad."

"This town can be so embarrassing sometimes."

"Yeah, but some of the quirks are what keep the property prices down. If everyone who came to visit stuck around, we'd all get squeezed out."

"True," he said.

I greeted the other brunch guests, then stationed myself in the kitchen, putting garnishes on the mini quiches.

Frank watched me, his small, hooded eyes narrowing. His pointy, crooked chin shifted from one side to the other, like the carriage on an old typewriter.

Finally, he could take it no longer, and smacked me on the back of the hand.

"Zara Riddle, you've got dirt under your fingernails."

"It's just dirt," I said. "Dirt is good for you. It's got microbes."

"I'm perfectly happy to have you help, but you need to wash up."

"You're *perfectly happy*, are you?" I raised my eyebrows. Frank and I always used that phrase to mean the exact opposite, the way most people did, only we were aware of it.

"Fine. I'll *tolerate* your help, but only if you remove your microbes."

He pointed emphatically at the sink.

I got scrubbing.

"We'll have no microbes on the mini quiches today," he said. "You're like a wild animal."

"I'm not that bad."

"Honestly, I'm surprised you haven't been banned from the community garden, considering what you did last weekend."

"Hah! Not only am I not banned, but they all pitched in to reimburse me for the rental fee on Betsy-Boop-Boop. It just goes to prove that old adage: It's better to beg forgiveness than ask permission."

"That's dangerous wisdom to have," Frank said.

"It also proves that other old adage: People do not see the value in renting heavy-duty mechanical equipment by the hour to clear an overgrown garden until they've tried it one time."

"Now you're just making up adages."

I held up my hands for inspection. My fingernails had never been cleaner.

"Good enough," Frank said.

"Mrs. Puddikin misses you. She says you never pop in anymore."

"That's not true. I pop in all the time to look at the silk ties. She's the one who's never there anymore."

"What? But she's practically a fixture at that place. Are you going in on the weekends? That's when she's in the garden."

"No. Weekdays on my lunch break, like usual," he said.

"Maybe she's avoiding you because you hurt her feelings when you rejected paisley."

"Parsley! That's it!"

"What?" I'd said paisley, not parsley.

"The pesto," he said. "I almost forgot. Brunch would have been a disaster."

He got the basil and parsley pesto from the fridge.

We all had a fantastic brunch, with many laughs.

116

I had never really bonded with Frank's friends before this, but that Saturday morning I revealed a few of the quirks I'd learned about him during my stay. Everyone howled with the delight of recognition.

After cleaning up—to Frank's quirky specifications—we all bundled up and went outside to take the haunted hay ride.

The fog stayed rolled in all day.

The hay ride event was good, but not as memorable as the previous year.

Call me an old-fashioned witch, but haunted hay rides aren't nearly as much fun without half your party barfing over the sides of the wagon.

CHAPTER 15

Sunday, October 14th

On Sunday, I went with Frank and his friends to the corn maze.

I bumped into Liza Gilbert, and her scurry of chipmunk bridesmaids. She greeted me with high-pitched squeals, like she was reuniting with a long-lost friend, and had also been sucking on helium balloons. Her bridesmaids, who were in their regular clothes, made their chipmunk sounds.

I hadn't seen her since the wedding day, so I asked, "How was the honeymoon?"

"So, so, so good," Liza gushed. "Hey! You should join me and the girls for one of our girl dates. We girly-girls do so many interesting things." She grabbed my hand and leaned in to say, "It's hard being married to an actual man. I do love my time off with my girls."

"Oh, yeah. I hear marriage can be a lot of work."

"It is." She rolled her eyes. "So much work."

"My condolences."

She bounced up and down on the spot. "So? How are you? Seeing anyone?"

"Just enjoying my time as an empty nester."

She gave me a funny look. "You're into... bird stuff?"

"Am I? I'm an empty nester. It's what people like me are called when our kids have left for school. When they've flown the nest."

She made a sour face. "I don't think that's okay to say these days."

"It's not?"

"Because of... *you know*." She whispered, "Because it's insulting to people who can't get rid of their adult children. Like that they aren't able to be birds, you know?"

"Uh, that's not what that saying means."

She furrowed her brow. "You need to do your research."

Her chipmunk bridesmaids grew bored of standing by while we talked, and dragged her away, along the corridor of corn rows.

Frank, who'd been observing the interaction, said to me, "That generation is really sensitive about bird metaphors."

"I don't get it."

"Of course not." He snorted. "You let your daughter dress up as a budgie for Halloween."

I paused. "Was that offensive to you, as a bird shifter?"

"Me? No. But I'm not like the young people. The whole bird thing has really gotten out of hand."

"I had no idea. Zoey speaks the same language as me."

"When she's around you. I bet she's completely different around people her own age. It's like they're from another planet."

I pulled out my phone and checked. No new messages from Zoey. But that was fine. No news was good news. She was having a normal college experience. Just like she'd always wanted.

"Come on," Frank said. "We need to get out of this maze and claim our hot cinnamon cocoa before it's all gone."

He pulled me in the opposite direction of where I'd been headed.

"This is the fastest way out," he said. "I flew over a few times when they were setting it up."

I went with him.

"Frank Wonder, what would I ever do without you?"

"You'd get lost and wander around this maze until nightfall, and then call me to rescue you."

"Call for rescue? I'd sooner burn it all down."

"Sounds about right," he said. "Are you coming to Becky's Roadhouse with us after this?"

"I can't," I said.

"But she's got another new local beer. And darts."

"I promised to help the gang finish up that new area in the garden."

"But it's almost winter. Can't it wait until spring?"

"We'll be way too busy in the spring if we don't get on top of things now."

We were whipping through the corn maze now, Frank leading the way.

It wasn't until we were out of the exit and standing in line to get our prize beverages that I realized we'd missed out. The whole point of a corn maze was to get lost in it, not to sail through it like it was nothing.

Frank was older than me, but he wasn't always wiser.

* * *

After the corn maze, I joined my gardening group, and we lost ourselves in our work.

All six of us worked together to finish tidying up the formerly wild area. It looked larger than ever now that it was cleared and ready for planting. The tough, thick-rooted plants—still unidentified—were now smoldering in a burn pile, fueled by dry, old dead wood from our fruit trees.

We stood around our bonfire, groaning about our sore backs and battle wounds—mostly scratches from thorns— like a bunch of army veterans.

There was nothing quite like a big, crackling fire on a cold autumn day.

As the fire died down, the other five packed up and left to pick up some fence supplies. We didn't need a fence, but it would enhance the look of the garden, and fall was a good time to plant certain things like fence posts. Legend had it that the spring's new shoots would feel more confident if the dormant roots had a full winter to admire a strong fence.

It never ceased to amaze me how much some regular people understood magic on an instinctive level. They felt the energy of not just living but inanimate things. It was strongest in those lucky sensitives who were able to detect magnetic waves.

I'd learned to hear the ultrasonic chatter of plants. Previous to discovering magic, I'd had no idea plants could even communicate, much less chatter. I was learning new ways to listen every day.

That Sunday in October, a fog-free day and a clear evening, I puttered around the fire, lost without being lost.

I poked at the embers to make them crackle. I could have extinguished the fire and gone home, but instead I added more dry fuel.

With the rumble of its engine, a red fire truck pulled up. It was not the big fire truck used for putting out fires, but a small passenger pickup that was also red, with the Wisteria Fire Department logo on the door.

The driver's side door opened. A big, burly firefighter stepped out, and walked up to me and the fire.

I stopped poking the embers and asked, "Am I in trouble?"

The firefighter, a fellow named Bon, said, "No trouble at all, Zara. I noticed you started an hour later than the time on the burn permit. I just stopped by to see if you needed any help."

"I appreciate your watchful eye." I gestured to our linen-covered table of refreshments. "Cup of tea?"

He rubbed his big hands over the fire. "I shouldn't. It's my day off, and I should get back to the Missus." He didn't leave.

"It's just tea," I said.

I poured two cups, and handed him one. The delicate china looked like a dollhouse teacup in Bon's large hand.

"Mmm," he said after the first sip. "Lemon balm."

"How are things going at home?"

He shrugged his big shoulders.

"Be patient," I said. "This is a big change for her."

"But it's what she wanted," he said with frustration. "Everything is exactly what she said she wanted."

"Ah. But what we say we want and what we actually want, those are different things."

Bon furrowed his brow. "I don't understand you supernatural women."

"People aren't easy. I don't think it's a trait that's exclusive to women, supernatural or otherwise."

"Things should be more simple," Bon said. "Predictable. Like a fire." He glanced up, then stepped to the side, just as the smoke changed direction and puffed through the spot where he'd been standing.

"Something tells me you'll figure it out," I said.

Bon had fallen for my friend Charlize Wakeful, the blonde gorgon who worked on and off for the Department of Water and Magic. She had decided that Bon was the answer to the question she hadn't known to ask.

The two had gotten married last Halloween—that was what I did for Halloween last year!—and now Charlize was pregnant.

It was what she'd wanted, and yet not what she'd wanted.

She'd asked for a baby, then found herself expecting triplets.

Triplets was a big deal for any woman, let alone one who'd never imagined herself being a mom until quite recently.

It was very nearly the definition of "be careful what you wish for," yet not shocking. Triplets ran in the family, and Charlize was one herself. If anyone could handle three babies, it was Charlize. She'd learned from the best mom: her own mom.

And so Bon and I talked about babies, and Charlize, and how wonderful life would be as their new future unfolded.

We poked at the embers and basked in their warm glow until the conversation had burned through all its fuel.

In the distance, Frogs were croaking their end-of-summer songs.

Bon handed me the empty teacup. There was a big smile on his face—one he hadn't arrived with.

"Thanks for the talk," he said.

"Give her a hug for me," I said.

He went to his truck, and I stayed where I was, not taking my eyes off the fire.

The fire went to sleep.

I poured water on it, and stirred the ashes.

Mixed in with the frog noises was another sound in the distance—music.

Had Mrs. Puddikin left behind her portable radio?

The darkness shifted, and a rabbit hopped into view and across my feet on its way elsewhere.

The music continued, distant yet familiar.

There was a rustling, and a sound of movement on the ground. Something was incoming.

All at once, I was surrounded by rabbits, a rushing river of rabbits, streaming around me.

They were all heading to the center of the newly-cleared patch.

I ran after them, just in time to see them vanish. They hadn't scurried into hiding places under bushes or wheelbarrows. They'd all gone straight down, into the earth. Like a river flowing through a field, and then suddenly swirling down the drain of a sinkhole.

I leaned over the dark hole.

The last rays of blue light from the disappearing sun went out.

Night had fallen, its silken cloak all around.

The frogs in the distance ceased their song.

The music, however, continued, emanating from the hole. From underground.

Since my arrival in the town of Wisteria, I'd seen an awful lot of unusual things, but not much in the community garden. The weirdest thing so far had been the unidentified plants, and their resistance to my feeble spells.

I had a theory that the garden existed in a dead zone. That would explain why nobody had developed the land into buildings, despite it being well located, walking distance to many of the town's amenities.

But now there was this mysterious hole that held a remarkable volume of bunnies, and music.

The DWM had facilities underground, but it was deep, deep underground. Multiple stories. And well protected.

I used some magic lip balm to turn the tip of my finger into a light, and slowly stuck it into the hole.

The opening appeared to be made of dirt, and just wide enough for a rabbit to squeeze through.

My heart was pounding hard. I was... scared? Excited?

I blew out my finger light, chuckling self-consciously. Talk about an OCW. Here I was, conducting an ultra-serious investigation of a rabbit's burrow.

But did rabbits listen to music in their burrows? And what was that tune? It sounded like an AM radio stuck between two soft rock stations.

I was low on magic lip balm, so I pulled out my phone. I switched on the light, and the video camera, and stuck it deeper into the hole.

Something cold and stiff wrapped around my wrist. It was dry, not metallic but not a plant root or vine.

I managed to not freak out... until the thing squeezed my wrist.

Then I let out an embarrassing OCW shriek, and yanked my hand out of the hole.

I jumped back, ready for the hole's next move, magic pooling in my palms.

A minute passed, and nothing emerged.

The music was gone. Had it ever been there at all?

My wrist was dirty, but unharmed.

However, I had lost my phone.

From a distance of a few feet, I cast an object retrieval spell on my phone. It didn't come flying out of the hole. That wasn't too surprising, considering the spell barely did anything without levitation.

I inched closer to the hole, and in my most polite voice, I said, "Please, may I have my phone back?"

My phone flew out of the hole, and straight into my hands. It was undamaged, except for some smudges of dirt.

"Who's down there?"

No answer.

"Frank? Is that you down there? Or someone I know? It's me. Zara."

Still nothing.

And then, just when I'd started to believe I was hallucinating the whole thing, the hole closed.

Now, over my years as a witch, I had built up a high tolerance to the heebie jeebies, but I still got them from time to time.

The heebie jeebies came on with a shudder.

I wanted to review the footage on my phone, but not there in the dark, formerly wild part of the garden.

I checked the firepit one more time, grabbed my bag, and headed for home.

CHAPTER 16

Later that Night

The intercom in my apartment buzzed.

"Intercom," I said on the way to the unit. "Intercom. Intercom."

I was nervous. The video on my phone had been unsettling. I was trying to be cool, pretending I wasn't rattled, but apparently I was talking to myself, and repeating myself.

I pressed the small, black button to unlock the door, then the orange button. "Come on up. Third floor."

There was no click. My visitor had not opened the exterior door in time.

I pushed the orange button again. "What's going on down there?"

"You tell me." It was the voice of our town's detective, who was also my half-sister. "Aren't you going to ask who it is?"

Just hearing her voice was already helping my nerves enough that I could goof around.

"Whooo is at my door?" Imitating my coworker, Kathy, always cracked up Persephone. "Whooo could it beee? Whooo doth buzz the intercom after darkness has settleth on the land?"

There was no laughter. "It's me, Persephone."

"But how do I know? Anyone could say that."

"Zara, it's me."

"Prove it. Hold your badge up to the intercom."

There was a rustling sound. She was doing what I asked her to.

I said, "You know this thing doesn't have a camera, right?"

"How should I know that? Cameras are tiny these days. Almost invisible. It's a huge problem, you dummy."

I pressed the button for the door. "Just come in already. Stop messing around. You'll get me in trouble with the landlord."

There was a click over the intercom as the front door opened.

I opened my door to the hallway, and waited.

Detective Persephone Rose came bouncing up the stairs, pink-cheeked, with her dark ponytail swinging.

She wore bright-colored athletic gear, but didn't smell of sweat. She'd probably been running in her fox shifter form—something she lived for. Well, that, and dating guys who were bad for her. Those were two of her passions in life, right after solving crimes.

My dark-haired sibling barely hugged me hello before dumping her sporty backpack on the floor. She gave the new apartment an inspection. A full, detailed inspection.

She'd been too busy to attend my housewarming, so now she scrutinized every corner. She sniffed loudly, then pressed aggressively on a section of paneling. The wall let out a crisp CRACK, the sound of an old paint seal being broken, and a hidden cupboard sprung open under her fingers.

"It never gets old," Persephone said with satisfaction.

"Have you been here before? How did you know?"

"It's the scent. I can smell hidden cupboards."

"Oh, really. And what do hidden cupboards smell like?"

"Like the inside of a sailboat in a windstorm on Friday the thirteenth," she said, and then she inhaled deeply.

I hadn't been expecting an answer at all, let alone one so oddly specific.

The cupboard wasn't empty. It held a selection of glass marbles, tin soldiers, old smoking pipes, and a single walnut, unopened.

"I had no idea that space was there," I said.

"That's why I'm the detective and you're just a librarian."

"Ouch." I held my hand to my chest.

"Oh, come on, Zara. It's just a joke. It's no worse than what you say to me all the time."

"I tell you that you're *just a detective?*"

"You imply it."

"Do not."

"Do too."

"Not."

"Do."

"Nuh."

"Duh."

She went to my kitchen—it was only a few steps away —and started poking around.

"Not cool," she said. "You don't have anything decent for snacks."

"Gee, Persephone, I'm really glad I invited you over to my new place. Definitely not regretting it at all."

She finished ransacking the cupboards, and took a seat on the petite wingback chair, which was only petite for a wingback and not small at all.

She sat sideways, with her athletic legs hanging over the arm. She held out one hand and snapped her fingers impatiently.

"Let's see it," she said. "Let's see this little gopher infestation that you need my help with."

I didn't hand her my phone right away. I had to come clean about the story I'd told to get her there.

"It's not exactly a gopher," I said. "The phone line wasn't secure, so I didn't want to say what it really was."

She went limp in the chair, pretending to die of disinterest. Persephone had always been a bit of a thrill seeker, but living in Wisteria had really amplified those tendencies. That's why she loved solving crimes, running at top speed through the woods, and dating bad boys—often all three in the same day.

"It's a compelling video," I said. "The camerawork is shaky, but the cinematography is top tier."

"I don't understand why you didn't just send it to me."

"And deprive myself of your charming company? I notice you forgot to bring the customary housewarming present."

She grinned. "This place isn't bad," she said with actual warmth. "At least it's only temporary. As soon as you get all that cacodemon doodie with the insurance finalized, and you'll be in your new house in no time." She pulled a sports bar from her pocket and started unwrapping it. "Just don't buy in Fung's neighborhood. Everyone there is obsessed with collecting things."

"Oh, I got the cash. Ages ago. But with Zoey gone for college... I don't need all the hassle of maintaining a big house."

She squinted at me. "Hmm." She crammed the whole sports bar into her mouth.

She held out the empty wrapper, and I traded her for my phone. The video was ready to play.

She chewed on the bar while she watched the video, giving me a play-by-play in between chews. "Yup. I see your face. Nice. Up the nostrils. You're at the gardens. Wow. You guys really cleared that corner patch. Now it's dark, and—"

She jerked, and dropped the phone to the floor.

She sputtered and coughed. The sports bar was stuck in her throat.

I jumped up to give her the Heimlich maneuver.

130

She jumped past my arms in a flash of black fur. Persephone-Fox landed nimbly, swallowed audibly, and returned to human form almost instantly.

"Ha ha," she said as she picked up my phone from the floor. "Very funny. You totally got me. Can you send me this? I'll get everyone at work."

"It's not a joke."

"What did you use? Video editing, or practical effects?"

"It's real footage."

"But that's got to be Frank, or one of his friends. In a mask."

I shook my head.

She watched the video again.

"That's a skull," she said, growing serious. "It's a skeleton. A living skeleton."

"I'm not so sure about living. But it is animated."

That's what I'd encountered in the community garden.

A living skeleton.

That's what had been down in the hole, along with the bunnies, grabbing my wrist with its bony phalanges. And that's why I'd been pacing my apartment for the past hour, trying to play it cool until my sister showed up.

Persephone pulled her WPD-issued laptop from her backpack, and began typing.

I really didn't have much in my kitchen for snacks, but I put together what I had while I waited. It was two glasses of water, and the walnut from the hidden cupboard.

She glanced around. "Where is the ghost now? Is it in the room? Is it sitting next to me?"

"There's no ghost," I said.

She stared at me in disbelief. "No ghost?"

"No ghost. Duh. I'd have this whole thing figured out by now if there was a ghost."

She wrinkled her nose. "Really?"

"I'd have a few good leads, at least."

More nose wrinkling. "Without your intern here to do all your boring work?" She was referring to Ambrosia Abernathy, who was now off at college. Maybe the ghost had traveled to see her. I'd been working hard to refer all the local transparent people to the younger Spirit Charmed witch.

"I haven't come across a ghost in ages," I told my sister.

"But did you try any... you know... witcher-i-doo?" She gave me a triple eyebrow raise, then went into a terrible imitation of me. "Oooh, come to meee, spooky ghost. Come and climb inside of meee. I waaant to feel your ghostly fingers all ooover me. I'm so looonely."

I hit her with a pillow.

She laughed, and simply used the pillow to get more comfortable.

My cheeks felt hot and flushed.

She actually had hurt my feelings, but I couldn't let her know, or I'd have to suffer that imitation of myself with every visit.

Persephone got back to her research on the WPD laptop.

She kept typing as she reported, "No missing persons reports in the last six months. And nothing that's still open going back two years." More clicks. "Or even five years." She frowned. "The crime must not have been reported."

"You think the skeleton is a victim of crime?"

She stared at me as though I might be an idiot.

"Zara, you don't think skeletons just make themselves, do you? Like they're a species of magical creatures? And the mother skeleton carries a little baby skeleton inside her pelvis while it gets bigger and bigger, until one day she... reaches in and takes it out?"

"To be honest, I hadn't ruled it out."

She smirked. "Zara, there is such a thing as having a too-open mind."

I scratched my boiling-hot cheek self-consciously.

She returned to her laptop, typing in quick spurts between scrolling.

"I'll have to look into the cold cases."

"In your free time?"

She gave me another look, a you-are-definitely-an-idiot look. She would look into it officially. She didn't solve crimes and have capers for a hobby—though she probably would if the WPD did take her off the payroll.

"So... it's good that I called you," I said. "This is definitely something the WPD will be wanting to get involved with."

"It's not about *wanting*. If a crime happens in this city, it's our job to investigate. And if it does turn out to be out of our jurisdiction, I'll report to my partners at the DWM."

"Like if it turns out there's a species of skeletons living and breeding in the tunnels underneath the town? Hypothetically?"

She picked up the glasses of water I'd brought over, and drank both of them.

"Yeah," she said as she wiped her mouth. "I'm sure Agents Knox and Rob would *love* that."

"What do you want me to do? Canvas the area for witnesses?"

Her big, brown eyes, that drooped at the sides in a melancholy way, suddenly narrowed to thin lines. "You won't do anything, Zara. I'm the detective, and you're the librarian."

"I know, but I'm the one who found whatever this is."

"You want to be part of this?" She shrugged. "You can be part of it. You can tell your friends at the community garden that the whole place is a crime scene, and they can't set foot on the premises."

"What? No. Hang on. No way. You can't do that."

She shrugged again. "Fine. I'll tell them myself."

"No." I jumped to my feet. There was nothing to be done at that moment, but it didn't feel right to continue sitting. "I'll break the news."

"Thank you for your assistance," she said robotically.

"Let me know as soon as you find out anything."

She didn't say anything.

She did pick up the walnut, and then the toy soldiers, the glass marbles, and the old smoking pipes. She put them all in her backpack.

"Are those evidence?" I asked.

"No. I'm taking them so you don't start a collection. It always starts with one piece."

"But I just got those things. They're part of this apartment. They're mine."

"It's for your own good. If I don't confiscate these old relics, next time I come over, you'll have a curio cabinet full of eighteenth century carved whalebone figurines."

"I would not."

She gave me a knowing look, as only a sister could, and then she left.

CHAPTER 17

The Next Weekend

Sunday, October 21st

The day after I showed the skeleton video to my sister, the Wisteria Police Department put yellow tape around the community garden, and banned us all from setting foot on the premises.

They gave everyone the cover story that some "geological anomalies" had been detected. They also announced that the old, unused railroad tracks were due to be removed, so the site would be closed until all the work could be completed.

My fellow community garden members were horrified. They knew the tracks would have to be removed someday, but everyone assumed the permitting process would take another decade.

To compound the group's anxiety, nobody from the city was even working on the site that first week.

We had to watch helplessly from the other side of the yellow tape as our pumpkins got bigger and bigger. They cried out to be harvested. They really did. I heard them on their ultrasonic frequency. They wanted to become jack-o'-lanterns and pies.

The gardening club had to beg for permission, via several special permits, just to get access to the corner where our vine-ripened pumpkins were crying out all day and night.

We wouldn't have harvested at all if it hadn't been for newlywed Liza Gilbert pushing through the permits. It really did pay to have friends at City Hall. I would, however, have to endure a future outing with her and the chipmunks.

That Saturday, almost a week after my discovery—which I had not told my fellow gardeners about—work was finally beginning.

An excavation crew that secretly worked for the WPD was finally on site, starting their investigation into my skeleton.

It was a dark-gray, rainy day—the kind of day where the downpour was so heavy, the street puddles rinsed clean.

Mrs. Puddikin and I shared an extra-large golf umbrella to protect us from the rain that came from above. It did very little to stop the rain that came in sideways.

Rain soaked us relentlessly as we stood watching the forensics team begin ripping up the garden.

This was nothing like the day I'd rented the heavy equipment to clear the wild patch. That had been fun. This was ten times the amount of equipment, but zero consideration for our planted areas.

Mrs. Puddikin squeezed my shoulders. "It could be worse, love. It could have happened before we got those pumpkins out."

I didn't say anything.

My focus was on Persephone. She'd been dodging my calls for days. This was as close as I'd gotten to the case since my first encounter with Mr. Bone-Jangles. I didn't know if the skeleton was even male, but Mr. Bone-Jangles was his name for now.

Persephone was everywhere at once, supervising the digging team, and checking that traffic on the nearby street had been diverted. She darted around like a fox in her shiny black rain slicker. She could probably dodge each raindrop if she wanted to.

One of the diggers—a man in an excavator—stopped his bucket, and shouted something urgent over the engine noise.

Persephone darted over, signaled for everyone to stop, then knelt in the mud to examine something.

When she looked up, she caught my eye across a sea of rain-battered plants. She raised a single finger to indicate *one*. They'd located one skeleton.

I started toward her, but Mrs. Puddikin caught me by the collar of my own rain slicker, and held me back.

"There, there, love," she said. "Nothing you can do now. Leave it to them with the strong constitutions. We pay our taxes so we don't have to suffer those sights."

I turned to her for further explanation. As far as she was supposed to know, the crew was checking that the ground wouldn't collapse when the railroad ties were being dug up.

I said, "What do you mean? About strong constitutions?"

Mrs. Puddikin said, "I didn't fall out of a sugar maple tree yesterday, love. They don't bring crime scene investigation vans to a simple municipal dig."

"Oh." I feigned ignorance, which, as you know, is very difficult for a knowledgeable person to do, let alone a smarty pants like yours truly.

"I know how things get done around here. There's always a story that doesn't quite match up to what you see with your own eyes, but people look the other way. And why wouldn't we? It's such a lovely town. We all enjoy having the bad things swept away behind closed doors, don't we?"

"What else do you know?"

"I know that people disappear all the time, but they're usually not the sort of folk who are missed." She leaned left and right, looking over my shoulder and through the rain. "Looks like they're putting something into a bag now. I reckon that's a body bag that they're going to tell us is just a bag for geological samples."

"Nothing gets by you," I said.

"You'd be surprised."

The heavy pour on our umbrella turned to pattering, then abruptly ceased.

Mrs. Puddikin tilted the umbrella away, shook it, and snapped it closed.

"Well, then," she said. "Fancy a spot of tea? You can come 'round my place. Even if I could get to it, I don't think my garden teapot's big enough to serve all the people here at this," she winked, "geological survey."

Just then, a large vehicle pulled up beside us, splattering us with mud.

"Oh, dear," Mrs. Puddikin said. "What's the water department doing here? I hope they haven't broken a line already."

The vehicle belonged to the Wisteria Department of Water, according to the logo on the door.

However, it was the Department of Water and Magic to people who were in the know. Also known as the Department of Wacky Monsters.

Two agents, Knox and Rob, stepped out of the vehicle. They were bird shifters, and competent agents.

Both looked my way, but discreetly looked away again just as quickly, not acknowledging me.

"What a kerfuffle," Mrs. Puddikin said. "Look at all these workers. And on the weekend, so it's overtime all around. No wonder our property taxes keep going up."

Even more vehicles arrived, and a gruff man in a reflective vest barked at us to go home.

"There's nothing to see here," he said, ironically using the magic phrase that only made people more curious.

A large van spun its tires in the rain-soaked earth, spraying both of us with mud.

Mrs. Puddikin gasped, right in time to get the next splash of brown water in her mouth.

I steered her away, and didn't stop until we were out of spraying radius.

"It'll be okay," I said. "Microbes, remember?"

She spat. "Yes, microbes. I'm fine. I'll put on the kettle, and we'll both be *in fine fettle*."

"Tea at your place?"

"Oh, no. I just remembered. The housekeeper is at mine."

"Then we'll go to my place, Mrs. Puddikin. I'll get us warm and dry there."

"Do you have tea?"

"Yes."

"Do you have whiskey?"

"Mrs. Puddikin!"

"Well? Do you have whiskey?"

"Of course I do."

CHAPTER 18

Monday Morning

Witches don't get hangovers—or at least not easily—so I was perfectly refreshed when I woke up for work in my bottom bunk.

Mrs. Puddikin, however, was not a witch.

If anything, she might have been part sprite—she certainly snored like one.

She had one arm and one leg hanging off different sides of the upper bunk. I manually adjusted her to a more comfortable-looking position, and left her to sleep while I made coffee.

Our "one" whiskey the day before had led to several others. We'd drank, ordered pizza delivery, and watched old movies until it had been too late for her to bother going home, even though it wouldn't have been far.

I'd also learned a bit more about the woman.

She was a widow—an official, recognized one, unlike me or Carrot Greyson.

Her husband, the cheater, had been ill for many years, and he'd passed away peacefully in his sleep on the night of the tornado.

"'Twas a blessing, that tornado," Mrs. Puddikin had said. "A blessing that ended his suffering."

She'd sounded so sad about his passing. She'd never stopped loving him, in spite of what he'd done to test their marriage.

I couldn't tell her about my experience with the tornado, let alone how her blessing had been my curse.

Few people know that a man named Theodore Bentley lost his life that night, sacrificing himself to save my daughter. We'd kept it from the news. The official report at the police department was that the detective had taken early retirement, and left for another town.

Chief Fung had the cover story written that way because it was simpler than declaring someone dead without a body, and having all the unwanted attention of an investigation.

Zinnia confided in me that they'd done it that way as a favor for me—as though it might somehow make things less terrible, as though it were better to leave him in the twilight zone of possibly being alive, even if it was just on paper.

Talking about the tornado had definitely accelerated our drinking the night before.

Mrs. Puddikin lived alone, her children having moved out years ago. She kept busy running The Chintz Boutique during the week, and gardening on the weekend, but she wanted more. She'd gotten all wistful about achieving greater things, and the limited time she had left.

I'd offered her a volunteer position at the library, even though I had no right to do so, and the waiting list was a mile long anyway.

She hadn't been interested. She must have had something truly amazing in mind. Good for her. Dreams were free.

As I puttered around the kitchen, the smell of coffee did its job, and lured Mrs. Puddikin out of bed.

She must have been embarrassed to be there. She managed to drink a full mug in one go, then quickly excused herself to go home.

She was only gone a few moments before she buzzed my intercom, and came back up.

"You're going to laugh at me." She patted her cardigan pockets. "I have my keys, but I can't remember where my car is parked."

She lived right across the street, so her car shouldn't have been far away.

I asked, "Did you drive it yesterday? It was raining."

"Ah, that's it, love. My car's by the body."

"By the body?"

Her cheeks reddened. "By the garden, love. It's by the garden. Assuming all those municipal vehicles didn't run over the poor thing like they did our pumpkin patch."

She thanked me again for the fun evening, and for washing all her muddy clothes while we watched movies in pajamas.

After she left, I stared at the door for a long moment. I did a lot of my best thinking staring at closed doors. Not as much as in the shower, but good thinking all the same.

Why had she said her car was *by the body* and not by the garden?

Now that I thought about it, she had been the least surprised out of the group when the excavation had been announced. Her main concern had been the pumpkin patch.

Did she know something about Mr. Bone-Jangles?

And should I have let someone I didn't really know that well have full access to my apartment while I slept? Protective wards didn't do much if you invited the evil inside—case in point, my mother's long visits.

I quickly shrugged off any suspicion.

Nobody outside of a BBC crime series would suspect a sweet old British lady with buck teeth of burying bodies in a community garden.

CHAPTER 19

I got to work at the library only a few minutes late. It would be the day of the Big Kiss—more on that later.

I told my two curious coworkers everything I knew about the excavation in the garden.

They'd already heard about the animated skeleton the previous week, so this Monday morning they both looked disappointed in my tales.

"It's feeling a bit anticlimactic," Frank Wonder said.

"Sorry my life isn't delivering the usual thrills and chills," I said.

"Where's the skeleton now?"

"I don't know."

He wiggled his fingers. "Do one of your location spells. I'll get a map."

"No spells," said Kathy Carmichael, our head librarian and resident sprite. "No magic in the library. We don't have any room in the budget for you two and your shenanigans."

Frank frowned. "Does that mean I won't be getting a raise?"

Kathy scowled. "You can raise your butt off that chair, and get to the circulation counter."

"Boo," he said.

Kathy said, "Speaking of boo, let me see that video again."

I handed her my phone. She didn't want a copy of her own, but she would demand to see it on mine. She watched it yet another time, finishing with a shudder.

"My father might know something about skeletons," she said.

"Why's that?" I asked, intrigued. Kathy usually changed the topic whenever her father came up.

"Never mind," she said hurriedly, and she left us alone in the break room.

I asked Frank, "What's that all about?"

"Kathy doesn't like introducing her friends to her father."

"Why? Is he really gross?" I imagined a hybrid between the two sprites I knew, Kathy and her cousin Karl Kormac.

Frank's eyes twinkled. "I really couldn't say."

"You could if I put you under my spell."

Frank pointed to the new sign that Kathy had printed out for the break room. It had large, red letters and read NO SHENANIGANS.

She couldn't use the word *magic* because we had a bunch of non-supernaturals as volunteers.

"Come on, Frank. Tell me what's going on with Kathy's dad. Is it the tongue?"

"I really couldn't say," he repeated, pretending to zip his lips, then immediately unzipping them to eat stale cake from the weekend.

"What do you know about the Wilds?"

"Doesn't ring a bell," Frank said. "But what would I know? I try to stay in my own lane. I only enjoy vicarious thrills, like the ones I get from you. It's no fun being at the center of the storm, no offense. Speaking of which, are you ready for the Monster Mash? It's only eleven days away."

"I should talk to Vincent Wick," I said, still on the subject of the Wilds. "He's got eyes all over town."

Frank finished his cake, and licked icing off his plate. "I know this is the last thing you'd ever expect to hear from Franker the Pranker, but maybe you should sit this one out."

I threw my hands in the air. "What do you think I've been trying to do?"

Frank glanced at the clock on the wall. We should have started our shift already.

"Our boss is going to think we're up to shenanigans," he said.

"Gossip isn't shenanigans. Plus I was only talking about it because you two pounced on me the second I walked in."

"Is that how you saw it?"

"I've been sitting this one out, I swear. I walked away from that sinkhole, even though I could have tried a dozen spells. I'm perfectly happy to let Persephone and the others deal with whatever this is."

"You are?" He blinked repeatedly. "*Perfectly happy?*"

"Yeah." I played with my hair.

"Speaking of happy, do you love the bunk bed?"

"I do," I said, reluctantly accepting the topic change. Work was waiting. "I love that wacky bed, and I love you, Frank Wonder."

I grabbed his face in my hands, put my palm over his mouth, and pretended to kiss him passionately.

I'd never kissed Frank before, but our pretend kiss triggered something magic between us. It wasn't romantic, but I did feel great *joining-up* power pulsing within me, like a tandem spell. It intensified through our contact points, and shot out, sparking in the air.

I tried to pull away, but I was strangely stuck to him. His lips and my lips were separated only by my hand, which was now the filling in our face sandwich.

Frank must have tried to shift into his flamingo form. Pink feathers rained down around us.

At that exact moment, our volunteer staff member for the morning walked into the break room with a big cardboard box.

She saw us in a scandalous embrace, surrounded by pink feathers, standing right underneath the big sign that said NO SHENANIGANS.

She dropped the box. It was full of cut-out words that were meant for the new poetry wall.

The magic of our false kiss rippled out, caught the words, and flung them everywhere.

Individual words soared like confused birds trapped indoors, colliding in mid-air, forming phrases and even haiku before settling on the tables and floor.

The volunteer was beyond shocked.

By the look of Frank's eyes, which were mere inches from mine, he was in a similar state.

CHAPTER 20

After some struggle, Frank and I extracted ourselves from our magical embrace.

The loose words formed a few more poems on the tables and floor—a magical encore—then finally stopped moving.

Frank and I apologized to each other profusely, even though neither of us had done anything wrong. Yes, I'd been the aggressor with the Big Kiss, which was a violation of any sensible workplace's code of conduct, but, in my defense, Frank did have a very kissable face. My daughter often lengthened his last name, Wonder, to call him Mr. Wonderful for a reason. He was a wonderful specimen of a man, for his age.

There was a simple explanation for what had happened between us. Two coworkers working in close proximity, bantering steadily over years, getting to know each other's secrets, could create a build-up of energy. That energy could sometimes reach its flash point, and begin to behave like a creature. Magic has a mind of its own, as you know.

We'd both heard of this phenomenon before, but, as with so many legends and dire warnings, you never think it will happen to you. We'd all laughed about it, right up until the Big Kiss.

The phenomenon had a very stupid name. It was a Willthey Poltergeist. It came from the "will they or won't they" trope about romantic liaisons between characters in a sitcom. Or maybe the connection went the other way around. The Willthey Poltergeist had been documented in some very ancient texts. Just like the romance plot dangled in sitcoms, it had the power to unite or destroy.

Stupid name aside, that was clearly what we had accidentally created.

We banished the newly-formed entity within minutes with a simple cure. Frank and I looked each other in the eyes, and both said "Ewww."

That part was easy enough.

However, it took the entire rest of the day to convince our shocked volunteer that Frank and I were not having a secret affair. And also that it had only *seemed* like a magical entity had made mid-air poetry in the break room that morning.

Frank got annoyed by the volunteer, and disappeared for the entire afternoon. He claimed he was reorganizing the board games section, but Kathy saw him playing a board game for at least two hours with a group of little kids. After, the board games section was even more chaotic than usual. It wasn't my favorite section. Compared to books, where every part was sensibly attached and glued along a central spine, games were kind of a nightmare.

We had a steady flow of patrons, and I got so busy with my regular librarian duties that I didn't get a chance to badger Kathy about the Wilds, or find out what her father might know about skeletons.

I finished my shift, and clocked out my time card with the usual KERCLUNK. It was as loud as ever, ringing through the quiet building.

We'd recently tried to replace the library's old-fashioned punch-card system, but it had been a disaster.

From the day we replaced it, things had started going wrong.

It was small things at first, like three books in a row being returned with uncooked bacon tucked between the pages as bookmarks. Three in a month, let alone three in a row, was a significant increase from the typical occurrence of what we called Baconating.

Then the houseplants on top of the shelves had formed factions, battling each other after closing. Even the fake, plastic ones.

Finally, the roof had blown off. Literally. During a mildly breezy afternoon, the roof had simply unfastened itself from the walls, and sailed off like a kite. It was never found.

There had been a lengthy investigation by the DWM, in conjunction with the coven.

We determined that our beloved library was sitting on hexed grounds, and the old punch-card system was an effective counter-hex mechanism. Or at least it had been, before we removed it. That explained why the machine had been covered in so many DO NOT REMOVE notices.

Kathy used her connection with the town's metal recycling department—Vincent Wick—and got the old machine back just in time before it had been melted down for its base elements.

After the repairs, everything went back to how it had been, but with one lasting change. The new roof had been a rush job with rush surcharges. We'd obliterated the library's contingency fund, and half of the annual operating budget.

Kathy had to painstakingly reconfigure the entire operating budget, cutting back on several services.

Thanks to the cutbacks, some of the previously paid roles were being filled by volunteers. Sadly, many of these volunteers were not quite worth the zero dollars we paid them. But, with enough patience and time, Kathy believed that even the most eager ones—the ones who were the most troublesome, with all their "bold, new ideas"—might become helpful members of the team.

Even with the difficult changes, the library was still a wonderful place to work, and I loved my job.

After clocking out, I patted the old punch-card machine with genuine affection, and said, "Thank you for your service."

I may have been feeling the lingering effects from the Big Kiss, because I was in high spirits that Monday afternoon when I stepped outside.

The chilly October weather and dim skies didn't dampen my mood at all.

As I unlocked the passenger door of Foxy Pumpkin, I pondered going for a drive up the coast. There was nobody at my place, nobody waiting to complain about dinner to me, so why not check out the view from the mountains? The leaves were still changing to orange and red, and it would be a lovely drive.

A large, white vehicle lurched into the empty parking spot beside me. The driver had pulled in backward, and rolled over the concrete divider, so he was right beside me.

The driver's window lowered. The driver was a smooth-cheeked young man who looked all of seventeen.

"Ma'am, you need to come with me."

He was in a service vehicle from the Water Department. He was probably a DWM agent, but I didn't know him, I didn't like his driving, and I didn't care for his tone.

"I don't think I do," I replied.

True, there was nobody waiting at my place, but that didn't mean I wanted to spend my evening in the DWM's underground headquarters. They always promised full catering for dinner-hour meetings there, but then it was just a disappointing paper plate of carrot and celery sticks with bean dip.

"Ma'am," he said with forced bravado, his voice deep but his upper lip trembling. "You need to come with me."

"On what grounds?"

"B-b-because those are my instructions."

"I didn't get any instructions. And I'm a free citizen."

"Just get in the van."

"Or what?"

The nervousness evaporated, and he said with some force, "You need to come with me right now, Ma'am. There's no time to explain."

"You watch too many movies," I said. "That's not how it works in real life. Who do you report to?"

He reached for something beside him, and suddenly I was looking at the business end of a DWM weapon.

A cocoon gun.

I didn't let him see my fear.

"Don't you dare pull that trigger," I said coolly.

"It's safe," he said. "Unpleasant, but safe enough. This is what you get for not listening."

"Looks like the original model. Did they at least fix the problem with the air holes?"

"What?"

"I'll show you."

Before I could get closer, he pulled the latch that removed the safety pin.

"Stay back," he said.

"Careful with that thing," I said. "At least hold it upright. Look at that. You're squeezing the bottom, and you're dropping larvae all over yourself. Euch. Disgusting. Look at those little guys. And so close to the family jewels."

"Huh?"

The cocoon gun didn't use live larvae, but my story worked. The kid looked down.

While he was distracted, I reached in through his open window, and dropped a half-dozen sparking fireballs inside the vehicle.

The kid's reaction was both instant and chaotic. As intended.

While he dealt with the active fireballs, which I'd set to fireworks mode, I climbed into my car, fired up Foxy Pumpkin's magically-enhanced engine, and drove away.

I put a few miles between myself and the DWM agent quickly.

Had that actually happened?

Had that baby-faced young man actually called me *Ma'am*?

The nerve of some people.

CHAPTER 21

Nine O'Clock That Night

The intercom buzzed.

"Intercom," I said to myself as I ran toward the buzzing. "Intercom." I pressed the button. "Intercom?"

A male voice came back. "I think you mean *hello*."

In a robot voice, I said, "Hello, and thank you for your interest in selling us aluminum siding. We'll get back to you if we have any questions. This... is a recording."

"Zara, it's me. Rob."

"Official business, or pleasure?"

"You know I always make it a pleasure to do official business. Buzz me in. I know it's late, but I brought the catered dinner with me."

"What's the magic word?"

"Is it... *intercom*?"

"Sure." I buzzed him in.

Agent Rob entered my apartment. The protective wards relaxed to allow him, but they still had some elastic kick to them. His straight black hair flew up and stayed up, full of static, until he smoothed it back down.

I stared at the open doorway, expecting to see his usual partner, Knox, but apparently Rob was on his own.

"Great place," Rob said. "Here's dinner."

He handed me a package. It was a cardboard tray full of carrot and celery sticks, plus bean dip.

"The chef has outdone himself yet again," I said.

"Can I get a tour?" He didn't wait for me, and took himself on a tour, piling up questions as he went. "What's the deal with the shallow cupboard? Is this tub original? Are these shelves mahogany? Why does this bed have five posts? Are these kitchen outlets up to code? This wingback chair, is it from Zinnia's house?"

"I plan to use it for canned goods; no, but it is a hundred years old; some of them are; it's custom; beats me; and what do you think?"

He took a seat in the floral-print chair. Of course it was one of Zinnia's finds. How could it possibly have come from anyone else?

I said to the agent, "How are you? Am I in trouble? Is this about the skeleton, or the wet-behind-the-ears agent I dropped fireballs on?"

He said, "Can't complain; yes, as usual; and both. He had to get a skin graft from Doc Lund."

"The medical examiner?"

Rob nodded. "Among other things. You'll be glad to know the young man should have a full recovery." He sighed. "Some lessons are more painful than others. He'll be a better agent someday, thanks to this."

"You're welcome," I said. "Where's Knox?"

"Off for a few days to recover from some minor injuries he sustained during the retrieval of the O'Connor girl."

"You guys tracked her down?"

"Thanks to an anonymous tip from a guy named Captain Jiminy Whoozat."

I smirked. Xavier and my mother had been following up on some unfinished business as they traveled the globe.

Rob smirked back. "Is Captain Jiminy Whoozat a friend of yours?"

"If it was an anonymous tip, then obviously not. Why are you really here?"

"Honestly?"

"No. Keep lying to me, like you did about Knox."

Rob's eyes bulged, confirming my suspicion that his partner's injuries had been more than minor. Knox was too powerful to take time off work for anything less than a serious bone break.

Rob leaned forward with his palms up, wrists bared.

"Zara, I'm just here to find out everything you know about our little friend from the garden."

"Mr. Bone-Jangles?"

"Is that his name?"

"It's what I call him. Is he a *him*?"

"You tell me what you know first."

"I already told Detective Rose everything I saw and heard."

"Heard? Like what? There's nothing about anything you heard in the report."

"There was music playing down there. It sounded like soft rock, like a radio stuck between channels."

"There's no music on the recording."

"There isn't?" I pulled out my phone and played it again. Even though I knew to expect the sudden appearance of a skeleton face looming in from the darkness, it still gave me a fright. Good ol' Mr. Bone-Jangles.

There was no music on the recording, just my own heavy breathing.

"The music must have stopped when I got close to the hole," I said. "Before I pulled my phone out."

"Then why did you look in there?"

"Because it was a hole in the dirt. Who doesn't look into a hole like that?"

"It might have been nothing more than a rabbit warren."

"Exactly. I could have seen some cute baby bunnies. They breed year-round, you know."

"Something's not adding up," Rob said. "You heard mysterious music, then it stopped, and the first thing you did was stick your phone into a mysterious, dark hole." He leaned forward, his elbows on his knees. "Tell me what you were expecting to see, and don't say baby bunnies."

"I wasn't expecting. I was doing."

"And how's that working out for you?" He glanced around the small apartment. "Didn't you use to have a nice house, once upon a time?"

He was trying to push my buttons. It was what a good agent had to do. It wasn't personal, and yet it felt extremely personal.

I twirled my tongue and cast a self-protection shield, in case he had any other tricks up his sleeve, such as the cocoon gun.

"We're done here," I said. "Take your unwanted crunchy crudités, and go. If you have any other questions, you can speak to my lawyer."

"You've hired a lawyer?"

"I keep one on retainer." It was true. I'd hired one to get the insurance company to expedite my settlement, and I'd liked her so much, I'd kept her on for a small fee.

I handed him the business card for Blythe Delores Boomer.

"We don't need to involve any ambulance chasers," Rob said, wrinkling his nose at the card. "Let's keep this civilized. Would you mind humming the music you heard that day? To the best of your recollection?"

"I have a great memory, but it's not that good."

He reached into his jacket pocket. "I thought you'd say that. We have a new device that helps with memory retrieval. It's no more invasive than hypnosis."

Before he could retrieve whatever was in his pocket, I was on my toes, and so were the home's protective wards.

Agent Rob's black hair stood up with static as the force field pulled him from the chair, and whisked him out the door.

"It was worth trying," Rob said from the hallway.

"Take care now, bye bye."

"Always a pleasure." I closed the door on his face.

Had he really believed I would let him use one of the DWM's devices on my precious brain? I had to give him credit for his optimism.

Through the door, he said, "We should have coffee sometime."

"Send Agent Knox my regards."

He grunted acknowledgement, and left.

Alone again, I picked up my phone to replay the recording one more time to listen for any music.

I couldn't find the file.

It was gone.

Erased.

It was gone from my phone, and gone from the backup.

I ran to the window that faced the street, and yanked it open.

Agent Rob was getting into an unmarked vehicle.

"I know what you did," I yelled down to him.

He pretended to not hear me.

So, I did what any reasonable witch would have done.

I blasted one of his rear tires with a hex that would take effect when it was least convenient for Agent Rob.

When would those guys ever learn not to mess with witches?

CHAPTER 22

Tuesday, October 23rd

Pre-Sunrise

The sky was still dark when I stood outside the Carmichael residence, pressing the doorbell exactly three times.

It went ding-dong, ding-dong, ding-dong on the other side of the door.

I muttered under my breath, "Doorbell, doorbell, doorbell."

I missed having a doorbell. I was back to having the less-good version of the doorbell, the intercom. My visitors didn't make a ding-dong. They made a buzz-buzz, which wasn't nearly as pleasant.

These days I didn't have the hassle of worrying about maintaining a big house, but I did miss my ding-dongs.

From the other side of the door came my boss Kathy's voice. "Whooo could that possibly be? Whooo's ringing my doorbell three times?"

The door whipped open. Kathy sometimes reminded me of an owl, and today was no exception. She wore a brown velour house robe and fuzzy yellow slippers. Her pointy nose was beak-like, particularly when her round-framed glasses had slid partway down.

"Ah, fluffernuts," she exclaimed at the sight of me. "What's wrong now? Has the ground opened up and swallowed the library whole? I did hear some rumbling underneath us yesterday."

"Rumbling?" I hadn't noticed that, but I'd been floating from the Big Kiss.

"Just spit it out," Kathy said, flapping her elbows, and looking even more like an owl.

But I wasn't there with bad news. I lifted the lid on the box of pastries I'd picked up on my way. I waved the scent of vanilla and cinnamon, wafting it her way.

"Can't a friend stop by with breakfast for no reason?"

Kathy licked her lips. "Fresh pastries? But it's only Tuesday." We usually held off on such luxuries until Friday.

"May I come in? I'll be quiet in case your guys are still sleeping."

She waved me in. "Be as loud as you want. They're all out of town."

Kathy's husband and grown sons were all involved in professional sports. They were rarely home, which was why Kathy had so much time for craft projects outside of her full time job as head librarian. It also explained why the cupboards at work were crammed full of handmade pottery. She'd even made the NO SHENANIGANS sign herself at a screen printing workshop. There were also matching T-shirts.

I walked in, and squeezed through a narrow hallway. The walls must have been originally constructed at a standard width apart, but Kathy had shrunk the hall with her crafting and collecting. Both sides were covered in a base layer of hand-woven rugs and macrame, followed by old windows made into mirrors, framed embroidery, paint-by-numbers landscapes on canvas, decorative plates, novelty spoons, ceramic masks, wooden clocks, dried flowers, souvenir thimbles from around the world—Nova Scotia in particular—and a surprisingly large collection of acorns.

"Nice acorns," I said.

"They keep the invisible spiders away."

"Really? That actually works?"

"Well, you do have to hit the spiders with them."

"Ah."

We squeezed through the adjoining hallway that led into a tiny breakfast nook. It had once been a large, formal dining room, before the taxidermied animals. The stuffed birds and reptiles didn't take up much space, but the Grizzly bear—dark-brown with a fringe of white under its chin—dominated one corner.

We sat at the small table, and I commented, "Do you ever feel like you're being watched in this room?"

It was the same joke I always made, but only because I felt the same feeling every time I'd been there.

Kathy rolled her eyes as she stood again, and left for the kitchen.

The latin name for Grizzly bear is Ursus arctos horribilis. The *horribilis* part seems made-up, but I assure you, as a professional librarian with a bunch of education —it's very real.

My family had a personal connection to the fierce creatures, as Ethan Fung—my uncle—Uncle Fung?— turned into one when he shifted into his animal form.

His son, Fyrsil, wasn't named after bears. Fyrsil was a Welsh name meaning "bears the staff."

It was kind of a pun. The word *bear* was in the meaning, but it was a verb and not the animal bear. We all liked the pun. Now that we knew Fyrsil, we couldn't think of another name that could have suited him better.

The taxidermied bear in the corner continued to watch us with its lifeless eyes. I'd better not bring Fyrsil there without preparation. He'd be horrified by an inanimate, sawdust-filled version of his father.

Kathy returned, and we got settled with some beverages and plates for my pastries.

I said, "Aren't you going to ask me why I'm here?"

"I assume you're here to talk about the skeleton."

"Mr. Bone-Jangles, yes. I'm glad we're on the same page, so to speak, pun intended."

She blinked her golden-brown, nearly orange, owl-like eyes behind her owl-like round glasses. Pun intended? Game on. We played this game sometimes, though it was as much about metaphors as it was true puns.

"I know your playbook," Kathy said carefully. "And I can read you like an indexed periodical."

"Then my visit must feel... overdue."

"It's novel, but everything stacks up."

"Happy to help your circulation, unless you want to put me on hold?"

I waited for her to reply. Did she have one more in the barrel?

She slowly pushed her glasses up her sharp, narrow nose. "I apologize for my slowness. A book fell on my head. I can only... *blame my shelf.*"

I raised my mug to her. "I'm out. You win."

"What's the prize?"

"When we get to work, I'll tell Frank you're the Punmaster."

"Work?" She tilted her head. "We're closed today. Don't you remember? Budget cuts."

"Oh, right. We're closed on Tuesdays. Hmm. If only there were something we could do today, since we both have the day off from all our duties. Perhaps we could go somewhere, like on a field trip."

Her eyebrows twitched. "You didn't forget we were closed, did you?"

"I may not be the most dog-eared reference book in the canvas tote bag, but I do know my work schedule."

"Mm hmm."

"And I already know that the Wilds are real. They're part of the network of tunnels that run under the town. I've been up all night researching, and I'm ready to see it myself."

"Mm hmm."

"But I don't want to go down there alone. I need someone who's a natural in that environment. I need a sprite." I gave her my most imploring look, and my most beseeching tone. "I need you, Kathy."

She looked over at the taxidermied Grizzly, then back to me.

"No," she said.

"Please?"

"No."

"If you go with me, I'll take that crafting class with you."

"Which one?"

I couldn't think of any specific class. Kathy was constantly trying to enroll me in one thing or another.

For a while, Frank had been her constant companion, but the honeymoon had worn off—as so many do—around the twelfth month of their best-friendship. They were still close, but lately she'd been inviting me to more workshops while spending less time with him.

"The very next one," I said. "My word is my bond, as long as it doesn't involve hot glue or glitter, I'll take the next one."

"Hot glue?" She sputtered and snorted. "How dare you." Kathy would never use a hot glue gun, and I knew that.

Once she'd finally calmed down, she said, "Fine. I'll take you down there, but I'm not leaving you there."

"I should hope not," I said.

She refilled our mugs.

After a few minutes, I nodded at the Grizzly bear. "You've got to tell me the story behind that thing."

"It came with the house," she said.

"It did not. You're pulling my leg."

"Look at the pose. There's not a doorway in the place you could use to get it out in one piece."

"Who said it has to leave in one piece?"

She squirmed in her chair. "I like him," she said softly. "He keeps me company."

I shivered, even though the room was warm enough with the dawning light.

The stuffed bear kept her company?

I'd been living by myself for not even a full month now, but I was starting to understand quirks like that. Lonely people did things that non-lonely people didn't. There were the rigid routines, and the collections, and the obsessive behavior.

I wouldn't become that way, of course.

I enjoyed having my own space, but it would be nice to have something furry to soak up the emptiness in the shadowy corners.

As we prepared to leave, I looked at all the taxidermied animals and wondered if I should get one. Not a taxidermied one, but the live version of something with fur or feathers.

The conversation ended with Kathy standing up and saying, "I guess it's about time you finally met my dad."

I nodded at our pal, the Grizzly bear in the corner. "Is that him?"

She didn't even laugh. "I already regret this," she said.

She already regretted it?

I had never been more excited to go somewhere with Kathy.

CHAPTER 23

The sun came up as we drove to Kathy's father's house.

Kathy was driving, and we were in her car. The old, brown Honda was just as overstuffed as her house, and my seat was pushed all the way forward.

"We need to do something about this car," I said. "This mess makes you look like the sort of person who has overdue library books."

"How dare you," she said.

"This is the car of a monster who commits mayhem, and folds over the corners of pages."

"How dare you," she said again.

"If you squeeze a few more things into the back, and glue something on the hood, you can apply for a permit as a cultural landmark."

"Really?"

"Anyone can apply," I said. "That doesn't mean you'll get the tax break and special parking pass."

"I'd love a special parking pass," she said. "Deep down, it's what makes the world go 'round."

"Parking makes the world go 'round?"

"The whole thing. Being special, and getting a free pass to do something other people can't."

"Do you always get this philosophical at sunrise? I know I do."

She pushed her round glasses up her nose, focusing on the road.

A few minutes later, she pulled over at a nondescript patch of wilderness. There was no house, or anything to see except for local trees and shrubs.

Upon closer examination, which I did after stepping out of the car, I found a rickety wood fence, and a weather-beaten sign reading STAY OUT.

"My dad doesn't like people dropping in," Kathy said.

"I guess we should have called to let him know we were coming."

"He knows we're here." She lifted her chin deliberately, inviting my gaze to follow hers.

I didn't see what she was gesturing at until I cast a reveal spell, and there it was: security cameras hidden in an old bird's nest.

"We don't need to bother your dad," I said. "You could just take me to a different access point."

"He won't feel bothered." She pushed on a section of the fence, and it suddenly swung open silently and smoothly.

The fence wasn't what it appeared to be, thanks to a practical-effects illusion. People who didn't have magic wards could be so resourceful. Someone had installed a sturdy, iron gate, and disguised it as a falling-over fence.

Beyond the gate, there was even a well-groomed driveway.

I turned back to get in the car, but Kathy said, "It's not far. We can walk up." She pointed to the camera in the nest. "Plus it gives him a few more minutes to put away his weaponry."

"You two are on good terms, I hope."

"Why would you say that?"

"I guess because my relationship with my own father is complicated, and also because I hear you yelling on the phone sometimes, and it's not always Vincent Wick."

"Dad and I are on good terms," she said. "We just see the world in very different ways."

"That's parents for you."

"He sees the world wrong."

"That sounds familiar."

"He's hyper critical and unsupportive of all my beliefs."

"So, he's a parent."

She shot me a look of warning. "Promise me you're on my side, Zara."

"I've got your side, and your back." I saluted her, like I would the other members of my gardening group.

We walked up the driveway until we reached a quaint cabin made of logs.

"Adorable," I said. "This looks like Nick's place, up on the mountain over the zoo."

"There are lots of these old log homes around, if you know where to look. Mostly behind trees, on the double and triple lots that haven't been split up yet. Once upon a time, this was farm fields all around, before the subdivisions."

"Did you grow up here?"

"I did." She waved at some trees. "There's a treelibrary back there."

"Did you say *treelibrary*?"

She grinned. "Yes. Like a treehouse, but full of books." Her cheeks flushed. "I used to play librarian, and have my friends play patrons. I collected acorns as overdue fines."

I caught glimpses of something high up in the trees.

"Kathy, is that where you keep your secret stash of magical books?"

She stopped in her tracks, and covered her face with her hands.

I patted her on the shoulder. She could be so emotional. It had to be hard being on that constant roller coaster of emotions.

"Don't worry," I said softly. "Your secret book hoard is safe with me."

"I really should find a better place."

Up ahead, the front door—or possibly the side door—of the cabin opened.

An older man stepped out to greet us. It wasn't immediately obvious to me that he was Kathy's father.

He was younger looking than I'd expected. And way more handsome. Could sprites even look that attractive without a glamour? The ones I knew resembled the illustrations in old reference books—skinny of leg and potbellied around the waist—like bullfrogs.

Kathy did the introductions—the full ones, stating everyone's powers.

He was, indeed, a sprite.

It just went to show that stereotypes existed for a reason, but there was always room for exceptions.

Kathy introduced me as a "good witch." It bothered me that she'd felt the need to add the adjective.

Kathy's dad shook my hand with a strong grip.

"Always nice to meet one of the *good* ones," he said in a deep, rugged, no-nonsense yet friendly tone.

"Same to you," I said.

"All sprites are good," he said matter-of-factly.

Kathy made a tsk sound.

"Come on in for breakfast," he said. "The soup isn't ready, but I can rummage up something else."

"We already had breakfast," I said. "We're actually just..." I got a little tongue-tied.

There was something about the older man's face, and his unwavering gaze. I felt like I was being examined, or filmed by a dozen cameras for future examination.

Kathy said, "Dad, I hate to come by unannounced, but we need access to the tunnels."

"What business have you got down there?"

"Zara saw something down there, in the tunnels."

He moved slightly. It was a very small gesture, barely perceptible, and then he edged backward, back into the sturdy log cabin.

"It was a skeleton," I said. "I call him Mr. Bone-Jangles, but we weren't formally introduced. He grabbed me around the wrist with his bare phalanges, and that's all I know, because the DWM took over."

Kathy's dad looked at me steadily, unblinking, and said, "Whatever you think you saw down in The Wilds, it would be best to un-see it."

"I saw it, too," Kathy said. "In video, not in person."

He tapped his temple. "You two had best erase it from your mind."

"Funny you should say *erase*," I said. "One of the DWM agents paid me a visit last night, and deleted the footage from my phone. He tried to use something else on me, too. He said it was for accessing memories, but I wouldn't let him near me. The Department of Wacky Monsters doesn't have a great track record with other people's heads. I'd probably end up with a bad case of brainweevils."

Kathy's dad looked from his daughter, to me, and back again.

He was still in his doorway, neither in nor out. Like a groundhog preparing to face its shadow.

The smell of something simmering on the stove drifted out around him.

You never feel as shut out of a house as you do when you smell the food inside it.

Kathy glanced over her shoulder nervously, as though someone might have followed us undetected.

The crisp fallen leaves rustled. A mild breeze blew through.

Kathy's arms jerked up in the air. "What was that?" She whipped her head around, side to side.

"It's okay." I patted her shoulder, then explained to her father, "Your daughter's been on edge about mild breezes ever since one of them blew the roof off the library."

"Then you'd better come inside." He stepped in and aside. "It's a breezy day."

I stepped inside the log cabin.

CHAPTER 24

Kathy's father was Kent Alderman.

He lived alone in the log cabin, which he'd built himself when Kathy was a baby.

Kathy's mother hadn't been the stay-around type, so Kathy had been raised by her father, with the help of his parents, Kay and Ken.

Ken was the sprite in the family, and Kay had been a minor mage with some psychic abilities.

Kathy had told me about how Kay Alderman would get feelings about things, and more often than not, it would turn out she was right. The family matriarch had passed away years ago, along with Kathy's grandfather, but my friend reported feeling their presence around.

Since I had the ability to see spirits, the first thing I did inside the log cabin was look around for Grandma Kay and Grandpa Ken.

I didn't see any ghosts, but that didn't mean they weren't lingering, as a sort of psychic residue. The cabin had a great vibe, and the non-living enjoyed a lot of the same places the living did.

As for sprites, I didn't know them as well as I did ghosts.

I knew they had good hearing—when they felt like using it—as well as powerful digestive systems. Powerful in the sense that they had multiple stomachs, anyway. The sprites I knew often suffered indigestion, mostly from a compulsion to eat the exact types of foods they should avoid.

The most shocking thing about sprites were their tongues, which were long and prehensile, and could be used as whips.

I also knew that sprites were creatures of habit who hated disruptions to their routines.

That's why I said, "I'm so sorry we dropped in on you unannounced, Mr. Alderman. We've probably disrupted your whole day."

"That you have," he said gruffly.

We had not gone into a detailed discussion of the underground tunnels, let alone my encounter with Mr. Bone-Jangles. But it was still early in the day, and I had slightly more patience than an overcaffeinated teenager.

Kathy's dad and I stood in the rustic kitchen on our own.

Kathy had disappeared to tidy up her childhood bedroom so it would be ready for me to see it.

Kent Alderman was nothing like the storybook images of what we called a sprite, but some cultures called a troll. (Never, ever call a sprite a troll, unless you want a thorough tongue lashing.)

He was a sturdy man with thick, brown hair that was as straight as his daughter's was curly. He had watchful eyes, and a thick mustache that obscured the area around his mouth, making his emotional state less scrutable. Perhaps that was the whole point of mustaches.

He stirred an enormous pot of soup that sat bubbling on top of a very large, antique wood-burning stove that predated the cabin. In fact, it looked like the cabin might have been built around the stove.

He used the large, rustic wooden spoon to take a taste. He wrinkled his nose, then added two whole heads of garlic, unpeeled.

"It's pretty early to be making dinner," I said. "Most people haven't even had their breakfast yet."

"Good soup takes a full day," he said.

"It smells amazing. Is it some sort of seafood?"

"All kinds of seafood. Including lobster."

That figured. Sprites needed a high amount of chitin in their diet, and lobster was a great source, though not found locally.

He offered me a taste—from the same wooden spoon he'd just used—but I declined.

I wasn't too squeamish about a few germs, but I'd just eaten breakfast at Kathy's, and my mind was on the journey ahead, and going into the tunnels.

"The lobster is flown in from the east coast," he said. "I have a guy."

"Will you hook me up with your guy? If I ever have a dinner at my little apartment, lobster would make a strong impression. As would serving everyone their meals on TV trays because I don't have a dining table, let alone a formal dining room. But that's perfectly fine. Who needs a formal dining room, anyway? It's so old-fashioned."

Kent responded with a simple, "Yes."

"Yes to which part?"

"All of it."

I felt self-conscious about babbling, so I stopped talking to see what he might offer up. If you give people just a bit of space, they might tell you what they're all about. It can work better than questions, but it isn't perfect. Neurotic people can get overly worked up in silences.

After a moment, Kent said, "Would you like to hear the most terrifying phrase ever uttered?"

"Sure."

He used one hand to smooth his full, bushy mustache, drawing more space in the pause.

In an even deeper tone of his deep voice, said, "We're from the government and we're here to help."

"Ha ha. I take it you don't work for any of our local government agencies."

"I do not."

"But you must be a fan of *some* of the municipal organizations." I was hinting about the library.

"If I ever decide to become mayor, my first act will be to fire eighty percent of the government employees."

"But who will run the town?"

"I don't know what you mean."

"Won't it just be chaos if over half of the people who run the place disappear?"

"A river is not run by people and yet it runs."

"Sure, but a town is not a river."

"There is a place where two rivers meet at a right angle, and then carry on. Only ten percent of the water changes direction at the crossing. A river can run itself."

"Just because you're using the verb *run*, that doesn't mean the same thing as run when it comes to a town."

"I disagree. There is another place where three rivers —"

I cut him off. "But what about the roads, and the sewers, and the garbage trucks? And the traffic lights, and the signs? Say what you will about the permits department, which I'll admit is largely unnecessary, but not everything is the permits department. Roads and sewers are real. We need people to maintain those."

"And that is what the twenty percent is for."

I was starting to see what Kathy meant about the two of them having very different world views. And about his world view being wrong.

"It's fine to have some weird ideas, Mr. Alderman. But I hope you don't talk like that around your daughter. She's having a hard enough time balancing our operating budget as it is. She had three full meltdowns last week, and we didn't even have any popsicles in the book return."

"My daughter knows how I feel about that... dusty paper depository."

And there it was. He didn't support the library. No wonder Kathy didn't want to introduce us.

But I could be cool. I could keep my politics to myself and play the get-along game.

"You should meet my mother," I said lightly. "She really hates books."

"I do not hate books. On the contrary, I think we should have more libraries."

"Oh."

"But I would run them much better."

"We're always looking for volunteers," I said with a smile.

"Pass."

"You may not like my mother after all. She says that books are just dead words by dead people who won't let go and leave the stage after their curtain call."

"That is true of fiction," he said. "Your mother sounds like an intelligent woman. You have my permission to bring her on your next visit."

"She's a vampire."

"Of course she is." His dark, watchful eyes sparkled with mirth.

I put my hand on my hip. What did that mean?

Kent went back to tasting his seafood stew.

What was taking Kathy so long in her childhood bedroom?

The silence got to me. I asked, "What is it that you do, Mr. Alderman?"

"This and that."

I walked over to the wall behind the rustic wood kitchen table. It was wallpapered with swords and daggers from around the world. The display rivaled anything we had at the local museum.

"And do you do this and that with all this weaponry?"

He seemed to smirk under his mustache, but it was hard to tell.

"This explains why you have so much security around the perimeter," I said. "I bet this collection is worth a lot of money."

"I just... like how they look on the wall."

I tested the edge of a katana blade with my finger. It drew blood.

I instantly sealed the cut in my fingertip with a lick. Witch saliva didn't heal the wound—my body did that on its own—but licking it removed the blood that might have stayed on the surface, attracting unwanted creatures.

"They're pretty sharp for decorations," I said.

"I did not say they were dull."

Our conversation was interrupted by Kathy calling out, "Okay, Zara! You can come see my room now!"

Her father put the lid on the soup pot, adjusted its position on the stove, and said, "I'll go with you."

"I think I can see myself down the hallway alone, but thanks."

He rubbed his large hands together. "Into the tunnels. It's no place for a couple of girls."

"Mr. Alderman, I must remind you I am a witch," I said.

"I have not forgotten."

"I can fend for myself. And we Riddle women are tougher than we look."

One thick eyebrow raised slightly. "But the devil himself has taken back eighty percent of your powers."

"Eighty percent?" I scoffed. "He took levitation. That's all."

"Is it?"

"The levitation element did affect some of our other spells."

"Eighty percent."

"You can't put a number on magic. It's not like that."

He scoffed.

I scoffed back.

"We haven't been grounded or defanged," I said. "Despite whatever rumors you may have heard."

"All things can be quantified," he said. "That is the whole point of the invention of numbers."

I called down the hallway to Kathy, "Is your father always this argumentative, or did I get lucky today?"

She yelled back, "Dad, be nice to my friend!"

"I am," he said at normal volume. His voice was deep and resonant enough to reach his daughter without an increase in volume. "It is no kindness to lie to the delusional."

I felt a sting from his words.

"Mr. Alderman, are you calling me delusional?"

He nodded his head forward, foreshortening his face so that it looked even more square from where I stood. Like a giant roadblock.

Then he said, "Zara, do you see things that aren't there?"

"I can see ghosts, but they're still there."

"Are they?"

I remembered Bentley's ghost, and how I'd seen him for all those days, even though he hadn't been there, not even in ghost form. Maybe I did suffer delusions. But I wasn't suffering them all the time, and certainly not today. I may have had one delusion, once, but I wasn't delusional.

At my lack of response, he said, "Tell me about the snakes."

"Timewyrms? Those are real. I've seen them, and so have other people."

"The snakes," he said. "The ones attached to the heads of the pretty blonde girls."

He meant the gorgons, including my friend Charlize.

Perhaps he had a point. The snakes were not there, yet I could see them. But they did exist, on some plane.

Or did they?

"That's different," I said. "There are other planes."

"The plane of imagination," he said.

"I'm not delusional."

"With all due respect, Ms. Riddle—"

"Ahem," said his daughter.

Kathy stood in front of the wall of sharp swords and daggers, arms crossed, looking furious at both of us.

Kent Alderman continued, undeterred.

"With all due respect, Ms. Riddle, I will be coming with you into the tunnels. If not for your safety, then for my daughter's. She is the mother of my grandchildren, and they will require continued guidance long after I am gone."

Kathy scoffed. "Thanks, Dad."

Then I scoffed again, for no particular reason but that scoffing was in the air.

Kathy and I weren't just "two girls," and we didn't need an escort. Especially not one who saw the world entirely wrong.

CHAPTER 25

Before we set off into the underground tunnels, I got to see Kathy's childhood bedroom.

Kathy warned me as I stepped into the room, "It gets smaller every time I come home."

"Your dad's house is like mine was? You never told me that. Do the logs change size?"

"Not like that. I mean my room seems smaller as I get older."

I smacked my face lightly. "I always forget that my reality is some people's metaphors."

"Some people's metaphors are reality to them," she said.

"Now you're sounding like your dad."

She clasped both hands to her cheeks. "Heaven help me."

We giggled, and she showed me around the room.

Her father had kept it exactly the way it was when Kathy had moved out, so that when her sons stayed over with their grandfather, they could enjoy a room decorated for kids.

There were shelves full of the usual collectible toys from childhood, plus an impressive selection of leather-bound fairy tales on a sturdy bookshelf made of branches, but the most interesting part was the walls.

The bedroom was at the center of the cabin, so the walls weren't big, round logs like the exterior. They were regular, flat walls, perfect for a mural. And someone had painted an extravagantly detailed wrap-around mural on all four walls. It looked like the sort of thing we might install at the library, in the children's reading area, if only we had the budget. It was a forest theme, with all kinds of forest creatures perching on branches and peering out from underneath leaves. Some were local animals but there were exotic ones, too, from around the world. The animals were painted gazing off into the distance, or at each other, so the walls didn't give me the unsettling feeling of being watched—unlike Kathy's dining room at her house.

"Grandma Kay was a painter," Kathy said. "She also did illustrations for books."

"I'd love to see the books sometime. This mural is incredible. The sloths actually look slow, and the cheetahs look fast."

"It's the brushstrokes, I think."

"It might be magic."

"I don't know. Not everything that looks magic is magic," she said.

"Whatever you do, don't ever let your dad paint over it."

"What?" She puffed up, ready to let out a wail. Framed as she was in her childhood bedroom, I caught a glimpse of Kathy as a child.

"Hypothetically," I quickly added. "Don't hypothetically let him paint it. You can relax. He didn't say anything that would make me believe he's thinking about painting your room."

"He'd better not," she grumbled.

I went to the family of foxes lurking near a corner of the room—two orange ones and a black one—and examined them closely. They were only two-dimensional, created with paint, yet they exuded so much personality and attitude.

"This could be Zoey, my father, and Persephone," I said.

"Everyone is here," Kathy said, pointing at a pink flamingo who could have been Frank. "And she painted this thirty years ago. Isn't that amazing?"

"It reminds me of Carrot's work," I said. "Do the animals move around on their own?"

Kathy's eyes widened. "I should hope not."

Her father appeared in the doorway, clearing his throat. He looked ready to leave, with a jacket on, and a backpack on his shoulders.

I took one last look at the beautiful imagery that had been painted so many years ago by Kathy's mage grandmother, and left the bedroom.

We followed Kathy's father down the hall, and then down a narrow set of stairs.

We had our jackets and shoes on, even though we weren't going outside.

The entrance to the secret tunnels wasn't just near Kathy's father's house, it was *under* the house.

At the bottom of the stairs was a wooden door in a medieval style, made of multiple vertical planks.

"This is our cellar door," Kent Alderman said. "Cellar door."

He was a man of few words, so I knew he was making a statement by repeating himself.

"Cellar door," I said in an elevated tone. "The most beautiful phrase in the English language."

Being a librarian, or perhaps just being a word nerd, I knew about phonaesthetics, the study of beauty and pleasantness in the sounds of words. People who were not native English speakers admired the phrase *cellar door* for its beauty.

Mr. Alderman said, "Some people believe there is no such thing as objective beauty, and those people are wrong."

Kathy rolled her eyes.

"Some words are better than others," he said.

I held my hands up. "You're talking to a witch right here. You are preaching to the choir."

We ducked our heads to fit under the low arch of the doorway.

The root cellar's floor tilted down, so we weren't crouching for long.

The root cellar was, to my surprise, actually full of roots, fruits, and jars of preserves. Most of the root cellars I'd seen were full of dusty boxes of Christmas decorations, pots without lids, and lids without pots.

I saw a few of the same unidentified roots I'd encountered in the community garden.

Kathy closed the cellar door behind us, and then latched it on the inside.

If you've never been in a windowless, below-ground space and heard a door latch, I can tell you it is a worrying sound, even when it's one of your own adventure party turning the lock. The claustrophobia that sets in is more alarming than when a magical mask fits your face too snugly. It heightens your senses the way no caffeinated beverage can.

Her father led the way to another medieval-style wooden door, embedded in the floor.

"Trap door," he said, emphasizing the plosive P to contrast *trap door* with *cellar door*. "Trap door. Trap... door."

Kathy rolled her eyes again.

I gave her a light punch on the shoulder. She was being rude to her father. So what if he liked the sounds of certain words?

He used a big key to unlatch the iron lock, and lifted the trap door open.

Underneath was a pit of inky, shifting darkness that glinted like well water, sounded like a slow stream, and smelled like a swampy pond.

He pulled an acorn from his pocket, and dropped it in.

I expected a long silence, and the distant splash of an acorn landing in still water, but the sound was immediate, and it was a plop, not a splash.

It was the thunk-like plop of an acorn landing on dry dirt, not water.

"Look away, girls," he said to us.

Kathy squeezed her eyelids shut.

I turned my head, but not far enough. Out of the corner of my eye, I saw his square jaw open wider than should have been possible. A supernaturally long, prehensile tongue whipped out, snake-like. An instant later, it whipped back into his mouth, like the power cord being sucked back into a vacuum cleaner. He had the acorn between his teeth.

He put the acorn back into his pocket, and met my gaze.

I wasn't even pretending to look away.

He seemed amused by this, but it was hard to tell with the full mustache covering his mouth.

Kathy opened her eyes and gasped—she'd been holding her breath for some reason.

Her father gave us a nod, checked the shoulder straps for his backpack, and then hopped into the hole.

"Clear," he called out from below.

Interesting. The pit looked, sounded, and smelled of water, but had no water. This was a glamour, and one I hadn't encountered before. Very interesting.

Kathy was staring at me, blinking in a wise, owl-like way behind her round-framed glasses.

"You're enjoying this," she said. "You're enjoying my weird dad, jumping into dark tunnels, armed to the teeth, thinking he's fully prepared for what lives down there in the darkness."

"It's pretty fun. I haven't gone anywhere new since... uh... January before last, when I took the City Hall elevator to that other world."

"It's Tuesday," she said, shaking her head, making her long, brown spiral curls spin out like the seats on an amusement park swing ride. "We would be assembling a magnetic poetry wall right now if it wasn't for that mild breeze."

"I guess that mild breeze was an ill wind that blew us some good, after all."

She hitched her own backpack up her shoulders, and then hopped down into the hole.

"Clear," she called out.

I took one last look around the root cellar, admiring the neatly organized shelves. It was a lot like a library, but for natural foods.

My senses told me not to jump. I could see water, hear water, feel the moisture of water on my cheeks.

Was I sure about doing this? I could call the whole thing off. Both of the sprites seemed to be humoring me and my wishes. They'd likely be just as happy to climb back out of the pit—Kent probably had a telescoping ladder in his large backpack—and sit around the bubbling soup pot until dinner was ready.

Zara tries to be a good witch. Zara doesn't drag her friends and coworkers into shenanigans.

Who was that talking in my head, anyway? Was it me, or my inner OCW?

I jumped down into the darkness.

While in the air, I realized something profound. It was about caution, and how to use it at the right times, and that being called an OCW was no insult at all. Caution could be subjective, or it could be objective, like beauty.

Then I landed on the ground, saw my companions waiting for adventure in the dry darkness, and forgot all about it.

CHAPTER 26

Two sprites and a witch walked into a dark, dank-smelling subterranean chamber.

Not to get too carried away with self-indulgent, self-referential references that ruin a good narrative, but that last sentence sounds like the opening line from a roleplaying adventure module.

Back when I'd lived above ground—up until two hours ago—Agent Knox and I regularly joked about our lives being similar to the game *Dungeons and Dragons*. I had tried to convince him that my character's moral alignment was *lawful good*. He pointed out that I kept doing things that contradicted it. Mainly because I did. For example, throwing a hex at his DWM partner's tires. I wondered how far away from a service station Agent Rob had been when the tire failed.

Those two fellows would owe me a huge apology when I figured out the Mr. Bone-Jangles case.

Unfortunately, I wasn't much closer to any answers, and my nose was going smell-blind from the dank scent that dominated the underground chambers and tunnels. I dare say the dank scent was... *dungeon-like*.

As we walked, I told Kathy's dad about my encounter with the skeleton. Kathy did a wonderful job of dramatically explaining the now-erased video. In spite of all that information, plus his personal experiences in the Wilds, Kent Alderman didn't have any answers.

I kept asking, using different wording, hoping to jog his memory.

"That's enough," he finally said to me with some impatience. "Do not question me as you would a child. I would remember seeing a living skeleton."

"We aren't calling it that," I said. "For discussion purposes, he's Mr. Bone-Jangles."

Kathy added, "Living skeletons are already a real thing. They used to be kept in freak shows. They were people, men usually, with some disease or genetic disorder that made them very thin."

"And that's not even the best part," I said. "Did you know that many of them married the show's Fat Lady?"

That made Kathy's dad snort. "I'd pay to see that wedding," he said with a chuckle.

"Don't laugh," Kathy said. "Those poor, sad, unfortunate people. They didn't have access to medical treatments that could have helped them live healthy, productive lives."

"They were productive," he said. "They toured the country, bringing joy and entertainment to people during our nation's darkest moments."

"Dad!"

"Not everyone fits the same mold."

"But they didn't have to be freaks."

"Kathy, you can pretend the world is how you wish to see it, but I prefer to see the truth."

She groaned, and slowed down her pace until she was trailing along behind us.

"Don't wander off," her father said.

She muttered something unintelligible.

We took turns holding the lantern and being in the front as we made our way through the tunnels.

The lantern was *practical*—a word that Kent Alderman kept using to stress the usefulness of his supplies, because they weren't dependent on magic.

I'd had more than enough caffeine that morning to be able to power magic lights for three full days, but I didn't mind carrying the lantern. It was a lightweight model that directed the beam in one direction, like a headlamp. It could also be worn on the head, like a headlamp, but we didn't like that because it was too easy to accidentally blind one's companions when turning to them during conversation.

Whenever we reached a fork in the tunnels, Kathy would consult the paper map she'd brought, and her father would tell her she wouldn't need the map if she trusted him like she ought to.

The two bickered about everything. It made me miss my daughter fiercely.

On Tuesdays, Zoey had a literature class, and lacrosse —theory and strategy of the game, plus playing. She and Ambrosia joked about enchanting the lacrosse sticks so they could be flown like broomsticks. There really was no need; the game was already violent enough.

My phone had no reception down in the depths, so there were no updates from the girls.

The tunnels so far had fit my expectations. The walls were rock and dirt, fortified by thick wooden beams overhead. They looked exactly like the old coal and gold mining tunnels that most of them were. They didn't seem particularly magical, except for a few glowing patches of mosses that sprouted eyeballs to watch us pass by.

"Do not make eye contact," Mr. Alderman had instructed us when we'd first encountered them.

I'd taken a few peeks anyway. Nothing too bad happened, except I did have to fight the urge to go from eye contact to petting. The moss looked tempting to touch, like a wyvern's belly. However, I was just wise enough to know not to engage with it casually. Aunt

Zinnia had given me plenty of warnings about that creature. Its mating habits were unusual, to say the least.

We had just walked past a particularly large patch of seeing-eye moss when we stopped at a fork in the path.

"We're lost," Kathy said, unfolding and then folding her map noisily in frustration. "This fork isn't even on the map. I knew we'd get lost."

"We're not lost," Kent said. "Quiet."

He tossed an acorn into the dark tunnel on the left, and then another on the right.

"We must have come through here already," Kathy said, whipping out the map once more, and unfolding it noisily.

I was holding the lantern, so I lifted it to illuminate her paper.

"Quiet," Kent said. "Or, in a way you girls can understand, *shush*."

We both shushed.

"Listen," he said. "What do you hear?"

"My gurgling stomach," Kathy said.

"Besides that."

We held very still and listened.

Kathy's stomach, or multiple stomachs, gurgled loudly, then stopped.

I couldn't hear anything other than the sounds of our bodies—the sounds of breathing and digestion that you'd hear in the dead silence of a soundproofed room, or a tomb.

Kent took a pen from his tactical vest, and wrote on the corner of Kathy's map: *We are being followed.*

"Never mind," he said with a fake chuckle. "It's just Kathy's stomach after all."

Both of the sprites looked at me as though they expected me to do something specific.

Time for some witcher-i-doo. It was always nice to get a request from my fans.

I handed the lantern to Kathy, wound myself up dramatically, really hamming it up, then cast a threat detection spell.

The tunnel behind us, from where we'd just come, lit up like a Christmas tree.

The elder sprite was right.

We were being followed.

CHAPTER 27

The three of us turned left at the fork, and continued chatting as though we didn't suspect at all that we were being followed.

Then we set our trap.

I cast a modified sound bubble, similar to the one I used for occasional eavesdropping. For this one, I elongated with a sketchy spell that had been designed for lengthening the hem on trousers, so it had a foot-sized opening at the end.

We spoke into the bubble, which was now a tunnel within a tunnel, and it threw our voices.

Kathy and her father worked as a team, misting the air with one of their practical supplies, a canister of cover spray. It formed a dark one-way mist for camouflage. The formulation did use some magic, but I didn't argue with the sprites about that point.

We hid in a dark corner, and waited.

All three of us had weapons ready to use when our pursuers came into view.

Our frightening pursuers turned out to be... drumroll please... the size and shape of three little kids.

Were my eyes playing tricks on me in the dim light?

Deep down, I didn't want it to be three little kids. I willed it to be something more interesting. Our hunters could be the small-sized version of gnomes, like my nemesis Griebel Gorman. Or some other short but formidable creature. We could give them a real butt-whooping, and they could confess to whatever they had done to Mr. Bone-Jangles, then it would be case closed, party at my house.

All three of us held very still as the other party came closer.

The one in the lead, carrying a lantern, was a boy of about ten or eleven, dressed in a monk's robes.

Except it wasn't an actual monk's robe, but a brown terry-cloth robe, tied with a rope belt. It was the same style as the one I'd seen Kathy wearing that morning.

"You dummies are walking too loud," Monk said to the other two, only he used a more colorful word than *dummies*. Yes, they were regular young human boys, all right.

He called them a few more offensive words, then said, "It's toe-heel, toe-heel."

The second boy, who wore a green leotard covered in leaves made of felt—Bushy—whined, "My feet are sore."

The third boy, dressed in a red jogging suit with red demon horns, punched the second one in the small of the back. "Shut up, whiner."

Bushy whined louder, "Stop hitting me," then, "My pack is heavy."

Monk stopped abruptly, causing a pileup as the other two ran into him.

"Who's the leader here?" Monk demanded.

"Ozgarth the Demon challenges the role of leadership," said Red.

All three of the boys—Monk, Bushy, and Red—crouched in a circle.

Red pulled something from his pocket, and tossed it into the dirt.

It was a die, from a game. They were playing a game.

"Six," Red said. "I'm the leader now."

"Nuh-uh," said Monk. "You have to roll ten or higher."

The die was a high-numbered one, almost round from its many facets, like the kind used for playing Dungeons and Dragons.

Red suddenly shoved Monk by his shoulders, sending the boy rolling backward in the dirt.

Monk sprawled before the three of us who were still hiding, landing on his back with his eyes pointed directly up at us.

We'd been shielded from view by the cover spray, but not well enough to avoid detection at such a close range.

What the young fellow saw in the shadows must have been frightening.

It was an adventuring party of three people, much like his own, except not. For one thing, we were all adults. For another, two of us—the sprites—were holding sharp daggers at the ready. And, as if that wasn't scary enough, the two sprites also had their freakishly long tongues extended, partly coiled in mid-air.

CHAPTER 28

Monk blinked three times while the tableau registered.

Then he screamed and began moving, but he was untrained in combat, and disorganized, so he succeeded only in kicking up dust.

The other boys, Red and Bushy, hadn't yet noticed the three supernatural adults in the shadows, and interpreted Monk's frantic movements as an attack.

Red tossed aside his demon horns, made fists, and jumped on top of Monk as though he'd been waiting for this opportunity his whole life.

Bushy held back, hesitating.

He squinted in our direction.

Had he seen us? He gave no outward sign until he shrugged out of his leaf-covered backpack, dropped it, and ran off in the direction they'd come.

My sprite bodyguards put away their tongues.

Kent Alderman said gruffly, "I'll deal with these two ruffians myself. Zara, please retrieve that crying bush. He won't get far without a lantern." Then he instructed his daughter to circle around so the two boys couldn't escape the way their friend had.

I had so many options at my disposal that it would have been hard to pick my opening move, so I went with a standard.

I cast the shoe removal spell at Bushy.

With no lantern plus no shoes, he wouldn't get far at all.

I trotted off in the direction he'd gone, following the sound of his breathing. He was scared, and whimpering to himself, but—to his credit—he was brave or smart enough to keep going.

And he kept going until... he lost me.

I stopped in a wide part of the tunnel—a chamber. It was a connecting chamber, with five separate entrances or exits. The floor was smooth from regular traffic. The ceiling was covered in seeing-eye moss, all of its eyeballs looking at me with curiosity. I was somewhat aware of this plant and its hypnotic properties because it was prized by my aunt. She kept her refrigerator well-stocked with jars full of eyeballs.

I knew that the eyeballs could be helpful, if they felt like it.

"Hey guys," I said. "Did you see a little boy come through here?"

The eyeballs blinked at each other, and winked at me flirtatiously.

I knew what had to be done.

I stood underneath the fuzziest patch, and stuck my fingers into the moss.

"Ooh, so soft," I said. "Tickle, tickle, tickle."

I tickled the moss.

The moss twitched, and writhed with pleasure.

This was, weirdly, how it reproduced. To make more of itself, or possibly just for recreation, seeing-eye moss needed the fingers of a human to tickle it.

As you can imagine, most humans wanted nothing to do with such a thing. And some humans were a little too into it.

As for me, I was neutral.

As I tickled away, the eyeballs cloaked themselves in their mossy eyelids, vibrating in pleasure while the whole mass of green-blue moss made, to put it delicately, bedroom noises.

Finally, the eyes opened again, and they pointed in unison at one of the chamber's exits.

I thanked them, wiped my hands on a magic handkerchief I pulled from my bra, and ran in that direction.

It was the same tunnel I'd come through once before, but in the other direction.

My eyes weren't working as well as I wanted, but another of my senses detected something. The scent of bubble gum and peanut butter.

I found him wedged into a lichen-crusted crevice. His bushy costume matched his surroundings, plus he'd used dirt from the walls to darken his visible skin.

"Hello, Bushy," I said.

He kept his eyes clenched shut.

"You're very good at hiding," I said. "But you don't have to run away from me. You're not in any trouble."

His eyes flashed open.

I dropped the flashlight.

Can you imagine? I'd faced unspeakable horrors and held onto whatever I had in my hands. Then a little kid opened his eyes unexpectedly at me, and I dropped my flashlight like some amateur.

I leaned forward to pick up the flashlight, but he kicked it out of reach.

"Hang on," I said. "There's no need to be a little—"

He punched me in the stomach.

He punched me pretty hard, for a little kid.

Then he scooped up the flashlight and set off running again.

He switched off the light when he reached a bend in the tunnel, so I couldn't see where he'd gone.

I returned to the chamber with the seeing-eye moss.

With no practical illumination, I had to use magic to light the room.

I asked the moss which way he'd gone, but the moss was fast asleep, all of its eyes closed.

Now what?

If Bushy had been a gnome, or some other magical creature, I wouldn't have thought twice about blasting spells down the dark corridors.

I'd have relished hearing him shriek in terror or pain.

But, he was just a little boy.

I knelt in the dirt and looked for clues down low.

Luckily for me, Bushy's costume was failing him.

He'd dropped a pair of felt leaves a few feet into a tunnel.

I took that route, one magic-lit fingertip pointing ahead of me, and one on the ground.

I found another leaf.

It was, conveniently enough, just past another fork.

And then, at the next fork, there was another leaf.

The one was torn in half, as though someone had used strength to rip it from his costume.

The leaf hadn't fallen off by chance at all. That meant I might be walking into a trap. Wouldn't that be...

Bushy dropped onto me from above.

I shouldn't have been caught off guard by how strong he was, but I was.

I'd taken my witch powers for granted, and I'd forgotten that even as a relatively fit grown woman, I couldn't count on being the victor in hand-to-hand combat with an adrenaline-filled boy.

He didn't want to hurt me, at least.

"Let me go," he grunted as we wrestled. "Please let me go. I won't tell anyone, I promise. M-m-my word is my bond. I shall not tell."

Tell anyone what? That he'd been followed in the tunnel by a lady who seemed to have light coming out of her fingertips?

If he did break his bond, then whatever he said about the light, or my two friends holding daggers, I could deal with.

If I fought harder to detain him, using magic, I'd only be giving him more to talk about.

I let him go.

He ran off, barefoot thanks to my first spell.

I hoped he didn't step on anything sharp.

I hoped he got out safely.

What a ridiculous situation I'd gotten myself into, yet again.

It wasn't my job to police the tunnels, let alone apprehend local kids who were using it as a location to play a game of live-action roleplaying.

As I turned and headed back to where I'd left the sprites, I had a sinking feeling I'd made a terrible mistake.

CHAPTER 29

On the way back to the sprites, I found Bushy's shoes in the dirt. They'd fallen off right where I'd zapped him with my spell.

Shoe removal was one of those *bread and butter* spells that a witch could use with low risk of suspicion. To the kid, it would have seemed that both of the sneakers came untied and then caught on something at the same time.

Sometimes we witches even used it in non-combat situations. But mostly we used it on our enemies, or each other.

The hexed table where we held our coven meetings had been spontaneously removing our shoes all summer. There's been all sorts of accusations until we figured out none of us were doing it.

After that, we'd had to look for new things to fight about. The coven never did stage that intervention for me about my long face. I'd cheered up just enough from my gardening hobby to get my face into the acceptable range.

Meetings with the coven felt like distant memories down there in the tunnels, even though we'd just had a meeting the previous week. There was another one tomorrow, assuming I ever got back above ground.

I picked up the kid's shoes.

They were worn out on the bottoms, as though the kid had walked for miles. Or didn't have any other shoes to wear.

Either way, he would want them back. Returning the shoes would be a good excuse to check on him at home, to subtly make sure he hadn't seen too much.

What if he had seen too much?

There were forgetting spells, and devices at the DWM, but... I didn't want to think about that.

I carefully tied up the laces for the shoes. One shoe had been laced incorrectly. I fixed it.

It had been a long time since I'd tied up a kid's laces. Zoey would never have let her sneakers get so beat up and worn out, but it was probably typical for a boy. I'd always heard from parents of both that boys were a whole different game compared to raising girls.

I tucked the shoes into my purse—it was all I'd brought along—and carried on.

The two sprites, with their excellent hearing, must have heard me coming a mile away. They barely acknowledged me when I returned to them.

Father and daughter were alone, no sign of the two little boys whose physical altercation they'd been breaking up when I left.

"Dad, you don't understand how the world works," Kathy was saying.

"I understand it better than you," Mr. Alderman said firmly, his tone as square as his jaw. "People don't become less wise with age. I have seventeen years of experience on you, seventeen years of wisdom."

Kent was only seventeen years older than Kathy? No wonder he looked so... not old and gross.

The two continued to bicker.

Finally, I interjected with, "Where are your little boys?"

Both turned to me and asked in unison, "Where's yours?"

"He put up a good fight. I had to let him go."

Kathy said, "You did? Why?"

"It was either that, or use magic. I don't know about you sprites, but we witches try to avoid traumatizing minors."

"Same here," Kent said.

Kathy crossed her arms, and looked at me the way a baby does when a parent returns from an outing with a different hairstyle.

She said, "Are you feeling okay, Zara?"

"I think so."

"You look shaken up."

"I did engage in hand to hand combat with a cute little kid."

"Cute?"

I pulled his beat-up running shoes from my purse. "Look at these little shoes. Just look at them. It's like they're for an adult, but smaller."

Kathy said, "Did you hit your head?"

"Probably. It's okay. I've got a thick skull. Just ask my mother."

The two sprites exchanged a knowing look.

I got the sense they'd been talking about me in my absence. I didn't like it. I didn't like being outnumbered. We should have brought along at least one witch to even things out. Then she and I could exchange our own knowing looks right now. Plus, working together, we wouldn't have let Bushy go.

I changed the subject. "What happened with your kids? The one in the brown bathrobe definitely saw some things he shouldn't have seen."

Kent Alderman replied coolly, "We gave them a mild sedative, and sent them on their way."

"How? A potion?"

Kathy said, "It was in chocolate peanut butter cups."

"You brought chocolate peanut butter cups?" I held out my hand. "I could use a snack."

"They're laced with sedatives," Kathy said. "The crunchy bits aren't peanuts."

"Let's party," I said, my hand still out.

Then she named the sedative.

"Oh, no." I pulled my hand back. "But that will affect their memories. You can't give that to little kids." At a high dose, it would wipe out the entire day from their young brains.

"They'll be fine," Kathy said. "Dad gave it to me dozens of times when I was little, and look how I turned out."

"Are you kidding? Kathy, you've got a crazy temper. I've seen longer fuses on dollar-store birthday candles."

Her father said, "Candles contain a wick, not a fuse."

"My point stands," I said. "She's easily triggered, and her blood sugar plummets. We've had to force feed her Frank's teddy-bear crackers once a week since the volunteers started training. And you should have seen what she did to the bean bag chairs."

He waved one hand, brushing away the idea he'd had anything to do with her repressed trauma.

"Kathy was never harmed by a few well-timed naps," he said. "Her temper is genetic. It comes from her mother."

Kathy shrugged. "It's true. I've never seen Dad get mad."

Her father said, "Dogs get mad. People get angry."

"But not *my* dad," Kathy said, sounding like the little-girl version of herself.

I picked up one of the small backpacks the kids had dropped. It was red, where it wasn't filthy with dirt.

"Redford Robb," I said, reading the name tag. "This must be the little devil, Red."

"That name is familiar," Mr. Alderman said.

"I know that name," Kathy said. "He's one of the kids who's alway bugging Frank to play board games with them." She snapped her fingers. "Yes. That's exactly who he is. Those three always come in together, like a pack. And the one who ran off, he's... it's a weird name. Sometimes he comes in with his grandpa, but not lately."

Mr. Alderman was still mulling over the name on the red backpack. "Redford Robb. How do I know that name?"

"It's an inversion of Robert Redford, the actor," I said. "It's pretty clever, actually."

"The kid's not that clever," Kathy said. "He's on our Most Wanted list. Little Redford Robb currently has fifteen overdue library books."

"A Canadian dozen," I said, which was what Margaret Mills called the number fifteen.

"Of course he does," Mr. Alderman said. "When your organization, in all of its wisdom, drastically reduced overdue fines, you effectively killed any incentive for our town's young people to acquire the habit of returning things in a timely manner."

"Dad, we've been over this. The steeper fines were harming the disadvantaged families who need the library the most."

He made a square fist with one strong hand. "And you have only harmed them further with your maternalistic policies." He wasn't angry, but he was agitated.

"They're just little kids," she said.

"Every criminal was once a little kid," he said.

She crossed her arms even tighter. "Gee, Dad, it's too bad every kid in this town doesn't have the privilege of taking drug-coma naps in the back of your old car whenever they find out a bit of truth. It's too bad you couldn't raise every kid around here yourself."

"Would that I could," he said. "This town's future wouldn't be such a question mark."

I didn't want to get in the middle of their spat, but I couldn't resist asking, "What do you mean by that? What question mark?"

He gave me a surprised look. "The devil came here for a reason." He didn't blink. "And I am not referring to our little miscreant friend in the red costume."

"Oh, that."

"Oh, that," he said, mocking my nonchalance.

I said to Kathy, "I didn't know your dad was on the Endtimes bandwagon."

She frowned.

"I am not on any bandwagon," he said. "I am vehemently opposed to the Endtimes."

I waved a hand. "Don't let the devil get you riled up," I said. "He's always been here. Just because he walks the earth in the form of a young man named Atom Wick, that doesn't mean he only just showed up. Everything is as it always was, and always will be."

Very slowly and carefully, Mr. Alderman said, "You. Are. Delusional."

I pulled Red's backpack on my shoulder, and prepared to leave.

Then, rather than get into an argument with Kathy's father—who clearly enjoyed making other people angry to save himself the effort—I started to walk away.

Kathy called out, "Where are you going, Zara? You don't have the map. It's still a long way to the Wilds."

That was news to me. I'd thought the whole tunnel network was the Wilds.

Either way, I'd lost interest.

"Wait," Kathy said, then whispered something to her father.

I stopped walking, but kept my back to them. That way I wouldn't have to look at Mr. Alderman's face while he looked at my face for signs of my delusions. I was tired of people deciding things about me based on how my face looked. I wanted to wear a mask for a full day, and hide behind it. Halloween couldn't come soon enough.

Kathy said, "Are you mad?"

"Dogs get mad," I said, quoting her dad. "I'm not mad, or angry." Not entirely true. "I guess we should head back to the surface, and make sure those boys are okay."

"Quiet," Mr. Alderman said.

"Shush," Kathy said.

I listened. I expected to hear the boys, lost and disoriented from chocolate peanut butter crunchy sedative-hypnotic drugs. And that, kids, is why you don't take candy from strangers.

There were no voices, though. Just a low rumbling.

Kathy said, "We need to get out of here. It feels like the walls are closing in."

I had been in a few small spaces where the walls closed in. It had happened at my old house all the time. I knew that when it felt like the walls were closing in, sometimes they were.

I stretched out my arms, touching the walls with my fingertips.

There was a louder rumble, and my arms bent slightly at the elbows.

"The walls are closing in," I said. "It's gradual, but we should—"

The earth beneath us shook hard, and suddenly all three of us careened from left to right like actors in the movie set for a small spacecraft, filming the scene where they're going through an asteroid belt.

I did hit my head.

I didn't lose consciousness, but it did loosen the wisdom of a distant relative. Her words unspooled inside my mind in an ominous, third-person type of voice: *"Please consult your Elders before attempting any direct communications with the Spyryts. You don't want to accidentally conjure a portal to a Demon Dymensyon and release Hell on Earth! Nobody likes a Wytch who gets into trouble she can't handle or sets off the Apocalypse."*

Was the ground shaking because of me? Had I done this?

It might have been narcissistic as all-get-out for me to think the universe revolved around me, but it would be naive to assume all local disasters simply happened on their own, on some pre-ordained timeline.

Mr. Alderman broke free of the side-to-side pattern, looped his arm around my waist, and dragged me out of the way as two sides of the tunnel came together with a rumble.

CHAPTER 30

The rumbling ceased; the walls were no longer shifting.

After some panicked magic blasting—mine—and calm exploration—Mr. Alderman's—we determined that the tunnels had become stable again.

We would later find out the cause of the shifting, and we would laugh and laugh, but I'm getting ahead of myself. We're not there yet.

We did figure out, through knocks and whistles, that Kathy was alive and well on the other side of what was now a dead end.

On the plus side, we weren't in immediate danger of being buried alive.

On the minus side, our party of three had been split up, and everyone knows that's a bad sign.

We could independently find our way through the maze to reunite, but first we would try to reopen the connection manually.

We hadn't brought along anything as sturdy as a pickaxe, but we used what we had. Kathy was digging on her side, and we were digging on ours.

It wasn't going well. I didn't like how Kathy's father kept picking a different spot on the wall to dig.

"Mr. Alderman, if we work together, and stick to one spot, we can get through this wall faster."

"Faster isn't necessarily better."

"Are you always like this? Questioning every single word people say? No wonder Kathy has such a hair trigger to criticism."

He raised a dark eyebrow. "Is it really Kathy you are speaking of?"

I handed him the long-handled spoon I'd been using on the wall.

"Maybe you want to dig by yourself while I map out the area for Plan B."

He said nothing as he switched to using both tools, one in each hand. He'd become warm from the effort, and had removed his outer layers, revealing a strong body. He was nothing like any pot-bellied male sprite I'd ever seen.

"This is not working," he said to the rocky wall.

"I know it's not," came the muffled voice of Kathy from the other side. "Every time we dig it thin enough that I can see your lights, the hole closes up, and I swear the dirt is twice as dense."

"Three times as dense," he said.

"Twice as dense," she said. "Three times would feel like solid rock."

"Some of it is solid rock," he said.

While the two of them bickered over the density of the wall, I did an exploration of our route options.

I regretted not getting more experience in the pre-Halloween corn maze. I might have been more prepared, if I'd been allowed to get fully lost. But I did my best. I used the left-hand rule of labyrinths, keeping my left hand on the walls until it was time to use my right hand and return.

When I got back to my single sprite companion, he was packing up.

My heart sank. There was no point in digging at the wall. It really was reforming as we dug, denser and thicker, like scar tissue. I tried not to imagine that we were deep in the intestines of a giant creature, about to be digested. It would explain the dank smell.

"Kathy isn't far from the surface," he said. "She's able to go straight up. She'll be out in an hour or two."

"Then we'll go straight up, too."

He shook his head, and said what I'd already suspected. "It's solid rock above us. Kathy is beneath a fault line. She can go up, but we cannot."

"That's all on the map, isn't it?"

He nodded. It was indeed on the map—the map that was now in Kathy's possession.

I had taken a photo of the map on my phone for backup, but ever since my visit from Agent Rob, images had been deleting themselves when I needed them most. It was a technological hex that I had to admire, and that I would decode and recreate if I ever got back to the top side again.

"Okay. It's settled," I said in a cheery way. "We'll just go back the way we came in, and we'll be back in your cellar in time for dinner. Speaking of your cellar, did I see a jar of raspberry-rhubarb preserves?"

"We will return, by way of the Wilds." He hiked the backpack onto his broad shoulders. "We shall do what we set out to do."

"But, Mr. Alderman, what about your soup?"

"You may address me by my first name. Kent."

"Okay, Kent. What about your soup?"

"The worst that can happen is it thickens into stew."

I didn't think that was the absolute worst thing that could happen if we went deeper into the tunnels.

However, he did seem confident enough, plus we had come down there for a reason.

As we walked, we found more dropped leaves from the kid in the green leotard.

These weren't like the ones he'd dropped to mislead me, the obvious ones. These felt bits were at the edges of the tunnel, partly covered in debris. I only saw them because my light-casting spell had a tinge of ultragreen that made green objects glow white.

Please note: Ultragreen is on a magic frequency, and not supported by any scientific literature. Don't bother ordering it online. The so-called ultragreen lights commonly available are almost certainly fake, and will only give you a headache.

The mind-numbing sounds of our breathing and our movement were eventually cut through by a scream in the distance.

I recognized that scream. It was our little friend in green.

"Wait." Kent held me back with one strong hand. "It could be a trap."

"What do you think we're inside right now, *Kent*?"

He frowned, like a man regretting giving you permission to call him by his first name.

"You have so much to learn, *Zara*."

I didn't like him using my first name, either. It felt personal. Intimate. Everything felt personal and intimate deep underground, with only the sounds of your bodily functions for noise.

Bushy screamed again. He wasn't far away.

I cast my trusty threat detection spell, along with extra illumination.

The whole tunnel lit up like a fake outdoor street in Las Vegas.

Honestly, there wasn't much point in casting a spell like that when your other senses were already screaming.

The kid yelled, "Help! Someone help!"

Kent released my arm just in time before I made him release it.

"Go," he said. "Now. I have your back."

He had drawn a blade without my noticing.

I ran forward. The Las Vegas light show ran two paces in front of me, lighting the tunnel like an airport runway.

I suddenly stopped in my tracks, but the lights did not. They illuminated a horrific sight.

The child was there, or at least a child-sized shape. He was on the ground, covered in a writhing mass of exposed bone and burnt-looking meat.

Bone-crawlers.

CHAPTER 31

Bone-crawlers are supernatural creatures that don't belong in this world. I'm not sure they even belong in their own.

At first glance, they appear to be nothing more than a pile of nibbled-on barbecue meat, mostly short ribs, with some rack of lamb, and a few chicken wings. But they swarm and devour, like locusts, only much, much worse.

I had very little personal experience with them, but I did know about one terrifying encounter Aunt Zinnia experienced with them, inside the elevator at City Hall.

The hero that day had been a sprite, Karl Kormac.

He had unleashed his prehensile tongue, snapped up the crab-sized critters, and eaten every last one of them.

I stood aside, and let my sprite companion do what he did best.

Kent Alderman dispatched every single hideous, asymmetrical bone-crawler like they were boneless chicken wings.

When he was finished, he didn't meet my eyes.

"I'm sorry you had to see that," he said.

"I'm sorry we didn't have any blue cheese dipping sauce," I said.

"Oh." Kent licked his thumb. "That would be quite nice." He let out a burp, and apologized once more.

"You and your stomachs can have as many victory burps as you want. That was—"

"Hideous," he said. "I know how it looks. You should not have witnessed a feeding."

"That was heroic," I said.

The crumpled figure on the ground wheezed.

Our banter quickly ended when we realized the boy had been gravely injured.

Bushy's breathing was rapid and labored.

The creatures had chewed through most of his costume, and no small amount of skin.

He'd lost a lot of blood. Was still losing it.

I spat on my fingers and dabbed at his wounds as I held him close.

His feet in particular were ravaged. That was where they'd attacked him first. He might have been able to hold the creatures off longer, except someone had taken his shoes.

Why had I taken his shoes? And why hadn't I pulled away from Kent and gotten to him sooner? Why had I allowed him to become separated from the others in his group? Three of them, small as they were, would have had decent odds against the bone-crawlers. Especially if the other two were half as brave and resourceful as the boy who was slipping away in my arms.

His hands were so small. His ears, too.

He was hurt and bleeding because of me.

I let my guilt be fuel as I flowed my healing energy into him without restraint.

If he slipped away, I was ready to go with him. It was the least I deserved for allowing him to be harmed.

CHAPTER 32

I didn't slip away with the boy's soul.

He recovered, thanks to my magic, but the injuries would have been fatal if a witch hadn't been there. The same injuries that wouldn't have happened if a witch hadn't been there.

As he stirred back to consciousness, I pressed my fingers into his dark bruises, turning their colors like autumn leaves in another world, through shades of brown, purple, and green. They faded away.

He was whole.

"Good work," Kent said. "We'd best not linger."

"More bone-crawlers?"

"I did not detect the queen. She may be nearby with a second faction."

I tried to get up, but I stumbled.

"You are weakened," Kent said.

"How dare you." I tried to muster a fireball, but there was nothing. I had no magic left.

He pulled something from his backpack. A strange-looking sandwich, or possibly lasagne from another world. It looked a bit wet for my liking.

I didn't take the offering.

Kent unwrapped it, and shoved it toward my mouth.

I pushed it away. "No, thanks. I'd rather take my chances with the chocolate peanut butter cups. Let's start with one and see how I feel."

"Eat it," he said sternly. "Food is fuel, not entertainment."

The smell wasn't bad—or maybe it only seemed that way due to the pervasive dank smell in the tunnels—so I took a cautious nibble.

He pulled a chocolate peanut butter cup from his bag, and ate it in one gulp.

"That's no fair," I said.

"The sedatives don't affect my system," he said. "Much."

I finished the sandwich-lasagne thing quickly.

Bushy was slumbering peacefully, his head on my lap, as though he was a very large, very spoiled housecat.

Kent grabbed the kid under the armpits, and lifted him to his feet.

"You're all right," he said to the kid, who was still swooning.

Then he held a packet of smelling salts under the kid's nose.

The kid's eyes flew open, and he was wide awake.

Kent disposed of the smelling salts by eating them.

I was surprised, but after what I'd seen moments earlier, not shocked.

The ammonia-based chemicals were probably a spice to the multi-stomached sprite.

"You're like a goat," I said. "I bet you could eat a tin can."

"Easily."

The kid said, "Is he a goat?"

We both looked at him.

Bushy clarified his question. "Is he a goat shifter? You're a witch. I figured out that much."

Kent offered him a chocolate peanut butter cup.

"No." I put my hand between the treat and the kid, and told him, "Don't take candy from strangers. Especially this guy."

Kent ate the treat himself, and another packet of smelling salts.

I said to Bushy, "What do you know about shifters and witches?"

He lifted his chin. "I know that they're real. And so are vampires, and ghosts, and goblins."

"You have been misinformed," Kent said. "There are no goblins."

Bushy looked down at his tattered costume, then up at us with glistening eyes.

"W-w-what happened to me? What were those things?"

"Rats," Kent said. "Sewer rats. Everyone knows they live in the tunnels."

The boy shuddered. "Those rats could talk," he said. "They said they wanted to eat me down to my bones." He swallowed hard. "Until I was nothing but a skeleton."

Kent and I exchanged a look.

We were down there investigating an animated skeleton, and we'd found a creature made of bones that told their victim he would soon be a skeleton.

This was exactly the kind of break I'd been hoping would fall into my lap.

Now we just had to hunt down the queen of the bone-crawlers, have Kent eat her for dessert, and get back to the cellar before Kathy got nervous and called in the nosy DWM, who would take all the credit for closing the case.

CHAPTER 33

A sprite, a witch, and a little boy walked into a dark, dank-smelling subterranean chamber.

And then into a tunnel.

And another chamber.

Tunnel.

Chamber.

Tunnel.

Chamber.

"Do your magic again," Bushy said to me. "Cast the spell that takes off my shoes."

His shoes were back on his recently-healed feet again.

"I don't know what you're talking about," I said. We'd been trying to downplay the nature of our situation, for the boy's protection.

"I know you're a witch," he said. "I've been inside your house."

"I doubt that."

"The fences aren't very good. There's a gap on the side, and we go down there all the time."

Kent was staying out of the conversation, but he did shoot me a look of curiosity, his eyebrows lifted while the rest of his expression remained inscrutable.

Bushy was ahead of us, holding the lantern.

His name really was, weirdly enough, Bushy.

Yep.

His parents had named him Byzantium, after the ancient city that had been repeatedly sacked and renamed, like so many ancient cities.

Byzantium was a big mouthful for a kid, so his family had shortened it to Zan. Everyone assumed Zan was short for Zander, which was in turn short for Alexander, but only if you thought a Z was basically the same as an X. It is not.

The nickname Zan hadn't stuck, which was fine because the kid had a distant uncle named Zan anyway.

What did stick was Bizzy, which I agreed was a very cute name for a baby.

When Byzantium reached school age, he spelled Bizzy on his school papers as Byzy, B-Y-Z-Y. That had been great until he turned seven, and a character with that exact same name appeared on a popular TV series. It was a character that nobody liked, played by an untalented child actor who was the offspring of two much more talented former child actors.

Next, the kid had tried to get the nickname Butchy to stick, but absolutely zero people got on board with that.

Teachers and kids at school started calling him by his full name, Byzantium, or sometimes Chrysanthemum, or Doodieface. Kids could be cruel. He answered to any of those names until one day he auditioned for a school play, and everything changed.

The play had been a thinly-disguised allegory for war, and he'd played a hedge. A walking, talking, feeling hedge who helped narrate the play. He wore a green leotard covered in leaves for every rehearsal because the director was intense, and insisted that every rehearsal be a full dress rehearsal.

In those rehearsals, people spontaneously began calling him Bushy, and the name stuck.

That's how Bushy got his name.

Or maybe it is and always was Jayson with a Y, and I'm messing with you.

How would you ever know? And would it even matter?

Back to our adventure.

"Did you hear me, Witch?" Bushy had stopped, turning around to face me.

"Don't call me that," I said. "It's very rude."

"But it's what you are!" He put his small hands on my waist, and shoved me. "Tell the truth! Don't lie!"

I was off balance, unsure how to respond.

Kent Alderman said, "Son, do not make me punish you."

"You can't hit me," Bushy said, chin up defiantly. "Goatman. Goaty Goaterson. Mr. Goat."

"I am Mr. Alderman, and this is Mrs. Riddle."

"Miss Riddle," I said.

Kent did a double take. "Right. I keep forgetting because it's hard to believe a woman like you is single."

Bushy gasped. "Goatman loves Witch!" He sucked in a breath to yell it at the top of his lungs.

I shot the shoe removal spell at his feet.

His little shoes untied themselves, and whipped off, knocking Bushy to his butt.

His face registered the shock. Then he raised his little arms in triumph. "I knew it!"

I said to Kent, "Get out the chocolate peanut butter cups."

My sprite companion smirked under his thick mustache, and I laughed hard enough to make the muscles behind my ears ache.

We were having fun. Imagine that. I'd relocated my old laugh, and all it had taken was a trip underground, and a near-deadly encounter with bone-crawlers from another world.

I helped Bushy get his shoes back on again, and we returned to walking.

I asked him, "What do you mean you've been in my house? Were you at my Halloween party two years ago?" We'd had some kids earlier in the evening, before things had turned inside out.

"We go there all the time," he said. "Duh. That's how we get into the tunnels."

Kent and I exchanged a look. That did explain how the kids had gotten down there. They'd used the construction site where my house used to be. The town should have boarded things up better.

"But it's not my house down there," I said. "My house is gone."

"Ms. Riddle, the Red Witch House is still there. It's just... you know."

"I don't know. Tell me everything, or I'll zap your shoes off again. I'm a big, scary witch, remember?"

"It's in the Underneath," he said with effort, as though the truth was upsetting. "Your house is way down there, but... the windows don't work right."

"Is that what you kids call these tunnels? You call them the Underneath?"

"No." His walking pace slowed, like he was struggling to move and process mental concepts at the same time. He probably was. He was just a little kid. He was clever for his age, but he was only ten. And he must have been exhausted from all the walking.

I suddenly remembered the cardboard box of crafting supplies that had reappeared in my armoire at Ethan Fung's house.

Was my house still... somewhere? After all this time? Had it been sending me messages via objects, like handwritten notes in glass bottles, except way more cryptic?

Gently, I asked, "What is the Underneath? Is it the Wilds?"

"It's deeper," he said, then he let out a big, heavy sigh. "I only went down there once. It was too scary. I'm sorry. I'm so sorry."

He'd slowed even more, and was barely moving.

"You don't have to be sorry," I said. "But you shouldn't go down there anymore. Not without..." Without what? A witch and a sprite?

"I will go with you next time," Kent said. "I am not a goat, nor am I a shifter. I am a sprite." Then, with barely any pause, he said, "We will stop now for a rest. No arguing. My feet are sore."

I doubted his feet were sore, but I was grateful for the break because my proverbial dogs were barking.

Casting all the lights, plus the healing work on Bushy, had depleted my magical reserves. I shouldn't have even been able to remove the kid's shoes the second time. The silent words had fizzled on my Witch Tongue. The spellwork had only affected the shoes because the kid had wanted it so bad, self-powering it like a tandem spell by accident.

We had just reached a cavern that was as roomy as any of the chambers, so we stopped there for a rest.

We sat cross-legged, and passed around our food supplies.

It hadn't been very long in terms of hours since I'd last eaten, but the tedium of the dark tunnels made the prospect of putting something flavorful into my mouth much more appealing.

We shared the unusual but nourishing items from Kent's backpack, as well as some colorful candies from Bushy's.

When he was getting out the candies, I noticed a square object—a board game.

"What's that?" I asked. "Can I see it?"

Bushy smirked. "I don't know. *Can* you?"

He was lucky I was out of magic.

I tried again. "May I? Please, and thank you, and intercom?"

"What?"

"The magic word is *intercom*."

He did not get my joke. Which was fair, since it was a reference to my encounter with Agent Rob, so how would he?

I felt déjà vu.

I felt like I'd gotten ahead of myself. Like that Bushy *would* know the intercom joke, someday, but didn't know it yet. And we were all living through a time loop, like the kind my mother could cast, with dim memories of future events to be.

(Relax. We were *not* in a time loop.)

He handed me the board game.

I didn't recognize the publisher's name. Drexoll Games.

They sounded a tad evil, and pretentious. And the name itself? Drexoll Games? It was too similar to the name of a popular chain of drugstores to be a wise business decision.

It had to be a vanity publisher, the kind that takes money from unwitting game "designers" only to leave those hopeful people with a garage full of unsellable copies of a Monopoly rip-off.

But, when I opened the lid, I did not find the familiar Monopoly rip-off board.

It was a contemporary game, with high-quality components, and a board that could be reconfigured randomly for maximum replayability.

We had board games at the library, so the contents didn't shock me, until they suddenly flew out of the box, and up in the air.

"Wow," Bushy said. "So cool!"

Kent said to me, "You should conserve your energy."

"I'm not doing this," I said.

The tunnels around us rumbled.

The interlocking board pieces fell to the dirt floor between us, twisting and turning on their own.

When they stopped moving, the finished board appeared to match our real-life surroundings. Or so we all concluded based on what we could see, which was our current chamber. There was a matching tile on the board, representing our chamber, though it was labeled as a warren.

That central warren held three player pieces: a green tree, a white goat, and a yellow duck.

"Quack," I said. "Quack, quack."

Kent said nothing.

"I don't get it," I said. "Are we playing this game, or is it playing us?"

Kent had no answers, unless they were in his mustache, which he was quietly smoothing.

I said to the kid, "Clearly we are in some sort of Jumanji situation. Did you and your friends Jumanji all of us? How did you do it? What are your powers, anyway?"

"This isn't Jumanji," Bushy said, holding up the top of the box. It was a game called Warrens & Wyverns. There was a black warning label across the corner, which read:*Prototype. Do not play underground.*

"Great," I said. "You kids had to play it underground. Now you've Jumanjied all of us."

"Nobody's been Jumanjied," Kent said.

"Oh, no?" I picked up a tiny model of a skeleton. "It's pretty clear that we are Jumanji-ing as we speak. It all adds up."

"But we have free will," Kent said, his deep voice pitching up, as though he was struggling to keep the question mark off the statement.

I said to Bushy, "Why didn't you bring this out sooner?"

His cheeks flushed.

"Bushy," I said, using the tone I might use to crack my daughter during the rare circumstances that I suspected deceit from an otherwise good kid. "Why did you keep this from us?"

He looked down at the ground.

Kent said, "It's okay, son. I understand."

I didn't.

"I wanted to finish the adventure," Bushy said.

"And we will," Kent said.

He picked up the board pieces, leaving the tile with the tree, goat, and duck where it was. He shuffled the tile cards, then laid them out.

The ground rumbled around us, and the entrances and exits of our chamber, or warren, blinked in and out of existence.

Kent didn't like the new layout, so he shuffled the cards and laid them out again.

I said, "Why don't you just—"

"No cheating," Bushy said. "You can't look at the pieces before you put them down. That's cheating."

"So?" I didn't understand why we couldn't fit the pieces down one at a time, like a game of Carcassonne. Who cared if everything didn't come out square in the end?

"No cheating," Bushy said. "That's how you get to the Underneath."

I threw my hands in the air. Kent was shuffling the deck pieces for what had to be the tenth time now. How was that not cheating?

"There," Kent said as he laid down the final tile, completing a rectangle.

"Too easy," Bushy said.

"Not at all," Kent said. "We have three distinct puzzle doors to untangle before we exit the game."

"But no monsters," Bushy said.

I said to him, "You do know this is real, right? If we die in this game, we are dead for real."

He didn't look like he believed me at all.

Kids.

This was why they needed more than an internet connection and dry clothes.

"Puzzle doors are challenging enough," Kent said. "And they're good for team building. It teaches collaborative problem solving."

Bushy groaned, but he didn't put up any more fuss about the board.

We fit the pieces into the slim case that would preserve the layout, and set off.

As we traveled, the tunnels took on a library theme, the sides wallpapered in book spines, the books seemingly embedded in the walls.

A few of the warrens were downright cozy. One had a reading lamp partly embedded in a stony wall, and half of a comfortable-looking chair.

We reached the first of the series of challenges.

The first puzzle door was an old riddle. I solved it easily because that riddle was in every single old joke book we had at the library. (When is a car not a car. When it turns into a parking lot. Ha ha.)

The second required more teamwork. There were magnetic pieces that had to be harvested from the ceiling to solve a multi-layered puzzle that was also a poem. Kent and I took turns holding Bushy on our shoulders to harvest the pieces. The poem was about roots, and trees, and birds leaving the nest, and tumbling into the unknown.

At last, the third and final door was... thin enough to be kicked down by two adults who'd grown weary of reading the small print of game rules while being bossed around by a little kid.

With the final door out of the way, we stepped out into the area that had been represented on the Warrens & Wyverns board by a green line. It was the Outside.

We stepped into a ballroom, with checkerboard floors made of gleaming marble, and chandeliers high above us on the ornate ceiling.

We were in a castle.
Castle Wyvern.

CHAPTER 34

The ballroom was dimly lit, and mostly empty.

The only other people present were two Castle Wyvern employees, who barely glanced our way before getting back to work.

They were installing a big banner that read 171st Annual Monster Mash. The actual official name of the ball was written in fine print underneath, but lately they'd embraced the name everyone in the supernatural world called it anyway.

There was just one problem.

"Uh-oh," I said to Kent. "If it's Halloween already, that means we've been missing for ten days."

He walked up to the employees, and tapped one on the shoulder. They were a man and a woman in their fifties.

Kent said, "I am sorry to bother you, ma'am, but can you tell me the exact date and time? My phone is malfunctioning."

She answered in a French accent, "It is twenty-two, October. No, wait. Twenty-three. It is now... past midnight."

Kent shot me a look of relief. We hadn't jumped forward in time after all. The staff was just getting a headstart on preparations.

The middle-aged employee grinned at her coworker and said, "It is the overtime. We are making the overtime, Glen."

"I love this time of year," Glen said, giving her a high-five. "But I hate being here after midnight."

"Then get busy," she said. "Or do not get busy. I like to be in the overtime."

The two got back to installing the banner, not at all curious about why a dirt-covered trio had magically appeared in the ballroom.

I wasn't terribly surprised by Kent's ability to put the young workers at ease.

Sprites had a natural air of authority, which was why many of them worked in supervisory positions. Kathy was our head librarian, and her cousin Karl had managed the Permits Department for many years. I still didn't know what Kent did for a living.

Since the Castle Wyvern staff weren't alarmed by our presence, the three of us took over a table at the edge of the ballroom so we could regroup.

We must have slid through at least one spatial portal in the tunnels. Or been shuffled by the board game. There was no way we could have traveled on foot from Wisteria all the way up the coast to Westwyrd in a single day.

We were fortunate we hadn't skipped through time and worried our families. Or maybe we'd jumped forward but then backward the same amount. The universe did have its own system of checks and balances to keep out continuity errors—though it wasn't perfect. I still didn't understand the physics of the City Hall elevator key, or keys, plural, which moved through time like a snake eating its own tail.

I used some cleaning supplies from my purse to wipe the grime off Bushy's face. It would be easier to deposit him seamlessly into his regular life if he didn't look like he'd been dungeon crawling.

Kent took out Bushy's prototype copy of Warrens & Wyverns, and carefully dismantled the board.

The pieces let out discombobulated FIFFLE sounds.

All the magic of the enchantment drained away.

"Careful," Bushy said, squirming while I tried to clean his dirty chin. "That's the only copy."

"Correction," Kent said. "It *was* the only copy."

And then he ate the board game. Every single piece. As only a sprite could. He ate it like Kathy ate leftover birthday cake, and Karl ate imported junk food from the convenience store.

Bushy was too upset to speak. His cleaned-up eyes gleamed as his half-dirty mouth made silent fish lips.

"It's for your own good," I told the kid. "But, to be perfectly honest, it's mostly for our convenience."

Our phones had finally started working again, so Kent called his daughter.

"Kathy's got everything under control," Kent reported to me. "The other two kids are home safe and sound, sleeping in their beds."

He went back to talking to his daughter, walking away from our table for privacy.

I held my phone out to Bushy. "Do you know your phone number?"

He didn't take my phone.

"I'm staying over at Red and Monk's house. They're brothers but they aren't twins. They were born in the same year, so they're in the same grade. One of them has allergies, but I can't remember which one. I'm sorry."

"You don't have to apologize." I couldn't help but fix his hair, which was still damp from my cleaning supplies. He was a cute kid—most kids are. It's why we're always fixing their hair.

"I'm sorry about..." He looked at the spot on the table where his prototype copy of Warrens & Wyverns had been sitting up until a few minutes ago.

"You didn't do it on purpose," I said.

He squirmed. It wasn't the truth. He had known about the enchantment on the board game. But he had also learned his lesson. I would let his own guilt punish him.

I said, "If Red and Monk think you're with them, we'll drive you to their place. I'll cast some sort of spell so their parents believe you were there the whole time."

His eyes widened. "Can I watch?"

"There's not much to see."

"But I can watch, right?"

"Sure. Why not? You'll forget anyway when I scramble your brains."

His eyes widened even more.

"It's okay," I said softly. "You knew about me before this, and you kept it to yourself. That proves—"

"I can keep quiet," he said. "It can be our secret."

I didn't like the idea of keeping a secret with someone else's child.

"No," I said quickly. "It proves that your memory goes back way too far for me to wipe it myself. So, I'll let you roam free for now. But if I hear that you've been telling people things you shouldn't..."

He swallowed audibly. "My word is my bond, I shall not tell your story," he said.

I nodded. That wording was acceptable.

"How do you know all this stuff, anyway? Who are your parents?"

He yawned. "My grandpa told me."

"Do I know your grandpa?" I had a vague recollection of seeing the boy with an old man in the library. But it could have been my imagination making a composite memory. Lots of retired people visited the WPL with their grandkids. It was a perfect intergenerational activity, second only to a visit to the Atlantis Mini Putt and Water Adventure Park.

Bushy shook his head, no. Then he shivered.

"You're tired, and cold," I said.

"No." He shook his head. His lower lip was almost blue, like he'd been treasure-diving in the cold swimming tank at the Atlantis park for too many hours.

I channeled my inner stage magician, and yanked the tablecloth off our table. The cloth was plaid and flannel, almost a blanket. Using it, and my cardigan as a pillow, I set up a makeshift bed for the boy across two chairs. We would leave soon enough, but we had to wait for Kathy, or someone else, to get there by car.

Bushy protested about being put to bed like a child.

"I'm not a baby," he said. "I'm not a..."

He had already fallen asleep.

I tucked the covers around him tightly—a mother's muscle memory—while I looked at my phone.

I'd been missing, or, at the very least, out of contact for nearly a full day. It was nearing twelve-thirty, early Wednesday morning.

There were only three messages waiting for me. They were all reminders of an upcoming dental cleaning. My dentist was nothing if not thorough.

Nothing from Zoey.

Which was good.

No news was good news.

But did it feel that way? Of course not.

There's no way a parent came up with that saying.

Kent returned from his phone call.

"She's on her way," he said, referring to his daughter. "But not right away. She has to stop by the library."

"Unbelievable. She can't stay away from that place."

"Apparently the alarm system has been triggered. She mentioned something about a squirrel."

"Petey. Our local muffin bandit. He got in a few times when the roof was off. At least it keeps him from terrorizing people in the local limousines. He must think the library is the new good place to be."

"That is understandable," Kent said. "It is a good place."

"What's that?" I held my hand up, cupping my ear. "Was that a compliment about the library? All that taxpayer funding, all those operating expenses and heating bills for the wasteful lofted space, but it's actually a good place?"

Kent's head turned to the side, like he'd heard something worrying—even more worrying than a person teasing him about his politics.

I didn't hear anything.

His head turned the other way.

Now I heard it.

Screaming, in another room of the castle.

The two middle-aged employees who had been hanging up the banner were no longer in the ballroom.

I jumped up. My magic levels were still low, but I did have my trusty purse full of enchanted items and ready-made spells.

Kent grabbed the sleeping kid, rolling him up in the flannel blanket like a burrito, and threw him over his shoulder.

He followed me as I led the way toward the screaming.

You know, some people run away from the sound of screaming.

Not this witch.

CHAPTER 35

The screaming was perfectly understandable, and matched the tableau we found in a nearby supply room.

The two middle-aged employees from the ballroom were standing on top of a rolling dessert trolley, surrounded by our old foes, the bone-crawlers. The creatures skittered, rolled, and teemed, like a swamp covered in garbage that's trying to eat you.

Glen was instructing his French coworker, in between screams, on how to stave off the disgusting creatures.

"Frances, you're only helping them," Glen said. "You never listen to me. You're so stubborn."

"Glen. I am doing it. This is the best I can do!"

"Well, do it better! You've got to hit them with the soup ladle, not give them an express elevator ride to us."

Fran burst into tears. "I do not want to be in the overtime." She smacked bone-crawlers off the edge of the dessert trolley with her dented soup ladle. "It is not worth it, not even for the overtime. I am not ready to die. I have seen nothing that I long to see."

"Nobody's dying on my watch," Glen said heroically. "I'll be damned if—"

The bone-crawlers that had formed a megastructure dropped from the ceiling onto his face.

Three more—or maybe it was six—dropped onto his companion's face.

We had no time to waste as the two crumpled into heaps on the trolley.

My sprite companion did his tongue thing, and started eating the creatures, starting with the ones he plucked off the faces of Glen and Frances.

There were so many of them. But that tongue kept whipping, snapping up the creatures as though the sprite had been training for this his whole life.

He gradually slowed, and then stopped, holding his stomach.

"I can't take much more," he groaned.

"I've got this."

With no magic other than my own creativity, I got to work.

The rolling dessert trolley had four large wheels, and was weighted nicely thanks to the two employees crumpled on the top of it. The whole thing functioned like a drum roller.

A drum roller is, like a skid steer, very useful for getting rid of anything that stands in your way. It flattens organic material, such as bone-crawlers; it removes air pockets, such as the lung sacs inside bone-crawlers; and it creates a flat, buildable foundation decorated with, you guessed it, the broken body parts of your enemies. You can rent a drum roller wherever quality excavators are offered. Tell them Zara Riddle sent you. There's no discount, but I like the idea.

As the battle progressed, the charred-looking meaty bones looked less like leftover barbecue and more like roadkill.

The trolley did a great job as a drum roller, but it wasn't perfect.

Some of the bone-crawler bits stayed chunky in the wheel treads. They kept reanimating despite being split apart.

Even with the help of Glen and Frances, who were bleeding but thankfully not disfigured, it took us close to an hour to render all the bone-crawlers into pulp.

As the situation became less intense, and more like a work day, we chatted like we were all coworkers at the castle.

They were a married couple, a pastry chef and a personal trainer. It was very amusing that one tried to enlarge people's waistlines while the other tried to shrink them.

The couple did not see the humor in their contrasting choices of vocations. People can't see themselves in the broad, humorous strokes that others do. Comedy on the outside is drama on the inside. But comedy on the inside is tragedy on the outside.

Thanks to our chatter, we'd let our guard down. We were literally high-fiving each other when the doorway darkened with a hideous figure.

It was six feet tall, and insectoid. It bore very little physical resemblance to the crab-sized creatures we'd just squashed, but I knew immediately—thanks to the crown-like protrusions at the top of what seemed to be its head—that this was the queen.

"Careful," Kent said to me. "The queen is not like the others. Her head needs to be—"

The head in question rolled off the body, and toward us, like a bowling ball.

The head needs to be *what*? He hadn't said.

I had to assume, given its rolling nature, that the head was about to detonate.

I threw myself on top of the flannel-wrapped bundle we'd left on a small table meant for supplies.

Nothing was ticking, let alone detonating.

I cautiously looked up.

The remainder of the queen toppled forward into the room, limp and lifeless.

Behind the body stood our friend Kathy, with an absolutely enormous pair of scissors in her hands. Next to her was a pink flamingo standing on one foot.

I slowly pulled myself away from Bushy, who hadn't even woken up.

I said to Kent, "What were you saying about the queen?"

"Her head needs to be completely severed by two blades working together as one, such as the sharp talons of the iguammit, or..."

Kathy made a few snips in the air with her big scissors.

"You knew," I said. "You told Kathy to bring the scissors when you talked to her on the phone."

"Bone-crawlers always split into two equally sized factions," he said. "I'd hoped the second group had returned to their world, but hope is not an effective strategy against the enemy. Only careful preparation, and intelligence."

Kathy said, "I always keep these in my car. You never know when you'll need a good pair of scissors."

The queen's body turned to dust, but the rest of the flattened creatures remained.

Frank-the-Flamingo entered the room on his long, spindly legs.

He used his long beak to harvest and gobble up gooey, macerated bits of creature.

I'd seen a lot of unappetizing things in my life, but this topped the list. I wouldn't be hungry again for at least a few hours.

CHAPTER 36

After Frank-the-Flamingo had eaten his fill of otherworldly floor pizza, he shifted back into his human form.

When he changed, the two married Castle Wyvern employees simply shared a knowing look. They didn't have powers themselves, but they certainly knew about magic.

Frank patted his stomach. "What's for dessert?"

That elicited a dark chuckle from both of the sprites.

Frank shook Kent Alderman's hand. "Good to see you again, Kent. Shame about the circumstances."

"Always a pleasure, Frank. I am not one to comment on fashion, but I must commend you on your makeover."

"Thanks." Frank beamed with pleasure, and preened his winter-weight wool suit.

Kathy cocked her head and shushed us. "I hear skittering down the hall."

Glen said, "Our in-castle stand-up comedian does crab imitations. It's probably just him, skittering up and down the hallway for practice."

"That is rather odd," Kent said, frowning.

Frank looked around at the faces of everyone gathered. "What do we do now? I don't usually get to participate in the shenanigans."

Kent said, "We will conduct a thorough search of the castle." He made it sound very dry and un-shenanigan-like. Frank's posture slumped with disinterest.

They formed two search parties: Frank paired up with Kent, and his daughter Kathy went with Glen, the personal trainer.

Frances opted out of the search parties.

I stayed behind to keep an eye on Bushy, and to help Frances clean up the room.

I started sweeping in a corner.

"This isn't something I usually do," I said to Frances. I had made plenty of magical messes, but there'd usually been someone else around to tidy up.

"I can tell," she said dryly. "That's a mop, not a broom."

"I know that," I said. "I'm using a mop to sweep because the, uh, stuff over here is pretty wet. Also, do I really need to point out you're talking to a real, live witch? Trust me, I know what a broom is."

We worked in silence for a while before Frances finally said, "Mademoiselle, can I ask you a question?"

"Sure."

"That nice detective fellow, he did not transfer to another town, did he?"

"That information is classified," I said.

We exchanged a look, woman to woman, and she understood me completely.

"I am so sorry," she said.

"Don't apologize."

"He was a good man," she said. "When Josephine Pressman died here at the castle, I was so scared. I was like a little girl. So frightened. But he made me feel... he made all of us feel like... like..."

"Like someone was watching over you," I said.

She filled the mop bucket with clean water, and joined me in the corner.

"It has not been the same," she said. "It is not the same. The world, it feels like... like..."

"Like we've come to the end of something, the end of an era, and everything's a big question mark."

"The devil, he is walking the earth," she said with a shudder. "That is the end, no?"

"Don't tell me you're on the Endtimes bandwagon. You people really bum me out."

She didn't respond.

We mopped together.

We cleaned the whole room, and then disinfected the whole room.

The next shift would never guess what had happened in there, or how the soup ladles had gotten so dented.

Frances asked, "Mademoiselle, what was that *thing*?"

"It was the queen of a colony of bone-crawlers from another world."

"Not that. I am speaking of two years ago. At Halloween. That thing that was so big, and hideous."

"Oh, you mean the Pain-Body Cacodemon. It was summoned by accident, because a person was experiencing a lot of emotional pain. It wasn't her fault."

"That thing, it came from one person? Only one?"

"As far as we know."

"What if...?"

"Are you okay, Frances?"

"Never mind," she said. "It is just a stupid obsession of mine. I have the obsession up here." She tapped her temple.

"Go ahead. Say what's on your mind."

"What if a... many people were all experiencing the emotional pain? Everyone, together? What is... what would that be?"

I didn't have a specific answer, so I explained my perspective to her the way I might talk to my daughter.

"Everything's going to be fine," I said. "Scary things are always happening. It's a side effect of time passing.

Read any of the ancient texts from thousands of years ago. Those people always thought the apocalypse was going to happen any day now. It's actually pretty funny."

This seemed to cheer up Frances.

She said, "At least I do not worry about it when I am not here, not on the clock."

"You don't?"

"It is an enchantment," she said. "When we are on the castle grounds, we have different memories from when we go home."

"Exactly how powerful is this enchantment?" I patted my head protectively.

"It will not be the same for you," she said. "Not unless you have a timecard, a little paper card to punch in and out."

Another timecard machine at work. How perfectly mundane yet wonderful.

Kathy returned, on her own.

I asked, "What's wrong now? Give me a sec to grab my purse."

"The castle's clear," she said. "Glen's in the gym, and my dad's going to catch a ride home with Frank."

"You're dad's going to fly home on a pink flamingo, like some sort of Florida-based superhero?"

"Frank drove here in his car," she said. "I'll take you and the kid." She went over to check on the kid, fixing his hair as she got a better look at his face. "His name is Byzantium, isn't it?"

"Bushy for short."

"Not Bizzy?"

"Long story," I said.

"You can tell me on the ride."

We said goodbye to Frances, and then to Glen, who we found riding a stationary bike really fast, and we got into Kathy's car.

I'd never been so happy to see the inside of Kathy's Honda, though I would have been happier if she'd cleaned it out.

We rearranged her crafting supplies and made a bit of space in the back for Bushy, who was still asleep.

As Kathy drove us back to town, I caught her up on everything that had happened since we'd been split up by the shifting tunnel.

She was quiet. She was so intrigued by my exciting tale of adventure.

She brought the car to a stop near a familiar yet not-quite-right intersection.

She turned off the engine, even though we were in the middle of the street, and stepped out.

I checked on Bushy, then stepped out as well.

The night air was cold and damp, the opposite of the inside of the car.

"What are we looking at?" I asked, rubbing my arms. They were bare because Bushy was still using my cardigan as a pillow.

"I solved our budget problem," she said.

"Oh?"

She stared off into the murky darkness.

I followed her gaze, also off into the murky darkness, through what appeared to be a playground with no play equipment, just sandboxes.

Where were we? How was this barren-looking municipal park not more familiar? I knew the surrounding streets quite well.

And then I realized where we were.

Kathy had stopped her car down the street from the parking lot for the library.

It was now just a parking lot, and not *for* anything in particular.

The library was gone.

Not just the roof, or the little shed where the maintenance worker kept the lawnmower. Those were gone, too, but more importantly, the entire Wisteria Public Library was gone.

CHAPTER 37

FIVE HOURS LATER

Kathy's little brown Honda Civic was still on the street where she'd stopped, but it didn't matter. The WPD had blocked all the roads in a two-block radius to secure the site.

The library truly was gone. It hadn't been a glamour spell, or a trick of the lighting, or an exaggeration by me to create another cliffhanger.

My workplace, the WPL, with its unappreciated Brutalist style concrete walls, was gone.

Also gone were all the shelves of books and periodicals, plus the warring houseplants, Harry's haunted chair, our supplies of Motsenbocker's Lift Off, the bean bags from Grumpy Corner, the loud timecard machine, the rolling ladders, our winter-use space heaters, and even our brand-new display of Petey's Picks—heartwarming stories featuring squirrels.

Poor Petey.

Nobody had seen him since the library's disappearance.

He would be remembered forever in our hearts. Maybe not fondly by the many people who'd had their muffins stolen by him on outdoor patios.

Time didn't stop for tiny creatures like squirrels or budgies.

The world moved on.

The head librarian and I stood under a large tent in the parking lot, watching as various engineers and specialists inspected the site.

We had been there the last five hours.

It was raining, again, much like the drizzly day earlier that month, when I'd stood under an umbrella with Paisley Puddikin. We had watched the same crew dismantle and destroy our lovely garden. There wasn't as much for them to do this time around.

People kept asking me how I felt, and all I could say was, "Tired."

Kathy, however, couldn't even summarize her feelings into words, much less a single one. She had gone nonverbal, only hooting like an owl as needed.

But, that was to be expected.

Kathy was tough, and a sprite, but she hadn't been through the same struggles I had lived through in the last two years. She hadn't lost one house to an explosion, then another one to a tornado, and been magically evicted from the third for an innocent bathtub incident.

She wasn't even part of a community group, such as my gardening group, which had lost its purpose for existing.

She hadn't watched helplessly as a tornado took away...

Enough about me. Feeling sorry for myself had gotten real old.

I put my arm around Kathy. "Good work solving the budget issue, boss."

She didn't laugh, which was a real shame. I'd been saving up my callback to her announcement for five hours. Too soon was too soon.

Frank Wonder arrived at the site, dressed in a long trench coat and a fedora, looking like the investigator in charge. As he made his way to us, he had to shoo away several of the town's employees, telling them he wasn't in charge, despite appearances.

Frank joined us under the tent, removed his hat to shake off the raindrops, and said to Kathy, "Good work solving the budget issue, boss."

Her face cracked, and then Kathy cracked.

She laughed so hard at Frank's version of the joke that two medics ran over to see if we required assistance.

I was so jealous I felt myself turning ultragreen.

I told the medics, "She'll be okay after she gets some rest," and shooed them away.

Frank yawned, muttered about needing coffee, then wandered over to the deluxe catering vehicle.

Catering vehicle?

Yes, we had craft services. It was all part of the cover story that a big Hollywood studio was shooting a film on location. They had accidentally caused a "structural accident" with the library's foundation. However, the building would be restored, and there was nothing for the citizens of Wisteria to worry about. *Nothing to see here, folks.*

Frank returned to us with mugs of coffee. Real ceramic mugs. The caterers were very high end.

Frank said, "If we put parking underneath, we can use this parking lot as a new annex."

"That's a great idea," I said. "But is it an annex if you build it at the same time?"

"Hang on, I'll just grab an architecture book from..."

He looked down as he trailed off, stuffing his free hand in his trench coat pocket. He hadn't been making a joke.

This situation would take some time to get used to.

I looked up the word *annex* on my phone. I was pretty sure I had the meaning correct, but I was disoriented from lack of sleep, and my magic still hadn't recovered.

I saw some cute photos of boots on the screen, and forgot what I'd been looking up.

"Annex," Frank said.

"Right."

"Never mind," he said.

"No. No. I've got this." I scrolled across a vintage dress that would go perfectly with boots.

Frank leaned over my shoulder. "Get that," he said.

I showed Kathy the photo of the dress, paired with the boots.

Kathy said "Whooo." It was all she could manage.

Frank and I chatted away for an hour about shopping.

We did eventually look up annex. It meant what I'd thought—an addition, or a previously separate space that became joined through a connecting structure.

"That enchanted board game could have had an A name," Frank said. "Annexes & Alligators."

"Start working on a prototype," I said. "But make sure it's set underneath a fictional city, not Wisteria."

"Right."

We moved on to chatting about our new dream library. It would have a modern HVAC system, and those fancy shelves that run on tracks so they can collapse against each other to optimize space while providing new opportunities for the local ghosts to freak people out.

The sun came up.

We refilled our coffees, and got bagels from the catering van. They were piping hot, from a genuine wood-fired oven.

Our day felt so much like a regular day at work that we barely noticed how odd it was when Kathy said, "I suppose one of us should get to the circulation counter. It's time to open for the day."

She handed Frank her empty mug, and then walked out into the rain, to the sandy spot where the central counter had once stood.

We would have run out after her, but her husband got to her first. He had flown back to town as soon as he'd gotten the news. He put his arms around his wife's shoulders, and escorted her away.

Frank and I waved at Mr. Carmichael, but he wasn't interested in us.

"She'll be okay," Frank said. "Did you get much sleep?"

"Zero. Both of us were here all night."

"And?" He indicated the site, which was bustling with people, measuring and digging small holes with shovels, seemingly at random.

"And what?" We'd already filled him in on the details.

"You must have a theory."

"Well, Ribbons has been acting up. He showed up in the garden one night, accusing me of summoning him. He even said something about warrens."

Frank's small eyes opened wide. "Really?"

"My working theory is that everything, including the skeleton, happened because of that board game. The kids have been playing it off and on all month, but it didn't cause as much trouble when it was just them. I'm guessing the library got shuffled away when Kathy's father shuffled the tiles to get us out."

Frank stroked his off-center, clean-shaven chin. "Are you saying the library got Jumanji-ed?"

"Not officially. Sony Pictures would sue us for trademark infringement."

"But still."

"Yeah."

"Are we sure?"

I turned to look him in the eyes. "Are we ever sure?"

Frank's expression softened. "It's going to be okay," he said. "There's a balance in the universe, remember? I'm sure something good will happen any minute."

Just then, an older, loud, buck-toothed British woman came running up to us.

"Oh dear, oh dear, oh dear," she was saying. "Oh dear, oh dear, oh dear."

"Nobody got hurt," I said to her.

She held both hands to her chest. She was soaking wet. "Are you sure?"

"The library was closed, and all the staff and volunteers are accounted for."

"What happened?"

Frank and I exchanged a look, and then he told her the cover story about the movie so I didn't have to lie to my friend.

After he was done, she gave me a skeptical eyebrow raise.

"I know that's just a cover story," she said.

We did not confirm nor deny.

"It must have been from the tunnels," she said in a hoarse whisper.

Frank and I leaned in. She knew about the tunnels? The warrens? The annexes?

She said in a confessional tone, "Someone has been using a tunnel boring machine underneath this city. They've been at it for years. It's like Swiss cheese down there." She burst into tears, which mixed with the rain already pouring down her cheeks from her hair.

Frank shrugged one shoulder. A tunnel boring machine was a decent cover story.

"Looking for that darned treasure," she sobbed. "The treasure that probably doesn't even exist! I bet if you found the box, and opened it, inside it would just have a note saying *Peace on Earth*."

Frank and I exchanged another knowing look.

This was why the DWM and WPD created cover stories. If you didn't give people a plausible explanation for strange occurrences, they became hysterical and invented their own stories.

Mrs. Puddikin abruptly stopped crying.

"I know," she said.

We braced ourselves for more crazy ramblings.

"You can set up a temporary library in my shop. I have way too much space, and it's too much inventory to keep track of. I'll run a clearance sale starting today. I'll invite Zinnia, and all my regulars, and we'll make space for the library."

I grabbed some cloth napkins from the catering van—I told you it was fancy—and dabbed the rainwater from Mrs. Puddikin's face.

Frank got a muffin from the caterers, and handed it to the woman.

"That's very generous of you," I said. "But you don't need to—"

"We'll take it," Frank said. "That's a wonderful idea, Mrs. Puddikin. I love it. Zara, isn't it a wonderful idea?"

I wasn't so sure.

Frank said, "We can ask for materials from the other libraries in our network. Oh, and we can call in all the overdue titles with an amnesty on fines. We can run the circulation program through any old computer. Mrs. Puddikin, do you have a working barcode scanner?"

"Of course," she said.

"Perfect," Frank said, beaming at me. "Zara Riddle, are you in, or do I have to kiss you?"

"Eww," I said. "Of course I'm in."

"Happy now?"

"Sure," I said.

Frank tilted his head. "Then what's wrong with your face?"

"Something's not quite right." I was still heartbroken about something, but I couldn't remember what.

Just then, a squirrel dropped from the interior supports of the tent. He landed on my arm, grabbed the fresh muffin from Mrs. Puddikin's plate, and scampered off with it.

I let out a sigh of relief.

Petey the squirrel was okay. He hadn't been inside the library when it got shuffled away by Warrens & Wyverns.

Now I could be happy.

The rain stopped, the clouds parted, and the sky brightened.

CHAPTER 38

Friday, October 26th

Chintz Public Library & Boutique

Soft Opening Day

I was all alone in the new space we'd created for the library, in half of what had previously been all Chintz Boutique.

My coworkers had all run out for last-minute supplies. The truth was, they were too nervous to be there, and they'd been driving me nuts, so I'd sent them out for snacks. It was, after all, Fresh Pastry Friday.

I unlocked the door.

Five minutes passed, and I was still alone.

My coworkers weren't the only ones who were nervous.

What would people think? Would they walk in and laugh at us? Would we have to shush laughter all day?

And who did we think we were, putting a library inside half a clothing and housewares store?

Another minute passed, and then four more.

Ten whole minutes and nobody had come in yet? That would have been unusual at the old location, where people often waited at the door, tsk-tsking about the time.

Was my spell even working? I checked the drawer. My miniature dolls were in alignment, so any minute now...

The front door opened, and a person peered in nervously.

"Welcome to the Chintz Public Library & Boutique," I said to the would-be patron, sounding like a barker at an old-timey carnival. "Come on in. Don't mind the chaos. We're still getting things settled, but you're welcome to come in, and browse, or check out materials from our growing collection."

The would-be patron, a woman, slipped in hesitantly, looked around, and then relaxed and gave me a huge smile.

Any nervousness I'd had about how the mini library would look to a non-librarian evaporated immediately.

Our first patron was the elegant and ageless Mia Gianna, the owner of Mia's Kit and Kaboodle, the consignment and second-hand shop. Her store was just down the street. I was a regular shopper there, though I hadn't been in lately. We three librarians had all been too busy to do any extracurriculars. We had thrown ourselves into pulling together a temporary library location in less than three days.

"The rumors are true," Mia said with a teasing smile. "Zara, you've been cheating on me with Mrs. Puddikin."

It was true. Being around Mrs. Puddikin's selection of handsewn dresses had proved more tempting than expected. I was wearing one of her signature garments that day. A nice thing about working at a library is that everything's free, so you don't spend your paychecks before you get them. Sharing space, as we did now, with a boutique full of eclectic wardrobe and household temptations, was not the same.

"I'm afraid it's much more serious than that." I held out my hands, one pointing at the Boutique part of our name at one side, and one hand pointing at the Public Library side. "We've moved in together."

Mia circled the display tables of books, moving counter-clockwise, exactly as I'd anticipated when setting up the tables.

"I feel so betrayed," she joked.

"I'll still be able to see you at Kit and Kaboodle. Mrs. Puddikin and I are not exclusive."

"It won't be the same." She heaved a sigh that sounded only half joking. Her store was much larger than Mrs. Puddikin's, and we hadn't asked her for space, or any of the other local stores.

"It's only temporary," I said apologetically.

Mia said, "Well, I suppose we'll always have our memories of picking out Zoey's prom dress. How is she?"

"Thriving, apparently. Getting along perfectly well without her mother."

"They always say that, and it's never true." She perused our new selection of Petey's Picks. "I get books sometimes, in estate sales. Can I bring them over here?"

"Absolutely."

"Only the books that are in excellent, like-new condition, of course."

"We are... not that fussy."

"Oh. Okay." She backed up toward the door again. "I really should get back to my shop." She raised her hand and wiggled her fingers. "I just acquired some very special belongings that need to be rehomed."

"How's *that* going?"

Mia Gianna was a Belongings Mage, and had recently become aware of the full extent of her powers.

It had thrown her for a loop at first. She'd left her fantastic shop in the hands of an assistant and disappeared from town for a six-month sabbatical, traveling the world, only to return and announce that she belonged there, and there was no point in *denying a belonging*.

"I have accepted my fate," she said cryptically, just as she had before.

"Haven't we all," I said. "Sure beats complaining about it."

She put her hand on the door. "I really should go. Why is it that the conversation only gets started for real when a person is at the door?"

"It's a type of magic," I said.

"That figures. Anyway, I just wanted to drop in and give you my blessings."

"Bless away." I bowed my head, and held my hands forward.

She made a gesture, and I felt her blessings.

I thanked her.

She left, and I greeted the two patrons who slipped in while she exited.

When those two left with their checked-out materials, four other patrons came in.

After the four, came eight.

And so it went, with the traffic doubling, until our new library was packed.

The windows fogged up on the inside from all the warm, breathing bodies inside the small space.

We were in danger of having too grand of an opening, and today was only supposed to be a soft opening, to work out the bugs.

I opened a drawer on our new circulation counter, and adjusted the tiny dolls I'd used to cast a welcoming spell. We wanted traffic, but not all of it at once.

Kathy came up to relieve me at the end of my shift, and I was surprised at how much time had flown by.

"It's all going so well," I said. The welcoming spell had ended, but people kept pouring into the tiny shop.

The head librarian frowned like I'd just cleaned all her favorite acorn treats out of the mini-fridge.

"I know," Kathy said, her brow furrowed. "It's terrible."

"It is?"

"My father was right," Kathy reluctantly admitted. "We can serve the community just as well, with a much smaller footprint."

I shook my head. "We must never tell him."

"Never," she agreed.

"But it is going very well."

"Shush," she said.

"I promised I wouldn't tell."

Her eyes flashed. "Shush," she said again, with urgency.

I turned around to find her father, Kent Alderman, standing behind me.

"Busy place," he said.

"It's too small," Kathy said. "Tooo, tooo, tooo small."

"Hello, Mr. Alderman," I said. "What brings you here? Are you interested in our selection of board games? They've all been sprayed with anti-hex plus deodorizer."

There was a smirk under his thick mustache. "Not today. Tell me what you know about the local fishing spots."

"We have a guidebook," I said. "More of a brochure, really."

I pushed my way through the crowd to get to our local guidebooks, and found the item I'd had in mind.

I handed Kathy's father a folded single sheet of paper.

He accepted it cautiously. "This is your best guidebook?"

"I'm afraid so. Technically, it's just a hand-drawn map on the back of a paper placemat, but it does fit the basic requirements for a periodical because Arden Greyson draws up a new one every month."

"That will suit our needs."

We pushed through the crowd again, back to the circulation counter.

He pulled a vintage paper library card from his pocket. It was salmon-pink, and had a little metal piece, stamped copper. I hadn't seen a card like that in decades.

I ran the card through our machine, and checked out the paper placemat, coded in our system as *Greyson's Guide to Sea-Monster-Free Fishing Holes*.

Mr. Alderman seemingly picked up the periodical with small, pudgy hands.

They weren't his hands, but those of our young friend, Bushy.

"Hey there, kiddo," I said, resisting the urge to fix his cowlick. "I'm sorry I didn't notice you in this big crowd."

"I'm in camouflage," Bushy said proudly. "That's why you didn't see me."

His shirt and pants weren't like any camouflage I'd seen before. The multicolored print could be wallpaper for a gentleman's study—all spines of leather-bound books.

"Very clever," I said. "Careful we don't try to put you on a shelf, or check you out. Is your weekend fully booked? Do you comma here often?"

Kathy put her hand on my shoulder. "Zara, you're punning."

"Am I?"

"You have to go home, and get some rest so you can work your next shift."

Kent said to his daughter, "Do you mind if I borrow your best employee?"

Frank suddenly jumped into our conversation to say, "I'm busy, but you can have Zara."

There were corny laughs all around.

I grabbed my jacket and purse, and I followed Mr. Alderman and Bushy out to the street.

Compared to the interior of the shop, the sidewalk felt practically abandoned.

The air was cold and dry, the opposite of the library. We would need an extra dehumidifier.

A tumbleweed rolled by.

Just a single tumbleweed.

It must have evolved from my former bridesmaid dress, taking its final form. That explained why the dress hadn't been on the clothesline where I'd left it.

The sprite and the little boy stood by patiently, and we all watched the tumbleweed tumble down the street and out of sight.

"What's the plan?" I asked them. "Is it time already for a reunion of our adventuring party? Please tell me you haven't found a sequel to that board game."

"Nothing like that," Mr. Alderman said. "We're going fishing. Above ground."

"That sounds nice," I said. It did explain why they'd come to check out a fishing guide.

"All *three* of us are going fishing," he said.

I looked around for the third person he might be referencing.

"You're coming with us," he said.

Bushy grabbed my fingers and pleaded, "Please? Goatman said I could pick any friend, and I picked you."

I might have been able to say no to one of them, but not to both.

We went fishing.

CHAPTER 39

Our fishing spot of choice was up on the mountain, above the zoo.

We weren't far from zookeeper Nick's cabin, which I learned that Kent Alderman had helped build.

Kent would have loved to have lived up there himself, away from the hustle and bustle of town. He had settled on the other plot of land, closer to other people, and the amenities of town, for his young daughter's sake.

It was a warm day for the time of year, but it was still October, and it wasn't long until we were above the snow line.

I would have been freezing or in need of a warming spell if I'd worn only the dress I'd worn to work, but Kent had brought extra clothes for me, from Kathy's childhood bedroom.

Thanks to young Kathy, I wore a pink ski suit that had been fashionable twenty-five years ago, and was also fashionable now. I took some photos to send my daughter, who was too busy to send back much of a response.

The hike up the mountain was in the sweet spot for hiking amateurs such as myself. It was a winding mix of flat and bumpy terrain with just enough climbing to keep it interesting. Some of the difficult spots had been upgraded by volunteers, who'd fashioned stairs and bridges out of the local fallen trees.

The local snowberries had already been harvested. It was customary for the coven to collect the plants' crimson-red, musical fruit after the first snowfall, which had happened early that year on Mount Woolbird.

When we passed through woolbird territory, we were careful to keep our distance, and to not let them sneak up on us from behind.

We were visited by a snowball vole, who jumped out of a snowy patch to cross our path in a white zig-zag pattern.

She may or may not have been the same snowball vole I'd been introduced to by a coven member. Fatima Nix wasn't with us that day, and I didn't speak to animals, so we had no idea what the vole was saying, but she did seem to recognize me.

I put my hand down to the ground, and she hopped right on my palm.

I held her out to Bushy. She lifted her chin while slow-blinking her red eyes at both of us.

"She likes chin scratches," I said.

Bushy scratched her chin. "They like it because it releases their scent glands," he said.

Kent and I exchanged a look. Our little human friend was knowledgeable.

I still hadn't figured out why Kent was taking him fishing, but I guessed we would discuss it over our fishing lines.

The vole rolled onto her back on my palm, exposing her white, silky belly.

Our little human friend wasn't *that* knowledgeable about creatures. He didn't know that one key lesson: the tummy was a trap.

He took the bait, and touched the snowball vole's tummy.

The trap slammed shut on his hand.

The vole dug into soft, human flesh—his and mine, but mostly his—with all of her sharp claws, and then delivered an epic warning nip with her razor-sharp teeth.

She jumped from my hand, shot me a red-eyed glance, and scampered off. She disappeared in the snow-dotted landscape instantly, her fur a perfect camouflage.

Bushy stared at his bleeding finger, in shock.

"You're okay," Kent said. "Use your other hand to pinch it and stop the bleeding."

Bushy was too shocked to move. He continued to stare at the blood as it pooled, his eyes growing wider.

Kent took the kid's other hand, and showed him how to stop the bleeding.

I could have stepped in, but this seemed like a valuable lesson. The kid was curious, and would find himself in trouble many more times in his life, and he wouldn't always have a witch around to mend his wounds.

After a quick bandaging, using supplies from the forest around us—bark and sap—we were on our way again.

We found the fishing hole, and cast our lines in the frigid waters.

I used the reflective water to take a few more photos of myself in my fashionable vintage pink ski suit.

Kent gave us a full lesson about fishing, showing us all the parts of the rod, particularly the hook, the line, and the sinker.

Bushy said, "Is that where that saying comes from? Hook, line, and sinker?"

"Yes, it is the origin of that metaphor," Kent said.

"It's also an idiom," I said. "An idiom is a phrase that has a meaning, as a whole, that isn't the same as a non-English speaker would guess based on the individual words."

"You two sure know everything," Bushy said, but in the little-kid equivalent of a "hoo-boy, I've got some real know-it-alls tryin' to teach me stuff over here."

We didn't catch any fish.

I could have caught plenty, but not without spells, and spellwork would have defeated the whole purpose of fishing.

As we packed up our gear, Kent said, "On the bright side, we can delay our fish-gutting and cleaning lesson for another day."

Bushy looked disappointed and relieved at the same time. I understood perfectly. I felt the same way.

We left the fishing hole.

As we walked, Kent said, "I must make a confession. I have been here a number of times. I know this area quite well."

I'd figured as much, since he'd spent so much time up there building the zookeeper's cabin, plus he hadn't needed to consult Arden Greyson's hand-drawn map once.

I said, "You didn't need a local guidebook from the library. It was just an excuse to drop in."

He smoothed his thick mustache. "My daughter would not have appreciated me checking in on her for no good reason."

"Any excuse to visit your local library is fine by me," I said. "We don't even ask for a reason, if you can believe that."

Bushy was walking between us, taking one and a half strides to each of ours, sometimes hopping to catch up.

I could no longer resist the urge to fix his cowlick.

It was, unfortunately for the kid, extremely resistant to fixing.

Bushy grew annoyed by my attempts to fix his hair, and ran ahead of us.

"Good idea, son," Kent said. "You run ahead and scout the way."

Bushy dropped his head, and ran even more quickly down the path.

"Careful," I called after him. "Don't fall down and—"

"And what?" Kent gave me an amused look. "And skin his knee? He's a boy, Zara."

"I know, but he's got a wound on his finger that's barely scabbed over, and there are *things* in the forest."

"There are things everywhere."

Bushy stayed well ahead of us, allowing himself to be seen from time to time, just long enough to give us a wave and an all-clear signal.

Kent said, "The boy's grandfather passed away at the end of summer."

"Oh, no. I'm so sorry. Did you know him?"

"The boy has been staying with the family of those other two boys. The Robb family. But they can't handle all three of them."

"What about his parents?" I asked, even though I'd already figured out from context that the boy didn't have parents.

Kent said nothing.

"Oh, no," I said. "That poor kid."

"He's going to be shipped off, to some distant uncle."

I read between the lines.

"And what do you want from me? Do you want me to write a letter on your behalf, recommending you as a foster parent? I can do that. And Kathy would, too, I'm sure. We'll leave out all the stuff about the chocolate peanut butter cups."

"He needs to be adopted," Kent said.

"Then I'll write you a letter for that."

"I'm afraid the agency won't let a single man my age take in the boy, not when there's a blood relative who's willing to take him."

"There's nothing quite like family," I said. "What about the uncle? Is he...?" I couldn't even finish the question. My jaw ached, and my eyes were sore. Kent Alderman didn't strike me as the type to insert himself in another family's business without good reason.

I remembered how our fishing rods had made those Zzzzzzz sounds as we'd cast the lines into the water.

"Zara, I know it's a lot to ask."

"You're right. It is a lot."

"But I wouldn't ask if I didn't think you were up to the challenge."

"The challenge," I said, taking two more steps. "The challenge?" Three more steps. "The challenge."

Just then, Bushy appeared from behind a boulder.

No, he *was* the boulder. He had turned his clothes inside out, to match the terrain.

He waved at us, grinning, and then took off running again.

"You won't have to do it on your own," Kent said.

I didn't like the sound of his voice. I didn't like how paternal he was being, as though he'd figured it all out already, and was simply breaking the news to me. As though everything had already been decided, and laid out for me.

"This isn't fair," I said, quickening my pace to run ahead, to not be beside him.

Kent caught up immediately, and grabbed my hand.

His palm was hot, and my fingers were as cold as ice.

I yanked my hand away.

It's not fair," I said again.

"Talk to me."

"You had your parents. They lived with you when you raised Kathy. You weren't on your own. You don't even know what it means to be on your own."

"I agree. I do not understand your life like you do. Only an individual can understand the depth and breadth of their own life, their responsibilities. We cannot ever, as it were, walk in each other's shoes."

He reached for me again, for my elbow.

I pulled away, and I ran ahead.

I caught up with Bushy, and walked down the mountain with him.

When he stumbled on some rocks, I reached out, and caught his small, pudgy hand in mine.

He didn't pull his hand away.

He held on tightly, and didn't let go.

And I admitted to myself then what I'd already known but hadn't yet been ready to say, even in the privacy of my own mind.

I'd fallen for the trap.

Hook, line, and sinker.

CHAPTER 40

Saturday, October 27th

My lawyer was able to squeeze me in for an appointment first thing Saturday morning.

Blythe Delores Boomer insisted that everyone call her Boomer. She was stockier than Margaret Mills, with a cherubic face and short, curly blonde hair. She dressed like a male detective from a film noir movie, and kept her office stocked with cigars.

She offered me a cigar when I sat across her desk in a visitor's chair that morning.

"No thanks," I said.

"These ones are chocolate," she said with her endearing, Southern hospitality. "I order them in special, for my non-smoking clientele."

I took one. It was more of a biscotti than a true chocolate.

Boomer's assistant whisked into the room with hot cups of piping-hot tea, then left us to our private conversation.

Boomer said, "First of all, I am so deeply sorry for the loss of our dear little feathered friend."

"Thank you. Marzipants will be missed."

"And you're sure he's dead? Once or twice when we were on the road on our way here, I thought I was going to have to pull over and give him mouth to beak. The ol' stinker was just playing dead."

"It wasn't a trick," I said. "He's gone."

Boomer bobbed her head and her short, blonde curls. "What about his G-H-O-S-T?"

"No ghost," I said. "And I haven't seen Minerva Pinkman around, either, so they've gone off together, to wherever it is they go."

"And where is that?" Boomer leaned forward over her desk, maintaining eye contact as she ate one of the cigar-shaped chocolate-dipped cookies.

I held my hands out, palms up.

"That's above my pay grade."

Boomer let out a big laugh, then leaned back and put her brown loafers on the corner of her desk.

She said, "We're coming up on the big day. Halloween. If you don't have a date yet for the Monster Mash, some of us single gals could go as a group. Be each other's plus-one's."

"I'm not sure I'll even go."

"Aww, but you have to go. You missed out last year. It was really good. All the local trouble-makers were over at the gorgon wedding."

"I know." I pointed to myself. "Local trouble-maker."

"No offense was intended."

"None was taken."

She gave me a wry look. "Right."

She swung her brown loafers off the desk and sat upright, more serious.

"Now, what can I do for my favorite client today?"

"Two things," I said, and I explained my situation to her for the second time.

Her office had already received a lengthy email the night before, but my guess was the assistant had only passed along the briefest summary.

When I finished, Boomer said, "As for the adoption, don't worry about a thing. I'm on it."

She pressed a button on her desk.

For an instant, I imagined that the button was a magical adoption button, and that simply by pushing it, everything would be taken care of, magically.

But the buzzer was for communicating with the lawyer's assistant, who came running in with a stack of papers. It was a lot of paper, as though they'd been up all night preparing for my meeting.

No. Not *as though*.

They had been up all night.

I realized this when I caught Boomer stifling a yawn by hiding behind her coffee.

She really was the best lawyer in town, perhaps in the whole wide world.

"Normally this sort of thing takes a year," Boomer said, sorting through the papers. "Six months, if you have a good team."

"Six months? But—"

"I told you not to worry, so don't worry!" She composed herself. "I apologize for snapping at you."

"No. I apologize for worrying when you told me not to."

Boomer nodded curtly. "Good."

For the next hour, she walked me through all the adoption paperwork.

The process varied across the country, but Wisteria had its own procedures that could be simple enough, if everyone agreed.

Boomer's eyes twinkled.

"There is one other thing," Boomer said. "I hear there's a form at the Permits Department that allows you to bypass some of these steps. A secret form. It would speed up this process considerably."

"I'll speak to my contacts at the department. How much would it speed things up?"

"A lot," Boomer said.

"I'll go see Liza Gilbert as soon as I leave here," I said. "Or, should I say, Liza Banks. Married name."

"It was a nice wedding. Her parents invited me. I loved the venue. The photographer was a bit much."

"I know, right?"

"The French," she said.

"But not all of them. You know who's sweet? Frances, the lady who works at Castle Wyvern."

"Oh, she's not French at all. She got hit on the head two Halloweens ago, and she developed that thing."

"What?"

Boomer stifled a yawn. "The thing where people develop a foreign accent after an injury. You didn't know?"

"I didn't think that was real. Is that real?"

Boomer shrugged. "It's above my pay grade."

She shuffled the papers around.

"That's about it for the adoption paperwork." She pressed the button again. Still not the Instant Adoption Button. The assistant returned, and traded the big stack of papers for a smaller one.

"Now, the other fun stuff." Boomer waggled her eyebrows. "Are you sure about this? It's a big commitment."

"Are you joking? I just signed up to adopt a kid."

Boomer grinned. "I am joking!"

"Oh, good."

"But this is a big commitment, too," she said.

I agreed.

Then I picked up the pen, and started signing the second set of papers.

CHAPTER 41

Monday, October 29th

I wasn't on the schedule to work at the library on Monday, but I wanted to share my good news with my coworkers.

The sun was up, but there were still two hours until we opened.

The new miniature version of our library had limited hours due to limited materials. We'd chosen to keep the same retail hours that were typical for the street. Not everyone was thrilled, but that's life for you. You can't make everyone happy, though librarians certainly do try their best.

I knocked three times on the back door before letting myself in. It took a while, since I had so many keys on my keyring.

As soon as I walked in, I sensed that something was wrong. The air crackled with tension.

Kathy Carmichael, who should have been there, wasn't.

Mrs. Puddikin was folding and refolding clothes that didn't need either.

I came up behind her, and startled her by walking too quietly.

She was clearly on edge, her hands shaking with adrenaline.

"What's going on?" I asked in a neutral tone.

"Oh dear, oh dear, oh dear," she said. "I've gone and ruined everything, love."

Frank, who, unlike me, was actually on the schedule that morning, came over and joined our conversation.

"Paisley, it wasn't you who ruined everything," he said to the owner of the boutique. Bitterly, he said to both of us, "It was Kathy." He shot me an exasperated look. "That sprite has one big mouth."

Mrs. Puddikin didn't react to the mention of Kathy being a sprite, except to refold a pile of chunky wool sweaters that didn't need folding.

I took one of the nicest sweaters from her hands. "Put this one on hold for my next paycheck. And will someone please tell me what happened?"

"It's all my fault," the buck-toothed British woman said. "I made her tell me. Don't blame Kathy. It was all me, the busybody. They say curiosity killed the cat, and I got too curious."

Frank sighed, and said in a softer tone, "It was bound to happen sooner or later. There's no need for anyone to be upset. We're all working in close quarters. Paisley, you're an observant woman. If Kathy hadn't blabbed our secrets at your little sleepover party, you'd have figured it out by Christmas on your own."

Mrs. Puddikin took my future sweater from my hands, and said in a business-minded tone, "Staff discount applies, of course. Would you like to wear it out today?"

"I must insist that you make me wait for payday," I said. "We need some semblance of order and normality around here. It's bad enough you know I'm a witch."

Mrs. Puddikin gasped, and dropped the sweater.

Frank shook his head. "Zara Riddle, you're one silly goose. Kathy didn't tell her *everything*."

I shrugged. "It's like you said. She would have figured it out by Christmas anyway." I pointed at Frank while I asked the woman, "Do you know what he is?"

"Of course." She stooped down, picking up the sweater. "You can't believe what the local authorities tell you. There's no way that a small local zoo has that many exotic animals escaping on a regular basis."

By the time she looked up again, Frank had shifted into his pink flamingo form.

Mrs. Puddikin shrieked, and dropped the sweater once more.

It was one thing to know something, it was quite another to see it with your own eyes.

He shifted back, and said, "You know what? I'm feeling much better. Paisley, I'm glad Kathy told you everything."

"Me, too," I said. "Now we can get up to all sorts of shenanigans behind the scenes."

Frank said, "Speaking of shenanigans, why *are* you here, Zara Riddle?"

"To share my good news. I'm buying the house."

Mrs. Puddikin said, "What house?"

I savored their curiosity and interest for a moment, like I was performing a one-woman show, then made my exciting announcement.

"Friends, you are looking at the new owner of the Mystery Mansion. I'm the first person to own it who doesn't have the last name of Myster."

"But it's much too big for you," Mrs. Puddikin said. "Take it from me, you don't need all those rooms to clean." She quickly added, "Oh, don't listen to me. I'm just a kooky old lady, set in her ways. This is wonderful news. I'm sure you'll be very happy."

Frank said, "This is not what I had in mind when I pranked you into getting that apartment." He rubbed his crooked chin a moment, then proclaimed, "It's so much better."

Mrs. Puddikin clasped her hands together. "Oh! You'll be my neighbor forever, and ever, and ever!"

I held out my arms, and we shared some group effervescence, jumping up and down.

I filled them in on the rest of the details.

The second set of papers I'd signed at Boomer's office were a generous offer to purchase the Mystery Mansion.

The Myster family had accepted the offer with no questions asked. They'd been waiting to sell the place, trying to time the market, but my offer was as good as anything they could hope for. Plus I'd promised to restore the home to its former glory rather than tear it down and build new.

I hadn't yet invested the funds from the insurance settlement for the Red Witch House, so I'd used that to put a big down payment on my new home. My father helped with the mortgage, as he had on my previous place. I'd hated to ask him, but he'd loved being asked, so it sort of worked out.

We weren't through escrow yet—even with my witchcraft, and the best lawyer in town, it would take some time—but the deal was as firm as could be.

It was more secure than my adoption of Byzantium—Bushy—which I hoped would go more smoothly now that I was a homeowner.

Until I heard back on that, at least the house would give me plenty of side projects to stay busy with. A witch with idle hands was a danger to everyone around her.

Frank and Mrs. Puddikin were over the moon, running around the boutique side like lottery winners on a shopping spree, gathering household items to give to me at my second housewarming.

"Hang on, you guys," I had to say. "Let's not make it too obvious that something's going on at the mansion. I don't want to freak out my tenants. The purchase is going to be a secret."

"Ah," Mrs. Puddikin said, struggling to hold a dozen candles and dish towels at once. "You're keeping the renters."

"I need the income more than I need the space. I hate to deceive them, but... secrets revealed are trouble unsealed. I've been hidden by a secret trust, and they'll deal with the management company, so they can keep treating me as an equal. Do you think that's the right choice?"

Frank raised an eyebrow. Since when did I canvas others for their opinions on my life choices? Since now, I guessed.

My two older, wiser friends—my mentors—assured me it was the right choice, and I could always reveal more down the road, but I couldn't do the reverse, putting the genie back in the bottle.

That was true.

Genies did not like going back into bottles.

There were three knocks at the back door, and then it opened.

Kathy entered with a hunched posture, looking guilty.

We told her the good news. She wasn't in trouble for gossiping, and now Mrs. Puddikin was one of us.

Then those three kicked me out, since it was my day off.

I had to go find mischief and shenanigans elsewhere.

I went straight to Mia's Kit and Kaboodle, and grumbled at her just like a real customer when she opened up her shop thirty seconds late.

CHAPTER 42

Wednesday, October 31st

Halloween

After an implausibly speedy escrow, I was the proud new owner of a dilapidated mansion.

It was a funny turn of events.

Many people rent a place expecting it will be temporary, then find themselves there much longer than planned.

By contrast, I had only paid a single month of rent before my circumstances changed. Well, they hadn't changed that much. I still had to pay on the first of the month, but the payments went to the bank, not the property management company.

The other tenants still didn't know the building had been sold, let alone that I was the owner. Secrets revealed were trouble unsealed, but secrets concealed were trouble avoided until some future day.

The only thing that would change at the house would be the loss of an upstairs utility closet that nobody used anyway.

The management company sent a notice to all the tenants letting them know there would be some noise and dust while the team of contractors added the utility closet space to 3B, my apartment.

The extra bedroom was necessary for my new roommate. I mean... uh... son?

My new *son*.

I hadn't gotten used to it at all.

But I had a bit of time.

He wasn't living with me yet.

He was out of town, visiting the distant relatives who'd offered to take him in if nobody else would.

Boomer had told me not to worry, so I wasn't worrying.

I was simply *thinking about* the situation a lot, and also imagining how it could go wrong. What if the other family members got attached to him? Was he really visiting because it was the most logical place for him to be at that moment, or were they trying him out? A try-before-you-buy situation?

I thought about this scenario, and others, a lot. I felt sick to my stomach when I did.

But at least I wasn't worrying.

I had my lawyer to do that for me.

Plus I had other things to keep my hands from becoming dangerously idle. Like renovations.

It was a blessing in disguise that all the local contractors were too busy to take on my small job of converting the third floor utility closet into a second bedroom.

That left me, and my limited knowledge of house renovation.

I'd owned an old house before, but I'd learned absolutely nothing. The house had used its own magic to shift walls and rooms around as needed. The Mystery Mansion—as far as I knew—possessed no such abilities.

And so, I lifted my new sledgehammer, which was heavier than it looked, and prepared to start the renovation.

I was stopped by a telepathic message.

"Do not do that, Zed." Ribbons was hidden from view, but the signal was strong. He was nearby.

"I should have known you'd show up. A fellow like you can't resist the lure of destruction. Show yourself. Let's see that ugly mug of yours, the one that looks exactly like heavily-peppered beef jerky."

"You have a face like a side of beef that is improperly cured for storage."

"You mean it looks like your butt?"

"You do look like my butt, Zed. That is where I know you from."

"Yep. It's all coming together," I said, barely paying attention to our roast battle.

I gently bumped the sledgehammer into the old lath and plaster wall.

To my surprise, it made a round divot, sending cracks all the way to the floor and ceiling. Oops. I'd only meant to tap the wall in warning.

"Do not," Ribbons said.

"Why not? Are you afraid I'll find your secret hiding place?"

"There is a pipe, Zed."

I set down the sledgehammer, and used my fingers to pry off a piece of plaster. Sure enough, behind the thin pieces of lath wood, there was a pipe in the wall, right where I'd been about to smash. The pipe had to be original, as it was highly decorated, as per the code during the time period the house was built.

"This isn't on the blueprints," I said, expressing my surprise and disappointment—whining, really. "This is drawn as a non-load-bearing, non-utilities-carrying wall. There can't be a pipe in here."

"There is a pipe, Zed."

"I can see that, you rodent-faced pencil sharpener!"

"You are welcome, soft human," Ribbons said. "You may repay your debt by procuring—"

"Maple syrup," I said. "I know the drill. Check the cupboard over the fridge. As if you didn't already know it was there."

In the hole of the wall, the gleaming black eye of a wyvern appeared.

The wyvern thrust his head through the hole, enlarging it, and then wriggled out the rest of his body.

He flapped over my head, to the kitchen.

His offspring, RJ, followed right behind him. RJ easily hopped through the hole without wriggling, and plopped onto the floor.

RJ didn't fly as his father had, but scurried along the floor like a duckling. He climbed over the toes of my boots as though I was nothing more than furniture.

I stared at the wall, and the exposed pipe.

It was definitely there, but that didn't mean it was functional. It could have been replaced by new runs and stacks, and left within the walls—orphaned—because it was easier to leave it where it was than tear it out and pay for disposal and patching. People did stuff like that over the years. I was no expert on renovating century homes, but I had heard a few things over the years, and they were coming back to me.

The wyverns slurped noisily on maple syrup in the kitchen.

It was a new brand, from Quebec, that came in cans, not bottles.

I would have to use my sledgehammer to reshape the empty cans, so my fellow residents didn't find my empty tins in the recycling bin and ask what kind of unusual can opener I had that left fang-sized holes.

The slurping in the kitchen stopped.

Ribbons flew over my shoulder, and straight into the hole again.

RJ used me like a tree, or a ladder, climbing my overalls to get to the hole, then disappeared after his father.

"That's it? You drink my syrup, and just leave?"

"It is Halloween, Zed. Change into your costume, and meet us at the castle. Everyone will be there."

"I don't have a costume," I said.

He didn't reply. He and Junior had already flown out of range.

Alone again, I had to laugh at the ridiculousness of what I'd said.

Zara Riddle, not having a costume?

My current wardrobe was diminished, but a good portion of it had been purchased during the spring cleaning sales of our local theater groups.

Oh, I had costumes.

And, since I couldn't knock down my wall as planned, I would have to keep my hands from growing idle by attending the ball.

I went to my closet and got busy.

I'd only been looking through my clothes a few minutes when the intercom buzzed.

"Intercom," I said under my breath as I ran to the terminal. "Intercom. Intercom." I pressed the button. "Hello?"

"It's me, Rob," said Agent Rob.

My least favorite—at the moment—DWM agent had dared to darken my doorway. He hadn't learned his lesson from his last visit.

I said, "You'd better stand back six feet. I have this whole place wired up to repel enemies with nefarious intentions. That means you. Stand back, or the light blue on the ceiling of the porch may be the last sky you ever see."

Another voice cut in. "It is also me, Knox."

"I'm not bluffing," I replied. "I will blast both of you into two piles of meaty feathers."

Rob said, "Really, Zara? I know you're mad at me, but *ixnay* on the *eathers-fay*. Is this even a secure line?"

Knox cut in again. "I brought you a housewarming present. Agent Rob put his name on the card, but he did not pay for it."

"A present? Why didn't you say so? Talk about burying the lead."

I pressed the button to allow them into the house.

CHAPTER 43

Agent Knox handed me a box.

Agent Rob said, "It's from both of us."

Knox said to his partner, "You said you wanted to get your own gift."

"And I would have, except my vehicle got a flat tire at the most inconvenient time."

"That's unfortunate," I said. "Were you really on your way to get me a gift?"

"Yes," Agent Rob said. "Why?" He rubbed his forehead. "I had no idea you were so obsessed with gifts. But I'm not great with girls, so what do I know?"

I didn't comment further, but I did make a mental note. Hexes often backfired. Even when they were deserved. I would try to restrain myself from using them in anger.

Knox said to me, "Open it. I want to see if you like it. I hope you like it."

I set the pretty, gift wrapped box on the coffee table, and opened it slowly.

"Nice wrapping job," I said. "The folds are so crisp."

Knox beamed with pride. "Thank you."

"I would have helped with the wrapping," Rob said. "But I was at the tire shop all day."

I opened the interior box, and pulled out the gift. It was a lamp. A new one, with a sturdy ceramic base and a delicate linen shade. No florals.

"This is really sweet," I said. "What a thoughtful gift."

"Zinnia gave me the idea," Knox said. "Zinnia says that you can never have too many lamps."

I turned the lamp over in my hands. It was very plain, unlike the enchanted lamp she had given me as a housewarming so many moons ago, back when I hadn't known about magic.

And here I was, with another lamp, courtesy of my aunt, sent through Knox.

With love.

I felt my eyes welling up.

I plugged in the lamp, and it made my place more cozy, more warm, more welcoming and full of love.

"Oh, no," Knox said. "It is not a good housewarming present." He tried to take it back.

I stopped him from unplugging it, and clutched it close to my chest. I sniffed back my emotions.

"It's perfect," I said. "I was just... it's my eyes. It's very dusty in here. You see that hole in the plaster? It's a construction site in here."

"There is a card," Knox said.

I opened the card. It was even sweeter than the lamp. Why was I getting so emotional? Was it all the big decisions I was making, all the new adventures and challenges I was taking on?

Probably just the dust from the wall.

"Thank you guys," I said. "Now, Rob, if you'll just restore my files on my phone, as a professional courtesy, I would appreciate that."

"I have something better," he said.

He ran back out to the hallway, and returned with a rolling suitcase.

He unzipped the case and opened it to reveal a skeleton.

"Oh, no," I said. "I just want the video I shot. I don't need to recreate it."

"You have to take it," Rob said. "Him. I understand you named him Mr. Bone-Jangles."

"No, thanks."

Rob said more vehemently, "You *have to* take it. Him. We've tried everything we can think of for storage. No matter what we put him in, he keeps getting out."

"It's true," Knox said. "One time, we put him in the incinerator."

"You put Mr. Bone-Jangles in the incinerator?"

They both nodded.

"He got out," Knox said.

"It was kind of a rough day for the department," Rob said. "With a flaming skeleton running around on the loose."

"I was not there," Knox said.

"We lost a lot of paper files that day. And curtains."

"Now I know you're making up stories," I said. "You guys don't have windows down there, and you sure don't have curtains."

"We have curtains," Rob said. "We're not monsters."

"We do have curtains," Knox said. "Not a lot of windows, but we have curtains."

I went to the suitcase, and got my first good look at Mr. Bone-Jangles.

"You guys, these aren't real bones," I said.

"We know that," Rob said. "We're not idiots."

Knox said, "I thought they were real."

"It's like one of those skeletons you use in a classroom," I said. "Except much higher quality. This isn't plastic. Is it a resin?"

"It's an unidentified material," Rob said.

"You had your best team on the case, huh?"

Rob frowned. "We do not have unlimited resources."

I closed the suitcase and zippered it again.

"Find someone else to take it," I said. "Maybe Fatima can use it at the vet clinic. Or see if Maisy wants some Halloween decorations for the coffee shop. Or..."

The suitcase unzipped itself.

Mr. Bone-Jangles climbed out.

Music began to play. It was strange yet familiar, hard to hold onto in my mind. Like a dream, unraveling when you wake.

The skeleton began to dance.

Agent Rob shifted into his bird form, and hopped backward to give himself space.

Agent Knox stayed in his large human form, backing up as well. He wore a big shoe on one foot, and a walking cast on the other. But even injured, he was a formidable foe.

The skeleton danced as though we were not even his audience.

He danced all the way over to the shallow hidden cupboard that Persephone had discovered.

He opened the door, used both bony hands to remove the canned goods and wooden shelves I'd recently installed.

Then he climbed in, settled against the back surface, and closed the cupboard door.

The seam around the door panel flashed, and the old paint resealed itself perfectly.

A visitor to the apartment would never guess that a skeleton was hiding within the walls.

Agent Rob shifted from bird to human again, and brushed his hands. "Glad we've settled that."

"I... You can't... I'm trying to adopt a kid, you guys. What if Mr. Bone-Jangles jumps out and does his little dance when the social worker is here for an interview?"

"He won't," Rob said. "That's the first time I've seen him get into something voluntarily. He's going to like living inside your wall."

"But what is he?"

Rob shrugged. "Just be grateful if he's the only skeleton you find when you renovate this old place. I bet there are endless surprises inside these old walls."

I groaned. "Old houses suck. I can't even get a plumber to come give me a quote. They all hate this part of town."

Knox said, "We will be your plumbers."

Rob tried to cut him off with a stern look, but Knox ignored his partner.

"We are both red seal certified," Knox said. "It is part of our basic training at the Water Department."

"Wow," I said. "You know, sometimes I forget that you guys also deal with the town's water supply."

"Supply *and* management," Knox said.

Rob shook his head, then reluctantly said, "Fine. I'll help with your plumbing. I do feel bad about... you know."

"About wiping the memory of my phone and then trying to wipe the memory of my... me?"

"You would have still been you," Rob said. "Just... fresher. With a bit less..." He looked pointedly at the rolling suitcase they'd used to transport the skeleton. "With a bit less baggage," he said.

I shuddered. "No, thanks. It's our baggage that makes us who we are."

The agents headed for the door.

"Wait a minute," I said. "Are you guys going to the Monster Mash?"

"We weren't planning to," Rob said.

"I like to go to the gym when it's quiet," Knox said. "Everyone will be at Castle Wyvern tonight."

"How about we all go to the ball together? We can be each other's dates."

They agreed.

I quickly picked out a dress, and we were ready to go to the ball.

As I closed the door to my apartment, I knew, thanks to a random blast of psychic certainty, that Mr. Bone-Jangles would remain in his cupboard.

And he did.

He remained there for a very long time, until everyone had forgotten he was even there.

But that's a story for another day.

CHAPTER 44

The party at Castle Wyvern was even more fun than I'd expected.

There was a wonderful DJ who played everyone's favorite songs.

With every song, someone in our group would yell, "This is my favorite song!"

It didn't matter that they'd declared three other songs their favorite already. That was the magic of a great DJ.

We danced, sang along, and enjoyed ourselves exactly as much as a bunch of supernaturals should enjoy Halloween.

Our group consisted of my dates, Agents Rob and Knox from the DWM, plus Kathy, Frank, me, and everyone from the Permits Department, including Zinnia, who'd left Fyrsil at home with his dad. We had one empty chair at our table. I kept meaning to ask the others who else was coming, but then the DJ played yet another of my absolute most-favorite songs.

Just before midnight, Zinnia asked me to come with her to the ladies' washroom.

I didn't have to go, but I went along. It was the least I could do, since I'd gone with the boys to her house and insisted she come with us.

The ladies' room was a gorgeous washroom with a lavender theme. Every surface was a different shade of purple.

We stood beside each other, and fixed our hair and makeup.

I was reminded of all the times we'd been forced to share a mirror. There'd been the time I'd lived at her floral-decorated house, before the tornado destroyed it, then our time at the hotel, and then at Fung's house, which was now her house. The one I'd been forcefully evicted from.

Was sharing a mirror with me really so bad?

If she'd hated it so much, why had she invited me to the ladies' room with her?

She missed me. That was it.

And now she was going to apologize to me for kicking me out so callously.

She would address the thing between us—the thing neither of us dared speak about.

She finally opened her mouth, and said, "It's a big commitment."

My inner thoughts did a hairpin turn. She was talking about the adoption. That was why she'd wanted me alone.

This was so like her, to be full of more warnings than encouragement. It's so easy to say no to ideas. They say cynics get to be right, but optimists get to be happy. Well, I was an optimist. I wouldn't let her cynicism weigh me down.

I tried not to show my irritation at her, but my face twitched, subconsciously telling her everything. I saw it in the mirror myself, as plain as writing on a page.

"It's not really a big commitment," I said, maintaining a light, casual tone. "Legally, it's only eight years. Getting a cat would be a bigger commitment."

I'd given that same answer to a few people now. Not the people conducting my adoption interviews.

Well, that's not true.

I had made the joke with them, but only the ones who I could tell could take a joke.

Well, that's not true, either.

I'd made the joke at the worst possible times, yet somehow it hadn't hurt my chances. All signs were positive so far that I would be the adoptive parent for the boy. In spite of my aunt's warnings, which I expected any minute now.

Aunt Zinnia didn't respond to my cat-commitment joke.

She said, "Can I try that lipstick?"

I handed the brand-new tube to her. "Can I try your eyeshadow?"

She handed me the eyeshadow, which was lavender, like the bathroom, but more sparkly. Sparkly eyeshadow wasn't recommended for women over thirty, due to it increasing the appearance of wrinkles, but she and I both ignored those age-based warnings. She could be an optimist about some things.

I said, "Speaking of cats, and long-term commitments you regret, how is Boa?"

Aunt Zinnia held her hands up to her chin like paws, and said, in a perfect impression, "Ham?"

"I miss her, but I do not miss the begging."

Zinnia patted her hips, and looked around like she'd forgotten something, some piece of herself.

"He's at home with your husband," I said.

"Ah, right." She tried on my lipstick. The color suited her perfectly. "This is nice. I'm glad I could be here for the Monster Mash. What a lovely event. How lovely that they do this every year, in spite of the danger. And the DJ is so good."

"You can't wait to get home, can you?"

Zinnia wilted, as only a woman named after a flower could. "Is it that obvious?"

"You don't have to stick around if you don't want to. We've got lots of people in our group."

"I know, but I wanted to be here for you. To let you know that you're not alone." She handed me back the lipstick. "And to let you know that, if I were in your shoes, I would do the exact same thing."

She would? You could have knocked me over with a swish of a cat's tail.

"Really? Even after...?"

"Aiden was a wonderful boy," she said, with the usual ripple of pain crossing her face at the mention of his name. The boy, an unofficial stepson, had passed away on Halloween. I had forgotten that detail until now, and suddenly I felt terrible for having insisted she come out to the castle. I could be so inconsiderate sometimes. No wonder she'd kicked me out. I was the worst.

"Aunt Zinnia, I'm so sorry. I..."

She shook her head, one hand up to shield my well-meaning apologies.

"He broke my heart, but at least he broke it open," she said. "We ought to be grateful for those who help us learn how to love."

She pursed her lips, so that they resembled a small rosebud. That reminded me of something.

"The heart is a rose," I said.

She tilted her head. "What's that? A poem?"

"Just something I heard. The heart is a rose. I guess because it opens?"

"You'll be a wonderful mother."

"Excuse me? I already am a mother. Have you forgotten about a young lady named Zoey?" I shook my head and joked, "Wow. If people aren't living inside your house with you, you forget all about them."

Aunt Zinnia smiled. "We ought to get back to the party."

"Tell me what you really want to do."

"I'd like to dance some more. They keep playing my favorite songs."

"I can create a distraction so you can escape home to put on your sweatpants. I could make one of the tapestries come to life, or set something on fire."

She leaned forward, and finished fixing my hair for me, since I hadn't fixed it properly myself.

Then she touched my cheek.

There was more to say. I had more to say, but I could never find the words, and it never seemed like the right time or place.

She stared into my eyes like she hoped that, whatever it was, I could keep it to myself just a little longer. Like she couldn't handle one more thing. The eyeshadow sparkles did make her look tired. Or enhanced the tiredness that was there.

We left the ladies' room.

"It's a shame Mrs. Puddikin couldn't make it after all," Zinnia said. "I wonder what happened to her."

"That's who's missing!" I suddenly felt terrible for forgetting all about our new confidante. "That's who the empty chair is for."

"Maybe she's running late." She checked the time on a nearby clock in the castle hallway. It was one of those large, freestanding grandfather clocks—the kind that lets out loud chimes on the hour. It reminded me of the fairy tale about the girl who goes to the ball, thanks to her fairy godmother, and then runs away at the stroke of midnight, leaving behind her slipper made of fur, not glass.

Zinnia said, "It's almost midnight, but I understand this event can go on quite late, if there's no..." She trailed off guiltily. It had been her own pain-body cacodemon who had ruined the ball two years ago.

Where was Mrs. Puddikin? She'd been so enthusiastic about officially joining the ranks of the supernatural and the knowing.

My aunt and I both came to a full stop in the hallway by the clock, as though we'd both had the same idea at the same time.

In unison, we said, "We should call."

Hallways were better for phone calls, after all. I would call Mrs. Puddikin, and she would call Fyrsil. Or someone who was big enough to answer the phone in the vicinity of Fyrsil.

I leaned against the castle's cool stone walls, pulled out my phone, and called Mrs. Puddikin.

Zinnia turned her back to me, and used her phone at the same time. She spoke to whoever answered in a sweet tone that she rarely shared with me.

Mrs. Puddikin answered my call with a shaky, "Zara? Is that you?"

"It's me. Are you feeling okay? We've got an extra chair saved—"

"My battery is about to die," she said frantically. "Zara, oh dear, oh dear, oh dear. I've been trying to call for help, and I couldn't get a signal. I don't know if it's really you, or if I'm hallucinating. I think I might be imagining this, love."

"Have you been drinking?"

"It's worse than that. I'm inside your house."

"Mrs. Puddikin, what's happening? Is there something wrong at my house?" My first suspect was Mr. Bone-Jangles, followed by the wyverns.

"Not your new one. Your old one. Zara, I'm—"

There were clicks and pops on the line.

She was gone.

I tried her number again immediately, but the call went straight to voicemail.

I waved frantically for Zinnia to finish her call.

She did, and said to me with irritation, "Now what?"

I explained what I'd heard, and what I thought was happening, but not why.

I didn't have any idea why Mrs. Puddikin would have gone underground, into the tunnels, via the hole in the ground where my former house had once stood. Where my house had existed before it had been inverted. Before it had gone inside out and upside down, underground.

Zinnia, however, seemed to know why.

She said with authority, "It's the heartstone."

"Tell me on the drive," I said, turning toward the exit. "There's no time to explain."

She didn't move. "What do you mean, there's no time to explain?"

"I mean there's no time to do it right here. Tell me in the car."

Zinnia caught my arm, and held me back from running out to the parking lot.

"She's after the heartstone," Zinnia said again, as though I was being deliberately obtuse.

"What's a hearthstone? You mean the flat rocks for a fireplace surround?"

"Heart-stone," Zinnia said carefully. "Not hearthstone. Heartstone. Heart plus stone."

"That's... that's what you tried to do to yourself with that potion. Turn your heart to stone. Did you give Mrs. Puddikin that potion? How could you? Or wait. Heartstone. Do you mean Codex, the AI? The thing that powered it? No. That was a living heart, from the droserakops, and Charlize turned it to stone... but..."

Zinnia's whole body twitched, like she was resisting the urge to slap me.

"Explain," I said.

"After the tornado, the salvage crew retrieved the cornerstones and the keystone from your old house, but not the heartstone. That was the source of its power."

"Are you serious?" I had never, ever heard of a heartstone. I hadn't even heard the word before. This was all completely out of the blue. Was she serious right now?

She blinked at me. Her hazel eyes were serious.

I'd been holding myself together, but my tide shifted, and I was furious.

I said through gritted teeth, "You knew what was powering my house, and this is the first I'm hearing about it?"

She took half a step back from me, as though I was twitching with witch-slapping energy. I probably was.

She said, "I only know because Ethan talks in his sleep."

I wagged a finger at her. "That's no excuse. We're family. I was your family long before him." I stopped wagging my finger at her, and switched to angrily tapping my sternum with all four fingers. "Me. I'm your family. I was here first. Me. What about me?"

I was here first. Me. What about me?

And that was it.

That was the thing that had been brewing between us for so long that I couldn't remember when it started, only that it hadn't ended. This monstrous potion had already been bubbling at a high boil the day she'd evicted me.

I'd known for a while that I would lose my place.

It was inevitable.

Cheerful inner voice: *It was a good thing!* It was good, that I would move down in Zinnia's life, and two more people would take their ranks above me. *It was good!* For her. But what about me?

Aunt Zinnia couldn't meet my eyes. I glared at her sparkling, lavender eyeshadow.

"I'm still here," she said, her voice soft, distant and present at the same time. "I'm right here. I'm not going anywhere."

I said something along the lines of *cacodemon doodie*.

She grabbed my hand, and held it between hers. Then she kissed her own fingers, which were still tight around my hand.

I pulled my hand away. We didn't have time for this, for whatever spell she was trying to cast to make it okay that she'd downgraded me out of her life.

"Mrs. Puddikin is in trouble," I said in a flat, surgical tone. "You can stay here if you want, but I'm going to extract her. I'll bring a whole extraction team. I'll take Rob and Knox. They're always good in a pinch."

"There's another way," Zinnia said. "A shortcut." She nodded at the stone wall.

This time, we were on the same wavelength. I understood exactly what she meant.

"A portal? Are you serious? After everything I've been through, with all the tunnels and portals?"

She grabbed my purse, and pulled out my brand-new lipstick.

She twisted the tube, extending the red waxy bit, and used it to draw an arched doorway shape on the stone wall of the castle.

The grandfather clock struck its first gong, its first hammer-strike on brass bells for midnight.

In front of us, the rocks split apart under the red lipstick line. They split, and a doorway opened.

On the other side, in the adjacent space, was a familiar sight.

My old living room.

It was upside down, and the furniture was on the ceiling, but it was my old living room.

"Hold the door," I said. "I'll go get the boys."

The grandfather clock continued to ring the bells for midnight.

"There's no time," she said. "It's only midnight on Halloween for..."

I didn't hear the rest of what she said.

I jumped through the doorway, just in time.

The grandfather clock rang its twelfth bell.

The portal closed with a soft POP right behind me.

CHAPTER 45

Exploring my old house was like a trip down memory lane, but inside a dream, with dream logic.

I might have felt right at home, except everything was upside down, reversed, inverted, or all three. Most of it was upside down. My once-familiar furniture was fixed to the ceiling, where it looked smaller than it had on the floor.

As I wandered through, I had to watch my feet, careful I didn't trip over the glowing bulges of light coming from the floor.

Most of my former possessions—and Zoey's—were still there, more or less where they had been before the explosion. All our clothes and household items would have been destroyed or at least damaged in the explosion, but now they were magically put back together.

I could reach the upper kitchen cabinets. When I opened them, one by one, each held a surprise—like a Christmas advent calendar, except instead of chocolate treats, there were swarms of insects, masses of white cocoons, empty cereal boxes decorated with cartoon characters I'd never seen before, and dishes that had been smashed apart then repaired with gleaming rivers of gold.

Beyond the kitchen, in an annex I didn't recognize, I found a wood staircase. It was my old staircase, or at least the same wood, deeply gouged by pets and shifters chasing each other up and down. In my above-surface house, the staircase had led up to the second floor, but this one led downward. Instead of a straight run with a landing, it was a tight spiral. There was no balustrade, just claustrophobically close walls.

Stepping on the inner side made my feet look enormous, and it didn't feel safe at all.

I realized I was rushing, and slowed down, moving to the wider part of the steps. I wouldn't be much of an extraction agent for Mrs. Puddikin if I tumbled down the stairs.

On the lower floor was a hallway, and a linen closet.

Something was scratching on the door from the inside.

"Mrs. Puddikin? Hello?"

More scratching.

I didn't want to open the linen closet, but I did what I had to do.

Before the door was even fully open, what was inside the closet came rushing out.

It was a tiny miniature goat.

No, two of them.

No, three of them.

The three goats charged out, ran over my feet as though I wasn't even there, and disappeared into the murky depths of the hallway.

I deeply regretted wearing open-toed heels to the Halloween ball. My toes would be okay after a quick healing, but my pedicure was ruined.

At the back of the linen closet was something interesting. It was the collection of cardboard boxes that had made the move to Wisteria, and had never been unpacked. They were stacked next to an aberration in the wall, a whirling hole in the wallpaper. Through the hole was black sky and pinpoints of stars. The wind whistled through the opening.

I didn't dare get too close, let alone stick my hand through it. The portal probably would have whisked me into the armoire in the spare room at Ethan Fung's house, but I wasn't ready to try my luck just yet. Plus I was on a mission.

My mind whirled as a breeze sucked my hair toward the hole at the back of the closet.

Wait. What had I been thinking about?

Something about a mission?

What a strange situation I had found myself in.

I couldn't remember how I'd gotten there.

Why was my house all changed around?

Why was I wearing a gown of blue, with a white pinafore?

Was I dreaming?

That had to be it. I was dreaming.

I walked dreamily down the hallway. The miniature goats returned from the other direction, running past me again.

I found a familiar door, and opened it to find my old bedroom. The bed was on the ceiling, and it appeared to be neither made nor unmade. It did look comfortable.

If I went to sleep inside a dream, what would happen to the dream I was already inside? Would I wake up somewhere else? How many levels deep would this dream go?

That was obviously my goal. My mission. To get myself into that bed on the ceiling and go to sleep.

And I might have figured out how to do that, if I hadn't heard the three little goats crying out for help.

I followed the sound of their bleating, down another spiral staircase, which led to another hallway, and terminated in a completely dark room.

The other rooms had been lit by lights at my feet and the occasional sconce on the wall, but this room was devoid of light.

My hand went to the wall on muscle memory, and my fingers found a familiar switch. I clicked it down, and a single light came on.

This room was another version of the same living room I'd seen already.

It didn't strike me as terribly odd that this dream-version of my house had more than one living room. My real house had changed itself many times. Sometimes this room had a fireplace, and sometimes it did not. This version had an enormous fireplace made of round river rocks. That was different. My fireplaces had been brick.

I walked around the room, standing on my tiptoes to switch on the lamps that hung from the side tables which hung from above.

I heard the goats again, except they weren't goats.

The sound was coming from inside the large, stone fireplace.

A woman was inside it.

Mrs. Paisley Puddikin.

I was shocked to see her there, with her clothes visibly dirty from crawling around in the ashes, and her hair disheveled.

This was no dream.

I woke up, and remembered what I'd forgotten.

I was wearing an Alice in Wonderland costume because I'd been at the Halloween ball at Castle Wyvern. I'd arrived at this place, which was not a dream, via a wyvern tunnel. And I did have a mission. Save Mrs. Puddikin.

There was a chair out of place in the room. She'd apparently broken a wooden chair free from the floor—or ceiling—and used it to climb into the fireplace.

She was curled around something. She was cradling in her arms... a big, lumpy stone.

"The heartstone," I said.

My voice sounded loud and croaky. It startled me.

Mrs. Puddikin opened her eyes, and looked down at me. Her eyes looked decades younger than the version of her I had in my memory. Even her face had fewer wrinkles.

"You found the heartstone," I said.

"I'm ready to go now," she said.

"Good." I held out my hand. She could step down via the same chair she'd used to climb up.

She asked, "Will it hurt?"

"Will what hurt?"

"Dying."

"Why would you die? Are you injured?"

"I know you're an angel, love. I know you're here to take me to the other side."

"I've been called a lot of things, but never an angel."

She tilted her head to the side, confused. "Zara?"

"It's me, Mrs. Puddikin. I've come to extract you from this... place."

"Purgatory," she said. "I know. You're an angel. I'm ready to go."

I checked her pulse. Her heart was beating strongly, and there were no physical injuries, but she was weak, confused.

I had a strong mind, and the inverted house had put me into a dream state. I could only imagine the power it had over a non-supernatural mind.

"Come with me," I said. "It doesn't matter where we are. We have to go."

"He wasn't with another woman," she said. "He cheated on me, but only because he was after... her." She looked down at the lumpy stone.

"The heartstone? Is this the treasure Mr. Puddikin was searching for?"

She nodded.

"It's not much of a heart," I said. "I mean, maybe, if you squint."

I reached for the lumpy rock. The instant my finger touched its dusty surface, everything around us shook. All the furniture in the room lost its grip on the floor-ceiling, and fell to the ceiling-floor with a great crash. The lamps shattered, and only a single light remained on the floor, partly shaded by fallen throw pillows. Dust filled the air.*Housekeeper's week off.*

"We really do have to get out of here," I said. "Come on." Taking care to avoid touching the heartstone, I tugged gently at her elbow.

"Save yourself," she said. "I'll stay here. I'm ready to see my husband again. I can't wait to tell him he was right. The treasure was always here, under our noses the whole time."

"Technically, it was under my nose. This is my old house."

She looked ready to argue.

I yanked her from the fireplace with more force. Words are powerful, but so are biceps.

We quickly discovered a problem.

She could leave the stony opening, but not with the heartstone. All attempts to remove the lumpy rock resulted in our surroundings falling apart. Some of the floorboards were now in broken pieces, on top of the fallen furnishings. She could keep the heartstone, or she could leave the underground. Not both.

I thought the correct choice was "bloody well obvious," to use her words, but she did not.

We were halfway out of the room when Mrs. Puddikin broke free of me, crawled over the broken furniture and back into the dark hole. She wrapped herself around the heartstone like a dragon around its golden treasure in a fairy tale. Or a wyvern around his secret stash of maple syrup.

"Pull yourself together," I barked at her. "You will see your husband someday, but not today. It's November first. Christmas is coming. You like Christmas, don't you?"

She blinked at me. "I like Christmas."

"Everyone likes Christmas. That's why we have it. Now get your butt out here right now. Stop feeling sorry for yourself. Your husband wouldn't want you to expire down here, underground. He would want you to carry on, to live your life above ground. There's plenty of time, infinite time, for you to be..." I couldn't finish the sentence. Dead. There was plenty of time for her to be dead.

The room had gotten so dim, but I could see everything clearly. I knew every inch of that room by heart.

I felt Theodore Bentley behind me. He was there. Down in the tunnels, beneath the city. He was below everything. He was part of all darkness now. All shadows.

But I belonged to the light.

And so did Mrs. Puddikin.

I pried her fingers off the stone, careful not to touch it with my hands, and dragged her out of the fireplace a second time.

I threw her over my shoulder, and immediately fell over from the weight of her. She wasn't large, but I was no big, tough firefighter. And I didn't have the body-lightening spell to make her manageable.

She was still conscious, though, so I held her hand while I pushed and dragged her out of the house.

We went up one spiral staircase, then another, and three more.

We finally found what appeared to be my front door.

It wouldn't open. I couldn't pull it toward myself. No matter how hard I pulled, it was as though the hinges were on the opposite side.

Because they were.

Everything was inside out and backwards and upside down and wrong, wrong, wrong.

I turned the handle and pushed.

The door swung open.

I'd already accepted in my heart that I'd be stepping out into blackness, into velvet-blue night sky with pinpoints of starry lights. We'd step into the void together, and we'd go where it went.

But there was grass below the porch steps.

Green, dewy grass.

There were houses down the street, their windows glowing warmly with regular light.

I had reached my former back yard.

My heart soared.

It was back! My house had sprung up behind me, restored to her former glory!

Holding Mrs. Puddikin's hand, I stepped off the porch, then turned to look at her.

There was no house. Even the doorway we'd come through was gone.

So much for that dream.

Mrs. Puddikin turned to me, her expression lucid again.

"I'm so sorry, love. I had to see if it was true. I had to meet her myself."

The ground rumbled ominously underneath us.

"No time for apologies," I barked, pushing her toward the slim opening in the fence. "We need to get out of here. I have to report back to—"

Headlights flashed across us, blinding us.

A vehicle came to a stop in front of us. It had four brand-new tires, the tiny rubber nubbins not yet worn off.

The driver was Agent Rob. Seated inside were Agent Knox and Aunt Zinnia. The boys looked surprised to see me there with Mrs. Puddikin. My aunt yawned.

They rolled down their windows.

My mind was feeling sharp. Sharp as a brand-new pencil straight from the pencil sharpener.

This was my moment. The right time to say something clever. The big payoff for putting my life in danger yet again.

I said to the people in the car, "What has two thumbs and just solved yet another case the Department of Water and Magic couldn't crack?" I pointed my thumbs at my chest. "This witch."

CHAPTER 46

After our successful extraction, my aunt went home.

She and I still had things to discuss, or maybe we didn't. Either way, the time and place would come along eventually.

Agents Knox and Rob didn't leave. They hung around with me at Mrs. Puddikin's house.

The two shifters watched her for signs she needed to be taken to the department's doctor, Dr. Ankh.

To everyone's relief, the woman made a rapid recovery. I was very glad we wouldn't have to deal with Dr. Ankh.

"Stop fussing over me," Mrs. Puddikin said. "I'm fine. If anything, I feel twenty years younger."

"Paisley, you do look younger," I said.

The fellows didn't know her well enough to comment, or perhaps they sensed that talking about a woman's apparent age would only backfire.

Even Knox, who could be startlingly honest, said nothing.

Mrs. Puddikin touched her face and asked, "Do I really?"

"Maybe not twenty years, but you look different, and that's saying something. After what you've been through, you should look older, not younger. You look very refreshed."

She ran to the main floor bathroom to look in the mirror.

"I do look younger," she said. She wetted a facecloth, and used it to remove fireplace ash and grime from her face. The skin underneath was pink and robust.

The three of us crowded in behind her.

"You must be younger," I said. "You feel it, and look it, so you must be younger."

Knox said, "Dr. Ankh will want to check her telomeres."

I said to him sternly, "Tell that witch doctor nothing of this."

Rob snorted. Dr. Ankh wasn't a witch, but I was, so of course that was funny.

"These are my husband's lost years," our British friend said with certainty. "She took these years from him, and she felt bad about it, so she gave his years to me, his widow."

She? I was confused for a moment, then I remembered Mrs. Puddikin had referred to the heartstone as a she. Sure. Why not? I'd called the skeleton a Mr.

The heartstone could be a Miss or a Mrs.

Miss Heartstone.

She sounded like a dominatrix—not that I'd know anything about that, say, from my early twenties when I'd needed cash to raise my kid. Nope.

Rob said to Knox, "It must be true."

"The fountain of youth," Knox said.

"Not *the* fountain, but *a* fountain," Rob said.

Neither of them made a move to leave the cozy mansion and run back to the site on Beacon Street.

There wouldn't have been much point. The hole had actually closed up with each step we took away from it.

The Wilds would no longer be enticing any groups of little boys with board games, let alone big boys with DWM tools.

I mused out loud. "I wonder if it's the same fountain of youth Kathy told me about. It was a long time ago, before I knew much—"

Rob interrupted, "Are you saying there was a time you didn't know everything about everything?"

"Ha ha," I said. "I didn't know about magic then. Kathy told me something about my house being connected to a fountain of youth. The old woman who owned it before me, Winona Vander Zalm, was really, really old, but nobody knew how old."

The agents exchanged a look that said they would keep this information to themselves, so they didn't get in trouble for not successfully retrieving the heartstone.

"Frank Wonder also knew Mrs. Vander Zalm," I told them. I was in full storyteller mode, delighted to be connecting so many loose threads. "He knew her for over thirty years, and he says she didn't age more than ten. Plus everyone thought Winona had served as a nurse during the war, but they couldn't figure out which war."

A hush fell over the group.

After a moment, Agent Rob said, "That could have been you, Zara. That house could have kept you young forever."

I felt cold suddenly, and crossed my arms.

"I wouldn't have felt right about that, staying the same age while everyone else got older. I'd feel guilty."

"Hah!" Mrs. Puddikin said. "I'd like to hear you say that when you reach my ripe old age." She put her hands to her chest, then under her chest, giving a test lift to a couple of body parts she probably should have left untested until the fellows weren't in the room.

"Huh," she said. "I really am younger all over."

The doorbell rang.

"Ding-dong," I said, running for Mrs. Puddikin's front door. "Doorbell!"

I yanked open the door.

My coworker and fellow dungeon crawler, Kathy Carmichael, stood on the porch, holding an armload of books. Frank stood right behind her, holding even more.

"Let me guess," I said. "You're closing down your old treelibrary?"

Kathy said, "A secret hiding place is no good if it's not a secret anymore."

Frank said, "It was a terrible location for keeping books. Just disgusting. No humidity control whatsoever. It's a wonder these books aren't disintegrated!"

Kathy rolled her eyes at me, annoyed by Frank.

Frank rolled his eyes at me, annoyed by Kathy.

It was a lot of eye rolling for people who had been up all night dancing at the Monster Mash, then fetching magical books. Like the rest of us gathered at the old mansion, they hadn't gotten any sleep.

Mrs. Puddikin joined me at the door.

"Come in, come in," she said to them. "Zara, love, we don't make our visitors stand out in the cold. Where are your manners?"

I stepped aside, inviting them in.

Mrs. Puddikin welcomed them to her home by bringing them on another trip to her bathroom mirror, to show them her newly de-aged face, and also her newly de-aged bosom.

"I'll get to make up my own cover story," she said with pink-cheeked excitement. "I'll disappear for a few weeks, then come back and tell everyone something unbelievable happened to my face."

"A facelift," Frank said.

"But a really good one," Kathy said.

"You need to change your hair at the same time," Frank said. "It totally throws people off. The hair change is the absolute, must-have red herring of cosmetic surgery."

All of us turned to stare at Frank. He'd gone from pink hair to silver hair, along with a clothing style change.

His cheeks reddened. "Me? No. I didn't do anything of the sort." He looked down at the floor. "Well, maybe a little something around my eyes, but not the whole face."

Kathy pointed at him. "I knew it! I knew you weren't visiting your sister for two whole weeks."

"Ah, but I was," he said. "I had it done in London. My sister knows a guy." He rolled his eyes. "Not that she has the sense to see him herself."

I could barely believe it. I hadn't even noticed the change to his eyelids, and I knew Frank's handsome face very well. I saw it more days than not. What else was I not noticing that was right under my nose?

We left the bathroom, and gathered in Mrs. Puddikin's spacious living room. She had a large, stone fireplace, just like the one she'd climbed into underground. That explained the river stones I'd never seen before.

This fireplace was a real, working fireplace.

She chucked several pieces of wood and kindling into the opening, and lit a fire.

"November first is the perfect day for a wood fire," she said over the crackling and popping.

We all got comfortable, and Kathy shared her books. We pored over them, looking for information about the heartstone, but then getting distracted by other rabbit holes of interest.

Agents Rob and Knox disappeared to the kitchen to make pancakes.

I closed my book, and ran across the street to my place to grab some maple syrup.

It was nice to see a familiar home with the furniture on the floor where it belonged, and no miniature goats hiding in the linen closet.

The skeleton was still in the wall as far as I could tell without using my sledgehammer.

Everything was exactly as I'd left it, including the hole with the pipe that Rob and Knox had promised to help with.

I searched my cupboards, and found two large cans of syrup from Quebec that hadn't been punctured and drained yet.

Then I returned to Mrs. Puddikin's house, letting myself in the front door. I had a feeling this was only the first of many times I would be letting myself in, and it was a good feeling.

You think that the good feelings in your life are going to come from huge events on the calendar, like weddings, or birthdays, or achieving some career or financial goal.

But the truth is, most of the good feelings come from things you've never given any thought to whatsoever.

Such as the feeling of rich soil under your fingernails, or having the first patrons walk through the door of your new library.

Or getting a phone call that you need to come to your lawyer's office to sign even more paperwork because the adoption is going through.

Or seeing a door that isn't yours, but knowing that you are welcome to open that door any time you need to.

I would need that door, and I would need Mrs. Puddikin, and all the others gathered around the crackling fire on that first day of November.

And it was a good feeling.

Not just to have people, but to need them in the first place.

For a full list of books in this
series and other titles by
Angela Pepper, visit

www.angelapepper.com

Printed in Great Britain
by Amazon

59442115R00178